"HANG HIM!"

The Kid heard the verdict without flinching. Billy Shay's gang had lashed his hands and feet. There was nothing the Kid could do but face death as firmly as he had faced a life of bare fists and quick-draw gun play.

Billy Shay stepped forward and barked, "Stand back! I ain't gonna ask any of you vultures to dirty your hands with hangin'. I'm gonna shoot this hombre myself!"

Slowly Shay lifted his ugly Colt and pointed it straight between the Kid's steel gray eyes. His finger tightened around the trigger. Then Shay paused for one more taunting word. . . . Suddenly the air sang with bullets; the ground trembled with the thunder of riders. Billy Shay never did squeeze that trigger, and in all his bloody life it was the worst mistake he ever made!

Books by Zane Grey

Amber's Mirage and Other
  Stories
The Arizona Clan
Black Mesa
The Border Legion
Boulder Dam
The Call of the Canyon
Drift Fence
The Dude Ranger
Fighting Caravans
Forlorn River
The Fugitive Trail
Lone Star Ranger
Lost Pueblo
The Lost Wagon Train
Majesty's Rancho
The Maverick Queen
Raiders of the Spanish Peaks

The Rainbow Trail
Riders of the Purple Sage
Rogue River Feud
The Secret of Quaking Asp
  Cabin and Other Stories
Stairs of Sand
Tappan's Burro
30,000 on the Hoof
Thunder Mountain
Under the Tonto Rim
The U.P. Trail
The Vanishing American
Western Union
Wilderness Trek
Wildfire
Wild Horse Mesa
Wyoming

Published by POCKET BOOKS

MAX BRAND

THE HAIR-TRIGGER KID

PUBLISHED BY POCKET BOOKS NEW YORK

Distributed in Canada by PaperJacks Ltd., a Licensee
of the trademarks of Simon & Schuster, Inc.

POCKET BOOKS, a division of Simon & Schuster, Inc.
1230 Avenue of the Americas, New York, N.Y. 10020
In Canada distributed by PaperJacks Ltd.,
330 Steelcase Road, Markham, Ontario

ISBN: 0-671-41570-0

First Pocket Books printing May, 1953

15   14   13   12   11   10   9   8   7

POCKET and colophon are registered trademarks
of Simon & Schuster, Inc.

Printed in Canada

CONTENTS

CHAPTER		PAGE
1	Plain Poison	1
2	The Kid Arrives	6
3	Battle Royal	11
4	Davey Rides	16
5	Three-card Stumbles	21
6	Watching	26
7	Treed	31
8	A Great Business	36
9	A Suggestion	41
10	Handmade Shoe	44
11	Callers	50
12	Notched Gun	55
13	Branding Iron	60
14	A Compact	65
15	Land Sharks	70
16	Storm Clouds	75
17	Bad News	80
18	A Volunteer	84
19	Two Reasons	89
20	A Challenge	94

CHAPTER		PAGE
21	Watching	99
22	The Chase	103
23	Compliments	108
24	The Law	113
25	Mixed Answers	118
26	Past History	121
27	Strange Tales	128
28	The Fifth Man	139
29	Cattle Lover	145
30	Down the Canyon	148
31	The Fifth Man Again	153
32	Milman Rides	158
33	Danger Ahead	163
34	The Approach	168
35	Hiding	173
36	Chuck	178
37	One Match	183
38	The Verdict	187
39	Davey Rides	193
40	For the Sake of Cows	198
41	Two Against Twenty	203
42	Heroes	208

THE
HAIR-TRIGGER KID

1
Plain Poison

Two THINGS waited for John Milman when he got West. One was his family, and the other was the spring. When he got to the end of the railroad, he could see spring eating its way up the mountains, taking the white from their shoulders and streaking the desert itself with green. But his family was not on hand with means to take him out to the ranch, and therefore he had to wait restlessly in the hotel, pacing up and down his room, and damning all delays. Sheriff Lew Walters was in that room, trying to help his friend kill time and uselessly pointing out that in an hour or two, at the most, the wife and daughter of Milman were sure to arrive. He might as well have read a chapter out of the Bible. Or better, perhaps.

"I haven't seen them for six months!" said Milman.

This was a proof that he was still, to a degree, an outlander. Real Westerners will not give way to their emotions so readily. They have picked up some of the manners of the wild Indians. But the sheriff, who knew the worth of this man, merely smiled and nodded.

"A lot of things can happen in an hour," said Milman. "I wonder what's kept them back? Elinore's as punctual as a chronometer, always. And Georgia would never be late for me! A lot of things can happen in an hour around this part of the world. How is Mr. Law, and old lady Order, his wife, Lew? They're still in your charge, I suppose?"

"They're recuperatin'," said the sheriff gravely. "They got a sort of shock and a setback a while ago, but they're recupera-tin'."

"What gave them the shock?"

"Well, typhoid fever, smallpox, diphtheria, delirium tremens and muscular rheumatism all hit this town together, one day, when Billy Shay turned up and opened his gambling house. I had old Law and Order out, taking the sun and the air every day, but now they don't dare to leave their beds till the sun's at nine o'clock, and they creep back in around about sundown."

"Who is Billy Shay?" asked Milman, willing to forget his trouble for a moment.

"Shay is poison," said the sheriff.

"What kind?"

"Skunk poison," said the sheriff inelegantly. "He's just one of those mean, low-down, sneakin' curs that has teeth and knows how to use 'em."

"Then why don't you run 'im out?"

"I can't hang anything on him. I know that everything crooked in the town depends on Shay, but still I can't get any information against him. He's slick as a snake, and he could hide in a snake's hole, if he wanted to."

"How does the town take to him?"

"How does any town this far West take to a chance to spoil its health, throw away its bank account, wreck its eyes, and quit work? Why, this town of Dry Creek is crazy about Billy Shay."

"Does everyone know that he's a crook?"

"Of course, everybody does. That won't hold your real hundred-per-cent Westerner from going to that gaming house and tossing his money away. Shay has such a good thing that he only has to use the brakes now and then to stop somebody on a big run. As long as a fool wins once in three times, he's sure to come back for more. And one player out of ten always makes something worth while. They do the advertising for Billy Shay."

He extended his hand, pointing across the street.

"There's Billy's house. He's gone and got himself the finest place in town."

"That's Judge Mahon's place, I thought."

"The judge has sold out and moved up Denver way. Didn't you know that?"

"News is six months dead to me," admitted the rancher. "There's somebody piling down the street in a hurry."

The horseman came with a rush and a sweep.

"Maybe news from the ranch—maybe bad news!" muttered Milman under his breath.

"Why, it's Billy Shay!" said the sheriff. "I never saw him ride in like that before!"

Billy Shay appeared to Milman as rather a hump-shouldered man with a long, lean, white face. As he got to the front of his house, he sprang from the saddle, without pausing to throw the reins, and as the horse dashed off down the street, Billy cleared his front gate with a fine hurdle and fled to the door of the house.

Then, as he fitted the key into the lock, he cast a frantic glance over his shoulder up and down the street and flattened his body against the door like one who feels the eyes of danger in the center of his spine.

A moment later he had disappeared into the house.

"Yes, that's a mighty hurried fellow," said Milman. "He doesn't act as though he's so dangerous as you've been saying."

"No, he don't," replied the sheriff. "He don't look bad enough to eat a raw egg, right now. But I've seen him—" He paused and sighed. "I'd like to know what's after Billy!" he continued, shaking his head. "Whatever is in his mind, I'd like to find out the nature of it. I'd like to discover the kind of mongoose that makes that cobra run!"

Then, distinctly, across the road, they could hear the noise of furniture being dragged—heavy articles which screeched against the floor. They even saw the door tremble as these things were piled against it.

"Dog-gone me if he ain't barricadin' himself in that house of his!" said the sheriff with a growing awe.

He laid his brown hand with withered, wrinkled fingers upon the shoulder of his friend.

"I got an idea that maybe we're going to see something, old-timer."

"See what?" said Milman.

"I dunno. A mob, maybe, that's after him. Once we can crack the shell and get at the news that's in that hound's life record, we'd have enough to raise the whole of Dry Creek, I suppose."

"You think there's a mob rising? I don't hear a sound."

"Mobs that mean real business don't make no noise at all," said the sheriff. "I've seen a hundred and fifty men wearin' guns and masks, and as quiet as a funeral. Funerals was what they was providin', as a matter of fact. Cheap funerals and a quick way out of the world to them that didn't understand the ways of the West, as you might say. How that Shay slicked off of his horse, eh? I never seen nothin' like it!"

"He's a badly scared man, all right," said Milman. "If the crowd should come to mob him, will you have to intervene?"

At this the face of Lew Walters turned grim.

"I'd have to," he declared. "The old days is gone, and Law and Order is supposed to be strong enough to walk right up and down the main street of this town night or day. I'm the escort. I've swore to do that job, and I intend to do it!"

He looked anxiously up and down the street as he spoke.

But there was nothing in sight that agreed with his grave imaginings of danger.

"Look at that dormer window in the roof!" exclaimed Milman.

The house of the judge, having been built as pretentiously as possible, had a roof like the crown of a Mexican hat, and on one side of it was a dormer window. The window was open, and inside it a mirror flashed a blinding ray of light, winking rapidly.

"There's a signal—that's heliograph work as sure as I'm a foot high, Lew. Can you make out the dots and dashes?"

"I can't make out a thing. I'm not a telegrapher. But I could guess the name of the fellow who's handling that mirror!"

"You mean Shay?"

"That's who I mean. He's sending out a message to pals of his somewhere, and I'd put my money that it's a howl for help."

"If we could get at the meaning of that message, we might be at the heart of Shay's private affairs—information enough to enable you to make your arrest, eh?"

"Aye, we might. Here's somebody coming. The mob, I'd say. And a mighty small mob to crack a nut with a shell as hard as Shay's. He's probably got half a dozen armed men in that house."

The dust cloud down the street dissolved, presently, to show two women and two men riding abreast, with led horses directly behind them.

"That's no mob, Milman," said the sheriff after a moment. "That's your wife on the left, there, if I ain't lost my eyes."

Milman, with an exclamation, made for the door, but the sheriff remained fixed at his post at the window, watching with curiosity-squinted eyes the flickering light from the heliograph that played in the dormer window. He quite agreed with Milman that this message might be useful to him in his work of ridding the town of the gambling nuisance. But he knew that by the time he had secured a telegrapher the signaling would probably have stopped. He could only sigh and watch, uncomprehending.

Still his mind struggled to guess at a solution of the mystery of Shay's fear. For the man, whatever his other faults of greed, low cunning, and knavery, was brave, and had demonstrated his courage over and over again. Yet here he had fled into his house, barricaded the door, locked the lower windows, and now was signaling—no doubt frantically—in an appeal for help!

The possible mob was the only solution that appeared to the mind of the sheriff. He loosened his Colt in its holster and set his mind sternly on the work that might be preparing for him. No matter what he thought of Shay, mob violence was something which he had put down in Dry Creek, and he was prepared to put it down again at whatever risk.

In order to get closer to the scene of action, as soon as the mirror at the dormer window stopped signaling and the window itself was closed with a violent bang, he went downstairs, and in the lobby found his friend, the rancher, with his wife and daughter beside him, looking as happy as any child.

Even with the trouble that was now in his mind, the sheriff could not help letting his eye linger pleasantly on the trio for a moment.

"Clean-bred ones," said the sheriff to himself, and being a man his glance lingered longest on the face of Georgia Milman. She was as brown as an Indian; she had the rounded, supple body of an Indian maiden, also, and Indian black was her hair, but her eyes were the blue which one sees in Ireland. She swung her quirt and greeted the sheriff noisily and heartily. They had shot elk together the season before.

"Father says that there's some sort of trouble brewing in the Shay house," said she.

"I dunno," answered Lew Walters, "but they's trouble buddin' and bloomin' over there. Come out on the veranda and have a look at the fireworks. Hello, Mrs. Milman. This here man of yours, he sure needed tyin' before he seen you down the street. Are you-all comin' out on the observation platform?"

They were. And the rest of the town seemed to be heading in

the same direction, so swiftly had the rumor of excitement spread.

2
The Kid Arrives

IT WAS not malicious curiosity that brought the crowd. It was the same impulse which draws men together to see a prize fight. There were perhaps fifty people already on the long covered veranda that ran in front of the hotel, supported by narrow wooden pillars, with a row of watering troughs on each side of the steps where a twelve-horse team could be watered at one time without unharnessing them.

"You're gettin' a new brand of trouble here in Dry Creek, sheriff," said an acquaintance.

"I've seen a lot of brands," said the sheriff. "What's the new one gunna be like?"

"The Kid is comin' to town, I've heard. Charlie Payson, he passed the word along."

"Which is this Kid?" asked Milman. "Denver, Mississippi, Chicago, Boston or—"

"This ain't any of them. It's the Kid," replied the sheriff. "You mean to tell me that Charlie Payson is handin' out that story? What would the Kid be comin' to Dry Creek for?"

"Yeah," said the other, "you'd say that Dry Creek wouldn't give him no elbow room, hardly. But that's what Payson is sayin'. I dunno how he knows. Unless'n maybe he got a letter. Some say that he was with the Kid down in Yucatan once."

"I've heard that story," said the sheriff. "How they went up the river and found the old temple and got the emerald eye, and all that. Is they anything in that yarn?"

"They's likely to be something in any yarn about the Kid."

"Who is the Kid?" said Elinore Milman.

"You never heard of him?" asked the sheriff.

"No. Never. Not of a man who went by just that nickname. What's his real name?"

"Why, that I dunno. But betwixt Yucatan and about twenty-five hundred miles north they is only one Kid, so far as I know."

"What sort of a creature is he? Young?"

"The sort of creature he is," said the sheriff, "is a hard creature to describe. Yes, mostly he's young."

"What do you mean by mostly?"

"Well, some ways they ain't nobody no older in the world. Maybe I can give you an idea of the Kid by what a feller told me he seen in a Mexican town in Chihuahua. When the word came in that the Kid had been sighted around those parts, they fetched in a section of the toughest rurales they could find, and they swore in a flock of extra deputies, and them gents that had extra-fine hosses. They led 'em out of town and sneaked for the tall timber, and the women that had pretty daughters, they got 'em indoors and turned the lock over 'em, and sat down in front of the doors with the biggest butcher knives that they could sharpen upon the grindstone. And the gamblin' house, it closed up and cached all of its workin' money by buryin' it real secret in the ground, and the big store, it closed and locked up all of its windows. It looked like that there town had gone to sleep. But it was lyin' wide awake behind its shutters, like a cat. Well, down there in Mexico, they know the Kid a lot better than we do, and that's the way they treat him there."

"But here in Dry Creek," Elinore Milman questioned, "you don't take all those precautions when this philandering horse thief, gunman and yegg comes to town?"

"Ma'am," said the sheriff, "you've heard that he's comin'. And ain't you standing out here with Georgia right beside you?"

She flushed a little, but the girl merely laughed.

"I imagine that I can venture Georgia," said the rancher's wife.

"Yeah," said the sheriff, "I see that you do. But if she was mine, I'd blindfold her and put her in a cyclone cellar when they was a chance of that Kid comin' by. Up here, on this side of the Rio Grande, we're all too dog-gone proud to be careful and that's the cause of a terrible lot of broken safes and necks and hearts!"

There was a distinct strain of seriousness in this speech, but Mrs. Milman, turning toward her daughter, smiled a little, and Georgia smiled in turn. They were old and understanding companions.

Murmurs, in the meantime, passed up and down the veranda.

"What's it all about, sheriff?" asked several men from time to time.

He merely shrugged his shoulders and continued to stare at the house opposite him, as though he were striving to read a human mind.

"The curtain ain't up," said the sheriff, "but I reckon that the stage is set and that they's gunna be an entrance pretty pronto."

"Here's somebody coming," said Georgia, gesturing toward the farther end of the street.

"Yeah," said the sheriff, "but he's comin' too slow to mean anything."

"Slow and earnest wins the race," said another.

They were growing impatient; like a crowd at a bullfight, when the entrance of the matador is delayed too long.

"We're wasting the day," said Milman to his family. "That's a long ride ahead of us."

"Don't go now," said Georgia. "I've got a tingle in my finger tips that says something is going to happen."

Other voices were rising, jesting, laughing, when some one called out something at the farther end of the veranda, and instantly there was a wave of silence that spread upon them all.

"What is it?" whispered Milman to the sheriff.

"Shut up!" said the sheriff. "They say that it's the Kid!"

He came suddenly into view, as a puff of wind cuffed the dust aside. His back was so straight and his stirrup so long that he seemed to be standing in his saddle. His head was high, and his glance was on the distance, like one who knows that his horse will pay heed to the footwork. But there was nothing unusual in his get-up except for the tinkling of a pair of little golden bells which he wore in his spurs.

Such a silence had come over the crowd on the veranda that this sound, small as the chiming of a distant brook, grew distinctly audible. The sheriff suddenly nudged Georgia.

"There's a horse for you," said he. "That's the Duck Hawk, as they call it. That's the mustang mare that he caught in Sonora. Ain't she the tiptoe beauty for you?"

She came like a dancer, daintily but smoothly, with a pride

about her head, as though she felt she were carrying some one of vast distinction. A king would have liked to ride on such a horse; or a general, or any mayor in the world, to lead a procession.

"She gets her name from her markings," explained the sheriff. "You see the black of her all over, except the breast and the belly is white. I never seen such queer markings on a hoss before. But that's the Duck Hawk. I seen her out of Phoenix once. I'd dig potatoes for ten years for a hoss like that, honey. How long," he added, "would you dig 'em for such a man?"

He turned with a grin as he spoke, and the girl smiled back at him.

"He looks all wool," she said most frankly.

So he did. The sort of wool that wears in the West, or on any frontier. Now, as he came up to the hotel and jumped out of the saddle, they could see that he had the strong man's shoulders, smoothly made and thick; and the legs of a runner such as one finds among the straight-built Navajoes. He had the deep desert tan, but his eyes were of that same Irish blue which made men look at Georgia Milman with a leap of the heart.

Their hearts did not leap when they stared at the Kid, however. Instead, glances were apt to sink to the ground.

The Kid took a bit of clean linen from his saddle bag and wiped the muzzle of the mare before he permitted her to drink, which she did freely but daintily, for Georgia Milman could see, now, that there was no bit between her teeth.

"Hello, folks," said the Kid. "Waiting here for a procession to come along, or is somebody going to make a speech?"

He picked out faces, here and there, and waved to them, but when he saw the sheriff he jumped lightly to the edge of the veranda between two of the troughs. The intervening people slipped hastily back, like dogs, Georgia thought, when the wolf steps near.

The Kid took the sheriff's hand in a warm grip.

"I'm glad to see you, Walters," said he. "I thought I'd drop in here at Dry Creek to see you. You've made my old friend Shay so much at home that I thought you might want me up here too."

"I'm glad to see you, too," said the sheriff instantly. "I've got a right good little ol' jail over yonder, Kid, and you'll find it mighty cheap here in Dry Creek to get a ticket to it."

"Never buy anything but round trips," said the Kid, "and I

hear that yours is only a one-way line. You're not introducing me to your daughter, Walters?"

"This is the yegg I was telling you about, Georgia," said the sheriff. "This is the same sashayin' young trouble raiser. The lady's name is Milman, Kid."

The Kid took off his hat and bowed to her with an almost Latin grace.

"I nearly borrowed a pair of your father's horses one evening," said the Kid. "But there were too many barbed-wire fences. Mighty bad thing to use so much barbed wire around horses. You tell your dad that for me, will you?"

He stepped back, replacing his hat upon the tangled, curly hair of his head. Georgia had nodded and smiled faintly, without embarrassment.

"He admits what he is," she said. "Don't your hands simply itch to jam him into that jail, Lew?"

"Yeah," said the sheriff, "and they'd itch a lot more if I had a bigger life insurance."

The Kid, in the meantime, had stepped down from the veranda again, and, breaking two matches, slipped them into his spurs so that the golden bells were wedged and silenced.

He talked to this curious and rather breathless crowd as he did this.

"Anybody know if my friend Shay is at home?"

"Yeah. He's at home," said one.

"He likes a quiet step," said the Kid, "because he says it's a sign of culture. A cultured fellow, is Billy Shay, you know. So I mustn't play bellwether when I go to call on him. I'll see you-all later on."

He walked across the street and through the front gate of Shay's house before the spectators realized, suddenly, what it was apt to mean.

Georgia phrased it in one gasping sentence.

"It's the fear of the Kid that's cornered Shay!"

3
Battle Royal

THE SAME IDEA came suddenly home to all of the watchers, and there was a stir and a bustle on the hotel veranda. Newcomers were running from either side to get to this natural grand stand.

"What about it, Lew?" asked Milman.

"I only got one thing to say," answered the sheriff dryly. "They both got only one life to give to their country, and they might as well do the giving today. Why, Milman, if you was to see a wasp and a hornet start a fight, which would you want to see win?"

This seemed the attitude of nearly all the watchers. They looked on with a smiling content.

"He don't know that they's half a dozen thugs in the house there with Shay," said one.

Georgia Milman grew excited.

"Lew, that ought to be stopped!" she declared to the sheriff.

"Because of the Kid's blue eyes, honey?" asked the grim sheriff. "No, ma'am. I ain't gunna stop it. If they was to blow the tar out of each other, it would simply save the State from lodgin' and boardin' 'em a good many years, or else usin' up a good rope to break their necks with."

Every one grew silent now. For the Kid had come to the porch of Shay's house, and was going swiftly up the steps. He went, not to the door, but to a window at one side.

There he worked for an instant.

It seemed to Georgia Milman that the windows of that house

11

were so many eyes, peering out at the stranger with serpentlike content.

"He's read the mind of that latch already," said the sheriff, for at that moment the Kid pushed the window up so softly that certainly no sound floated across to the people who waited and watched from the hotel.

"What are they doin' inside?" said some one.

"When you got a trap set, don't you wait for the critter to get inside before you spring it?" said another.

The Kid did not hesitate. The moment that the window was open he slipped inside—and then closed the window behind him.

They could see the glimmer of his raised hand and arm.

"He's latched it behind him!" gasped Georgia. "What possesses that madman?"

"Why, honey," said the sheriff, "he's as happy right now as you would be when you stepped into a dance hall and all the boys popped their eyes at you, and the music started up and you figgered that you had all of the other girls in that hall stopped four ways for Sunday. The Kid is just spreadin' his elbows at the board!"

There was not a sound from the house. The Kid had disappeared. The sun poured strongly and steadily down upon the roofs and raised from them a thin stream—the last moisture of the winter. Down the street rushed a whirlwind, white with circling dust. It passed rapidly, but the crowd on the veranda stirred and shifted uneasily and peered through the passing veil, as though they dreaded lest it might shut them off from some sight of importance.

But there was nothing to be seen. The house stood there, bald and open of face, with its windows black or bright in shadow or sun. The silence continued.

Said a voice: "Aw, it's a joke. Nothin' ain't gunna happen!"

And a whisper answered: "Shut up, you fool!"

For every one felt like whispering. The stillness in a church was noise, compared with this. Suspense drew every nerve taut. Georgia gripped the arm of her father; her face was cold, and by that she knew how pale she must be. Covertly she rubbed her cheeks and looked guiltily askance at the sheriff. He had prophesied that she would be interested in the Kid. She was ashamed even then of the depth of that interest.

She kept saying to herself over and over again: "He's just a bad one. He's no good. Everybody knows that he's no good!"

But the words had little meaning. They seemed to be brushed away by the bright beauty of the Duck Hawk, as the lovely mare lifted her head and listened to some far-off sound. She, it seemed, loved and trusted her master. Therefore he could not be all bad.

Then the silence of the Shay house was broken, and broken in no uncertain manner. Guns boomed hollowly and heavily within the walls, and a voice was heard screaming in pain, or fear, or both.

"Thunderation!" said the sheriff.

He burst through the crowd and started across the street, but Milman and two or three others grabbed him and pulled him back.

"You said the right thing before," said Milman. "It doesn't matter what happens to the rats in that den. We're not going to let you chuck a useful life away, Lew, old fellow."

"There's murder being done in there!" shouted the sheriff. "You fools, leave go of me, I'm gunna—"

"You're gunna stay here and stand quiet," said one of the men who held him. "If they's a murder in yonder, it'll be only a murderer that's killed! And what's the difference, as you was sayin' before?"

In spite of himself, the sheriff could not budge. He had to submit to the strong hands which restrained him.

The uproar in the house of Shay continued. Vaguely they could follow it. It seemed to dip from the first floor to the cellar. Then it climbed again.

Through the window by which the Kid had entered a man burst. Literally, he dived through.

He struck the porch, rolled headlong across it, and picked himself up from the ground. His face was a red mask, as he had been badly cut by the glass through which he had burst. Apparently he was half-blinded, for he stretched his hands out before him as he started running, and when he came to the side fence he collided heavily with it.

The blow knocked him down. He got up, climbed the fence, and ran on, out of sight.

"He's had enough," said the sheriff grimly. "That's Lefty Bud Gray. He's the one that killed Tucker and Langton on the Pecos. Governor Chalmers pardoned him—the fool!"

A frightful crashing and dashing now came from the second floor of the house as though furniture were being hurled about. Georgia Milman suddenly regained her breath and her color.

"Mother!" she whispered. "It's like seeing the rabbits come out when a weasel has gone down into the warren!"

Like rabbits, indeed!

And they came in a frantic haste! For now a door crashed at the back of the house, and an unseen man rushed out, screeching at the top of his voice.

The yells diminished as he turned a corner, but still they sounded, far off, floating like a wailing spirit in the air.

"I never seen nothin' like it!" said a puncher. "What's he done? Dynamited that old shack?"

Again the door at the back of the house slammed, and this time a double footfall could be heard rattling down the board walk at the rear.

The sounds of these fugitives diminished more quickly.

"That's four gone," said some one.

Silence came in the house of Shay.

And then, low at first, but more distinctly as their ears grew attuned to it, they could hear the groaning of a badly hurt man.

Mrs. Milman sagged suddenly on her daughter's arm, but Georgia caught her close.

"Steady, mother! Steady, dear!" said she. "It's not the Kid—I think!"

"That boy?" gasped Mrs. Milman. "Of course it's not he, but what's happening to the poor creatures in that house? That tiger —and those wretches who—"

At the very top of the house there was another wild outburst of gunshots, a continuous peal of them. Then the distinct sound of a door being slammed, and the dormer window from which the signal had flashed not long before was cast open.

Out at that opening slid the long, gaunt person of Billy Shay himself, and at this sight a whoop went up from the spectators across the street.

Billy was in a frightful haste. He acted as though he would die if he did not reach the ground.

He slid down the sharply shelving roof. There, at the eaves, he hung by his hands, swinging back and forth like a pendulum of a clock.

"Lemme go!" shouted the sheriff. "I gotta get there and—"

But still they held him helpless, for it seemed to all of those men a most foolish thing to risk such a life as the sheriff's in order to enforce the law among the lawless.

Billy Shay, twisting his legs in, got hold on a ledge below the eaves and climbed down like a great cat, reached the window beneath, and so down until he slid the length of one of the porch pillars.

He did not wait to look about him.

He fled across his barren garden with such speed that his long hair streamed out behind his head, and, reaching the fence at which the first man had had his fall, Billy Shay took it in his stride like a good hurdler, and twisted out of sight down the path beyond.

Once more silence fell upon the house of Shay, except for the dreadful groaning of the man on the first floor, as it seemed. A groan for every breath!

Then some one began to whistle, there in the attic of the place. The whistling grew dim, but still was distinguishable. It passed from the attic down to the second floor, and so down to the first.

There it stopped, and the groaning stopped, also.

"He's killed that poor devil" some one said between clenched teeth.

Georgia felt herself growing faint.

But now the front door of the house was opened, and out upon the porch stepped the Kid!

He stood there, teetering idly back and forth from heel to toe, while he made and lighted a cigarette, and then, smoking, he sauntered leisurely up the path.

At the gate he paused to remove the wedges from the bells at his heels, and as he crossed the street they clinked merrily in tune with every step he took making his way to the mare.

He gathered the reins.

"Billy had to go out, and couldn't wait for me, boys," said he. "Matter of fact, there was nobody home."

He swung into the saddle and added: "Except Three-card Alec. He was so glad to see me that he slipped coming down the stairs, and I'm mighty afraid that he's broken his leg. Any friend of his here to give poor Alec a hand?"

4
Davey Rides

Out of the town, as he had come into it, the Kid rode most leisurely. No one halted him; and only Tommy Malone asked him to have a drink.

He refused the drink, with apologies for the demands upon his time which made it impossible for him to linger, no matter how he wished to. But when he got farther down the street, a little freckle-faced boy of nine ran out into the street and shouted at him in a voice as thin and squeaking as the sound of a finger nail on a pane of glass. It was little Dave Trainor, "Chuck" Trainor's boy. Some of the neighboring women heard and saw what followed.

They watched, breathless. It was known that Trainor had made a lot of money in the mines recently, and it was more than possible that the terrible wild man, the Kid, might kidnap this child and hold him for ransom.

Old Betty Worth, who had fought Indians in her day, went so far as to get the old-fashioned Kentucky rifle, loaded with a bullet which contained an ounce of lead. This she rested on the corner of a window sill, and looking out through the branches of the honey-suckle vine, drew her bead and looked at the very heart of the Kid. At the first move he made, Betty was determined to shoot him dead. And she probably could have done it, for, even without a rest, she was known to have shot a squirrel out of a treetop only the year before.

The scene between the Kid and freckled young Dave Trainor progressed somewhat as follows:

16

"Hey!" yelled Davey.

"Hey!" yelled the Kid in return.

"Hello!" shouted Davey, waving.

"Hello!" shouted the Kid.

"Hey, wait a minute, will you?" said Davey.

"Sure I will," said the Kid.

He turned in the saddle. The mare, unguided, as it seemed, walked straight up to Davey and paused before him.

"Say, how did you make her do that?" asked Davey.

"Why, she reads my mind, most of the time," said the Kid.

"Golly!" said Davey; then added briskly: "Not that I believe you a dog-gone bit!"

"That's a mighty big word that you're saying," said the Kid.

"Yeah?" said dangerous Davey. "It's what I say, though. Are you the Kid?"

"That's what my friends call me," said the Kid.

"What's your real name?" demanded Davey.

How many a sheriff, deputy, editor, and hungry reporter in that wide and fair land would have been glad of an answer to that question.

"My real name depends on where I am," said the Kid. "You take one single, solitary name, it's hardly enough to spread over a lot of country the way that I live and travel."

"Why ain't it?" asked Davey, doubtful, but willing to be convinced.

"Well, south of the river the Mexicans like to hear a man called by a Spanish-sounding name."

"Like what?"

"Well, like Pedro Gonzales, say."

"Golly," said Davey, "anybody what called you a greaser name like that, you'd about eat them, I reckon!"

"Oh, no," said the Kid. "I hate trouble. That's why I change my name so much."

"Say why ag'in?"

"Why, to be a Spaniard with the Spanish, and a Mexican with the Mexicans. They used to call me Louis, up in Canada, when I was among the French Canadians."

"Didn't you punch them in the nose?" asked Davey candidly.

"Of course not. I was glad to have them take me in like that."

"What else are you called?" asked Davey.

"Oh, I've been called Johnson in Minnesota, and Taliaferro in Virginia, and a lot of other things. These States in our country are so big, old son, that a fellow has to have a lot of different names. What are you called, son?"

"Well, I'm like you," said Davey. "It depends on where I am. Over to the south side of town they just call me Red. I licked two of 'em last week for callin' me that, but still they call me Red. I don't care. I can stand it, I guess."

"I guess you can," said the Kid. "What's a name or two, anyway?"

"That's just the way that I look at it," said Davey. "I don't mind, and I get a chance to punch their heads once in a while. Down on the creek, all of the Banks boys—they got a great big place there, with the whangin'est swing that you ever see—they call me Freckles. When I ain't got a spot on my face compared to Turkey-egg Banks."

"Freckles is a good outstanding name," said the Kid.

"D'you think so? Well, they call me that, anyway, and they're all too big for me to lick."

"Are they? Maybe you'll grow to that, though."

"Yeah, maybe I will, but a Banks, he takes a pile of licking."

"Any other names?"

"Well, around here, they call me Slippy, account of me being hard to catch at tag. They's a lot that can run faster, but I get through their fingers, somehow."

"Slippy is a good name, too. I never heard a better flock of names than you carry, partner. Any more?"

"They call me Davey, during the school term, a lot of 'em."

"Yeah. That's a good name, too. Any others?"

"Pa calls me Snoops—I dunno why. There don't seem to be much meaning to it. Ma calls me David when she's feelin' good, and David Trainor when I ain't brought in the wood, or wore my rubbers on rainy days, or things like that."

"Well, Davey Trainor," said the Kid, "I'm mighty glad to meet you, sir."

"The same goes by me," said Davey.

He reached up and shook hands.

"Is it straight talk," said Davey, "that you can do all of them things?"

"What things?" asked the Kid.

"I mean, that you can shoot a sparrow right out of the air? There's one now up there on that telephone wire! And I suppose that you got a gun with you?"

The Kid looked at the sparrow, shook his head, and then

snatched out the revolver. As it exploded, the sparrow flirted off the wire and dipped into the air, leaving a few little, translucent feathers which fluttered slowly down to the earth—slowly, since they were not much heavier than the air through which they fell.

The Kid put up the heavy Colt revolver with a single flashing movement.

"You see, that's one thing that I can't do," said he.

"Golly, but you knocked feathers out of it, and you didn't take no sight nor nothin'."

"That was only a lucky shot," said the Kid. "Don't you pay any attention to people who talk about shooting sparrows at any sort of a good distance, Davey."

"What happened to the gun?"

"Why it went back home, where it lives."

Davey laughed.

"You're mighty slick, all right," said he. "Can the mare do everything, too?"

"Like what?"

"Come when she's called?"

"Yes."

"Walk on her hind legs?"

"Yes."

"Open a barn door?"

"Yes, if it's only to lift the latch and give a pull."

"Lie down when you tell her to?"

"Yes."

"Sit down, too?"

"Yes."

"Kneel for you to get on?"

"Yes."

"Golly," said the boy, "that's an awful lot. I can't hardly think of no more things for a hoss to do. What else can she do?"

"Oh, she can do a lot of things besides. She has brains, son. She thinks for herself right along, and she does a lot of thinking for me, too."

"Like what, Kid?"

"Why, like telling me if we're crossing a bad bridge."

"Can she tell that?"

"Yes, she can smell that. She's got a nose like a wolf. And I can sleep out, with her for company as safely as though I had the sense of a wolf myself. She reads everything that crosses her wind."

"My golly, my golly," said Davey Trainor, almost bitterly, "it must make you pretty tired to have to spend time with most folks, whan you got a hoss like that to be with."

"Yes," said the Kid soberly, "most people make me pretty tired, unless they have plenty of names."

"You wouldn't want to do something for me?"

"Why not? You've got about as many names as I have."

"Well, would you let me see her do something?"

"Of course I will. You tell me what."

"Well, make her stand up on her hind legs."

Davey could not hear or see a command or a sign, but the mare presently heaved up, her forehoofs flipping close to Davey's face.

Down rocked the mare again.

"Golly!" said Davey. "What else can she do? She's wonderful, ain't she? Could I touch her?"

"I'll ask her," said the Kid with gravity.

He leaned and murmured, or appeared to murmur, in the ear of the Duck Hawk, at which she reached out with a sudden snaky movement and plucked Davey by the ragged forelock, sun-faded to the color of burned grass.

"Hold on!" said the rider, keeping his eye fast on the boy's face. And Davey had not altered a trifle in color. He merely set his teeth and then grinned.

"Would you like to ride her?" asked the Kid suddenly.

"Why? But nobody but you has ever been on her back!" cried out Davey.

"You're there now," said the Kid.

He whispered something in the ear of the mare and rubbed her muzzle. And then young Davey rode the terrible fleet mare of the Kid across the road. She slid over the fence, unexpectedly, but as smooth as running water, and turning in the field beyond, she floated back across the fence again and halted beside her master.

"Now you know what she's like," said the Kid.

"Golly," said the boy, "now I know what heaven's like."

5
Three-card Stumbles

THE WATCHING population of Dry Creek had moved across the street to the house of Billy Shay.

It was not merely an interest in the welfare of the wounded man who had been groaning inside the place, but rather an inescapable curiosity to be on the site of the Kid's latest exploits. They were anxious to pick up first-hand details with which to furnish the stories which each and all of them would one day find an opportunity of telling to strangers.

In the Far West there is one thing which is more fabulously valuable then gold, even. And that is a story, whether it be truth or good, true-sounding fiction. Stories in the West are of two varieties. The first is the openly and the humorously exaggerated. These are not greatly considered except when they are really funny. But the staple Western story is one which clings so closely to the truth throughout most of its telling, that the embroidering of the main truth with fancy in the vital point of the tale will be overlooked by the listener. If only one shot is fired, there is no good reason why two Indians, Mexicans, or thugs should not be in line with its flight; but the narrator is sure to express astonishment before he tries to arouse yours, and he will carefully explain, with a false science, just how the odd position came about. There is the story-teller who never speaks in his own person, too. All of his stories begin, end, and are supported in the middle by "they say." "They" of "they say" is a strange creature. It has the flight of a falcon and the silent wings of a bat; it speaks the language of the birds and bees; it can follow the snake down the deepest hole, and then glide like a magic ray through a thousand feet of solid rock; it can penetrate invisibly into houses through the thickest walls, in order to see strange crimes; it can step through the walls of the most secretive mind in order to read strange thoughts. "They" has the speed of lightning, and leaps here and there to pick up grains of information, like a chicken picking up worms in a newly turned garden; "they" throws a girdle around the world in a fortieth of Puck's boasted time. Those who quote "they," who quote and follow and mystically adore and believe in "they," sometimes do so with awe-stricken whispers, but there are some who sneer at their authority, and shrug their shoulders at the very stories they relate. Such people, when questioned, yawn and shake their heads.

"I dunno. That's what 'they' say."

You can take your choice. Believe it or not. Most people choose to believe, and therefore the rare information of "they," thrice, yes, and thirty times watered and removed, is repeated over and over until it becomes a mist as tall as the moon and as thin as star dust.

There were gossips of every school in the crowd that poured into Shay's house. The moment that they drew open the front door, they found a scene which was interesting enough to charm them all.

The furniture which first had been piled against the door to secure this point against the entrance of the Kid, was now cast helter-skelter back against the walls. Much of it was broken. The legs of chairs seemed knocking together, or else they bowed perilously out. And one chair, as if it had taken wings, had become entangled in the good, strong chains which suspended the hall lamp near the door. For this was a very pretentious house.

Some strong hand had flung that chair!

No wonder that chairs had been thrown, though. For the ceiling, the floor, the walls, were ripped and plowed by many bullets. It looked as though half a dozen cartridge belts had been emptied here alone.

And at the foot of the stairs lay "Three-card" Alec, who no longer groaned, but had braced himself with his shoulders on the lower stair. His right leg extended before him with a painful crookedness, but he had a cigarette between his fingers, and he was smoking with deep, almost luxurious breaths, his eyes half closed. For "the makin's" is a greater thing in the West than whisky, chewing tobacco, and chloroform all rolled into one.

The crowd, entering, looked about with awe at that wrecked and ruined hallway. Turning, they could stare straight through the front wall of the house and see the little, white, round patches of daylight that streamed through the bullet holes. A long strip of plaster, loosened by raking shots from the ceiling of the hall, fell now with a noisy crash.

Some people grew afraid, and would not enter the place, even with such a crowd. There was a baneful influence still in the air, and the odor of gunpowder was severe in every room and hall from the cellar to the attic.

"Is there anybody else in the house?" asked the sheriff of the gambler.

"Say, whadya think?" replied Three-card Alec sneeringly.

The sheriff went on by him.

So did every one else, waiting for the "other fellow" to take charge of the hurt man. The "other fellow" is well nigh as ubiquitous and certainly of far better character than "they."

No one went near poor Three-card Alec to help him, until Georgia Milman squatted beside him and looked into his narrow, beady, winking, uncertain eyes.

Three-card looked like a bird—and a very bad bird, at that. His nose was long enough to make a handle for his whole face. Behind it his face receded toward the hair and toward the chin. The latter feature hardly mattered, and the face flowed smoothly, with hardly a ripple, into the throat. Three-card had two big buckteeth. Like all buckteeth, they were kept scrupulously white, but they looked, somehow, like the upper part of a parrot's beak. His mouth was generally half open, and he had the look of being about to give something a good hard peck. Three-card had little, overbright, shifty eyes; and he had a yellowish skin, and on his receding brow there were a maze of lines of trouble, pain, greed and envy. His body was as bad as his face, for it was starved, crooked, hollow-chested, weak-backed, humped, skinny, and generally half deformed. His only redeeming feature was his hands, and these were beautiful objects for even a casual eye to rest upon. They were graceful, long, slender and white—which proved that they were kept scrupulously gloved except when there was a need of them in action. Those delicate and nervous hands of Three-card were in fact his fortune, whether they were employed with cards, dice, the handle of a knife, or on the grip of a revolver. Three-card was only a wicked caricature of a man. There was hardly any good about him, but he had been brave as he was wicked, and therefore he was respected in a certain way.

Georgia merely said: "Is it pretty bad?"

For reply he stared at her and puffed on his cigarette again. There was no decent courtesy in Three-card.

"Do you want any special doctor? Doctor Dunn has his office just across the street, you know," said Georgia.

Three-card deigned to speak.

"I wouldn't let that crook mend a sick canary for me, leave alone put a hand on my leg. That leg is bust. I'll have Doc Wilton or nobody."

Georgia pulled out of the passing file of the curious a sun-burned young cow-puncher. His nose was toasted raw, which always makes young men appear cross but honest.

"Sammy, you go and get Doc Wilton like a good fellow," said Georgia.

The face of Sammy fell at least a block. He was enjoying this battle site. But Georgia was not a girl to be refused. With a sigh, Sammy departed for the doctor, and Georgia impressed four more men to carry Three-card into the little adjoining room, while she gingerly, with a white face and compressed lips, supported the broken leg. She had him put on a table, and placed a cushion under his head. She borrowed a whisky flask from another puncher and gave Three-card a good swig of it. She wiped the sweat of pain from his face. She unloosed the shirt at his throat. With unexpected skill, she rolled another cigarette for him and lighted it.

"You're a bit of all right," said Three-card, his bird eyes glittering at her suddenly in an unwinking stare, like that of a hawk.

"Are you comfortable? More comfortable, I mean."

Three-card closed his eyes. He did not answer, but began to chuckle softly.

"You wouldn't 'a' believed," said he. "I guess that he never pulled the trigger."

Georgia looked at the smashed window glass at the end of the room.

"You don't mean the Kid?" she said.

"Don't I?" snarled Three-card.

Then he seemed to remember that she had been kind.

"Yeah, that's who I mean," said he.

She tried to understand, but her mind whirled. With her own eyes she had seen the results of the explosion which occurred when the Kid had entered this house. She had seen men hurled out from it through windows and doors as if dynamite were bursting within.

"What did he use, if not a gun?" she asked.

"He used his bean," said Three-card.

This answer he seemed to think sufficient, and he nodded in satisfaction.

"Aces will always take tricks," said Three-card. "He was all full of aces."

He chuckled again. He seemed to forget his own predicament.

"He was always in the next room," said Three-card. "I wasn't proud. I went down into the cellar, but the cellar window was too narrow to squeeze out."

"Did the Kid follow you down there?" asked the girl.

She tried to make the picture bright in her mind, of the terrified men in the cellar, and the fear of the Kid upon them.

"All he done was to open the door at the head of the stairs and wait!" said Three-card, still chuckling in admiration of his enemy's maneuvers. "Somebody said that he was gunna throw a can of oil down and a lighted match after it. Then we charged up those stairs and crushed out through the doorway—and found that he wasn't in the upper hall at all! Then we bolted for the upstairs, because it seemed like the Kid was always just about gunna step through an open door and start shooting."

She caught her breath. She understood that nightmare fear which had possessed all in the house.

"On the way up I heard a sound. I looked back. I was the last of the bunch going up, and there was the Kid in the hall right at the foot of the stairs, with his gun ready. I pulled mine and turned to shoot, and just fell down the stairs and busted my leg. The Kid goes on up. Hell busts wide open all over the house. Pretty soon there's quiet. Down comes somebody walking, whistling. It's the Kid. He stops and makes me a cigarette.

" 'Hard luck, Three-card,' says he."

Three-card paused. He looked into the face of the girl.

"You'd 'v' liked to see," said Three-card.

"Yes," said Georgia beneath her breath. "I would!"

6
Watching

THE KID had stopped with red-headed Davey Trainor long enough to give him a ride on the Duck Hawk. Then he brought from one of his pockets a small knife. It had three blades of the finest steel, which he displayed and illustrated their uses. Then he mounted.

Davey stood by him, bending back his head and looking up at the picture of the hero against the blue sky.

"You wouldn't be comin' back here one of these days?" he asked.

"Sure I would," said the Kid. "Don't you be forgetting me."

"Me?" said Davey. "Golly, I should say not. So long, Kid."

"So long," said the Kid.

Then he took off his hat and waved it toward the window of a neighboring house, over which honeysuckle vines descended in a thick shower.

"Ma'am," said he, "you've been aiming too low."

With this he rode off down the street whistling.

Old John Dale saw him go by, with the Duck Hawk cake-walking in time and rhythm with the whistled tune. They seemed to be having a gay time of it, these two.

They crossed the bridge over the creek, and there they were seen by the Warner boys, Paul and Ned, who were fishing off the old ruined landing which had been built there in the placer days. They both got up and shouted—regardless of spoiling their fishing prospects for the rest of the morning. And the Kid turned in his saddle and waved down to them. He seemed in the highest and most childishly gay spirits, for he made the Duck Hawk rear so that she stood with her forehoofs resting on the edge rail which guarded the bridge.

That rail was made of old and time-rotted wood, and the boys held their breath at this madness of the Kid's.

Then he whirled the Duck Hawk away, and with a wave of his hand he disappeared, taking the Langton Trail through the hills.

That trail the Kid followed until after noon. By this time he had climbed the trail to a height above Dry Creek. He paused at a point where the trail looped out around the shoulder of a hill, so that he had a clean view of the path for a distance, going and coming. Moreover, this was a spot from which he could survey all the country lying back toward Dry Creek.

He watered the mare at a small creek, which had been one of his reasons for pausing there, and then he took out a pair of field glasses and first picked out the northerly hills, the mountains behind them, finally moving his view down again to Dry Creek, and its shining windows.

He smiled a little when he saw this town, as though of itself it were something of a joke; then he shifted his view out into the desert, lingering his eye along the smoky foliage of the draws, and particularly studying certain dust clouds which, by careful observation, he discovered were not wind pools, but clouds in slow motion toward Dry Creek.

There were three of these dust clouds. They might be riders, freighters, almost anything. Carefully estimating distances from point to point, away out there on the plain, he then timed each of the three dust clouds across certain stretches.

This had to be inaccurate work, for he could not estimate with any surety the distances over which the clouds were passing. Yet he knew that those draws were of about such and such dimensions. He could see, also, that two of the dust clouds slanted back, and one rose straight up like smoke from a chimney on a windless day.

He decided that the two slanting clouds were made of horsemen traveling either at a fast trot or at a gallop. The other dust cloud might be either quite a large party with their horses at a walk, or, more probably, it was the sweating team and the rumbling wagon of a freighter.

He put up his glasses and looked more intimately around him. This was the sort of country that he loved. It was neither the eye-hurting sweep of the dusty desert, nor the damp gloom of the great forests. It was a broken sweep of hills, pouring away in a pleasant variety of shapes, and dressed with patches of high shrubbery and low, while the forest proper was chiefly confined to the gulleys and the ravines between the hills. In such a region as this there were a thousand cattle trails weaving through the maze of hills; there were ten thousand modes of being lost in every ten miles of travel. It was a place where one needed to know the lay of the land, and have under one a good horse, with sure footing and a wise way of taking the ups and downs of a hill journey. The Kid knew this region well, and he had a wise horse beneath him, that knew how to take the constantly recurring slopes easily, but at a brisk walk, with a trot on the summit, and a break into a rolling lope on the downward slope, moving all the time so softly that there was no danger of battering shoulders to pieces. Such a horse can cover not twice, but three times as much ground as an animal not accustomed to the hill country.

But though the Kid knew this country well, he did not know it well enough to suit him. He never knew any stretch of land well enough. Nothing could exhaust the patient, the almost passionate interest with which he studied a landscape in detail. The position of every tree might be worth knowing, if he had time to get down to the most minor details.

This was almost his profession. The thick roll of his memory could unfold a scroll which was an endless map of desert, rolling plain, hills, mountains, wilderness of trees, the courses of rivers, the sites and the street maps of towns, dottings of ranches and ranch houses, intimate details of confused trails.

Like a hawk, when he flew into a new region, he first flew high, and from the summits of the high places he charted the lower regions with an exquisite precision. The result was that hardly any district could be strange to him for more than a day, and he had amazed certain ardent pursuers, over and over again, by his ability to disappear from under their very noses in a region where they knew, or thought they knew, every gopher hole.

So the Kid, as the mare grazed eagerly on the fine grass of that hillside, with the saddle and the bridle both removed, looked carefully and lovingly over this landscape. There were many creeks where one could find water, and by those creeks

were many dense thickets where man and horse could hide—
particularly a horse taught to lie down in time of need.

There were high points for spying in this landscape, and
there were crooked and straight ways across the country. That
is, there were safe and leisurely ways, and there were short
trails which condensed many miles of distances into a certain
amount of eerie twisting through ravines and flirting with preci-
pices.

All in all, he felt that this district was made for him. It was
"home" to the Kid.

He had other homes, of course, but they were not quite so
satisfactory for many reasons.

He took out his lunch. It consisted of a ration which an Arab
would have known and appreciated. That is to say, his food was
simply dates and old, stale, tough bread. A morsel of bread, a
morsel of date, he chewed them slowly, with the enjoyment of a
hungry man, for already he had ridden far on this day.

When he had finished his lunch, which was a meager one
even for such simple fare, he drank from the cold water of the
creek, and then sat beside it for a time watching the rippling
shadows which flickered over the sandy bottom, or the flash
and paling of the sun upon a quartz pebble.

It did not take a great deal to interest the Kid. He never had
found a desert so thoroughly devoid of life that it was dull to
him. Now, when he turned from the gazing at the creek, it was
to watch the arduous way of an ant through the grass, lugging
with it the head of a beetle twice its own size and four times its
own weight. Ten times the head fell as the Kid watched. Ten
times the ant picked up the burden and pushed ahead, forcing
between narrow blades and climbing then up and then down,
like a monkey struggling with a vast weight through an endless
forest.

Eight feet away lay the nest which was the goal! To the ant it
was eight miles of fearful labor.

A light, quick stamp of a hoof made the Kid look up to the
Duck Hawk, to find her standing alert, with tail arching into the
wind, and ears pricked.

The Kid did not delay. He slid bridle and saddle onto her
with practiced speed, and, running hastily down the trail, he
came to a rocky stretch, turned up among the rocks until he
came to a thick place of shrubbery and trees which perfectly
concealed him and the mare.

Here he waited, and after a time, sure enough, from down the trail, traveling south, he heard first the distant ring of an iron-shod hoof, striking against hard rock, and then the faint snort of a horse. Such sounds grew nearer and nearer, and around the corner of the mountain rode a man on a fine gelding of the mustang type, with two lead horses behind him.

This man carried a short-barreled repeating rifle, or carbine, which he balanced across the pommel of his saddle. He had two saddle holsters, from which the butts of revolvers appeared, and a capacious cartridge belt girded him.

On each of the two led horses there were small packs, but these were so light that it was obvious that he was using them as extra mounts rather than as pack animals.

The man himself was what one might call the true Western type; that is to say, he was tall, rather bony and thin from much exercise, and little fat from leisure. He had one of those thin, dark faces which one often sees, with a truly grand forehead, wide and high, and a little puckering at the corners of his mouth which made him appear to be smiling a great part of the time. But smiling he was not, as one could guess by a second glance.

This fellow was forty years old, with a back straight as an arrow, a head carried like a king, and a glance as bright as the Kid's own.

The latter smiled a little and watched with careful attention until the other reached that point along the trail where the Kid had lunched and where the mare had grazed.

The instant he came to these signs the rider slumped lower in the saddle, and tightening the reins, he slipped the carbine under his arm and whirled his horse about, scanned the rocks and the trees near him with the eagerness of a hawk and something of a hawk's hungry and fierce manner.

He seemed to content himself a little with this first survey, and then jumped from his saddle to the ground and carefully examined the grass that had been trampled down by his predecessor. By the movement of it, as it gradually was rising, he seemed able to tell that his forerunner had been there a very short time ago indeed. Therefore he straightened again, and scanned all that was around him suspiciously. Finally he leaped into the saddle again, and went on a tour of inspection.

7
Treed

WHAT WIND was blowing carried straight from the man hunter to the man.

Therefore the Kid carried out an experiment in which he could use the intelligence and the obedience of the Duck Hawk. He turned the head of the mare toward a gap in the brush to the rear, and through this, as he waved his hand, she went at once.

The noise she made was very slight. She walked like a cat, picking out her way. For horses who have lived a wild life where there is any amount of shrubbery and trees either learn the ways of silence or die young. Mountain lions are excellent schoolmasters in all such lessons. So the Duck Hawk went off with very little noise, and the wind which stirred was sufficiently strong to cover these slight noises of retreat.

Getting well beyond the patch of trees in which her master remained, she looked back to him, pausing, but he waved her on until she had walked over the brow of the hill, and disappeared.

Now that the mare was out of view, the Kid set about his own maneuvers. He could see that the stranger was skirting rapidly along the back trail which the Kid had made; and, in the course of the next minute, he was certain to arrive on the spot where they had made covert in the brush.

He decided this, and then slipped ahead for a few paces along the trail of the mare until he came to a good-sized tree. He swung into the branches and a dozen feet above the ground he stretched himself along a big limb.

31

It was so narrowed that it could not pretend to cover the width of his body. Without an instant's hesitation, he twisted himself around it like a snake. By the very strangeness of its posture, this body of his suddenly seemed unrelated to human-kind. By heel and arm and knee he clung in this difficult posi-tion. It would have exhausted another man in a few seconds; but the Kid had the strength and suppleness of a monkey. So he clung there, until he saw the fine, reaching head of the mustang come through the brush, and above it appeared the stranger, bent well forward, to study the fresh sign of the Duck Hawk.

At the place of covert, he remained only for an instant, then headed on. He had the look of something indescribably wild and wise as he bent above the hoof marks, reading them. The puckering at the corners of the mouth had increased into a greater resemblance of a smile, and the eyes of the Kid nar-rowed a little as he watched. It was an odd thing to see a man who acted so like a beast of prey. It gave him a fierce satisfac-tion to know that he was hunting the hunter.

The head of the stranger was down, but the keen mustang, when it was almost under the tree, noted something strange about the twisting branch overhead and looked up. That instant the Kid dropped.

Had the horseman been directly underneath, the matter would have been simple. As it was, he had to swing himself forward with his hands just as the horse shied. The rider jerked up his head at the same moment in time to meet the flying danger, but though his hand licked down for a revolver as fast as the dart of a snake's tongue, he was knocked headlong from the saddle.

Falling, he twisted in mid-air, to land on his hands and feet. But hands as strong as they were scientific gripped him and jerked him over on his back with a half nelson. Flattened out by superior weight and might, he stared at the young face above him.

"Hullo, Champ," said the Kid.

"Hullo, Kid," said Champ.

His eyes burned green, but he kept his voice as steady as the regular flowing of a river.

"I didn't reckon that the trees are shakin' down this kind of nuts this time of the year," said Champ.

"Lucky that I landed in good hands," said the Kid. "You haven't been hurt much by the tumble, Champ?"

"No," said the other. "Not a bit."

"Don't feel nervous?"

"No, I feel pretty calm," said Champ.

"All right," said the Kid. "I'll get up, then."

"Sure," said Champ. "Whenever you say."

The Kid, therefore, arose, moving cautiously and keeping a close eye upon the older man, who then got up in the same manner. They watched one another with an intense devotion and application. In spite of the quiet manner of his speech, those burning eyes of Champ and the strange puckering smile on his lips showed that he was close to violent action of some sort.

Yet he restrained himself. Sometimes there was a decided flutter and trembling in his right hand as it hung near the handle of his Colt, but the weapon remained undrawn.

"I didn't know that you were looking for me," said the Kid.

He whistled sharply, repeating the note twice. The mare, from a distance, whinnied.

At this the other nodded.

"She's more'n a hoss. She's a partner, that Duck Hawk," he declared.

"Aye, she's a partner."

"I wasn't looking for you. I was looking to see who had took to the tall timber when I hove in sight down the trail."

"Was that it?"

"Yeah."

The Kid nodded, smiling pleasantly.

In a way these frontiersmen were like excellent and long-trained actors, so perfect were their simulations. It began to be obvious that Champ had put away ideas of violent action for the moment, at the least.

"I just got off the trail to let a stranger pass," said he.

"Yeah?" queried Champ.

"I'll tell you how it is," said the Kid. "I'm a mighty shy sort of a fellow, Champ. I don't know that I'm very interested in having a flock of people move by and look me over. Besides, it takes a lot of time to exchange gossip on the trail. It makes the Hawk restless, too!"

He smiled a little as he said this, removing thereby all air of naïveté that might have adhered to his words.

"I understand," said Champ, and suddenly he smiled in turn. "I don't like to rub elbows with all the common bums on the trail either. Suppose that we go back and pick up my two hosses that I dropped there?"

"All right," said the Kid. "You've got a good outfit of horseflesh with you, Dixon."

"Aye," said Champ Dixon, "they're good enough to raise a mite of dust along the way. You need three when you're making long marches."

He looked up at the tree from which the Kid had fallen upon him.

"There ain't a branch there that would hide a squirrel," said he.

"I didn't hide," said the Kid. "I just sort of twisted myself out of shape around that branch there."

He pointed over his shoulder without turning his head, and Champ Dixon smiled and nodded again.

"You been among trees before," he announced. "There's a good many that are desert-wise and mountain foolish, but I reckon that you been around a while. There comes the Hawk, and a beauty she is, old son."

The Duck Hawk came up the trail with her lovely head carried high and her eyes shining toward her master, as though she inquired about the nature of this odd game in which he had been using her.

"I've got to eat," said Dixon. "You've had chuck already?"

"Yes."

"Come back and pass the time of day with me, then."

"I don't mind if I do."

They went back to the same spot which had been used by the Kid beside the stream. The horses grazed in a cluster on the good grass, and now a sleepy, dreamy content seemed to come over the Kid. He stretched himself out with his back against a rock.

Champ Dixon was eating parched corn and jerked beef with powerful and patient jaws.

"You've a fondness for climbin' game, I reckon?" asked Champ.

"Well," said the Kid, after a moment of lazy thought, "I'll tell you how it is. There's a fellow I met who said that one night he heard you talking about me, and talking sort of carelessly and free and easy. Well, that's all right."

"Who was the man that said I talked about you?" demanded Champ with a decisive click of his teeth.

"Who was it? Well, I dunno that I remember. I dunno that I'd ought to remember."

"Fools that repeat, they make a lot of trouble, because they always repeat wrong, and dead wrong, too!"

"They do," said the Kid seriously.

"They cause a lot of killings."

"They do," said the Kid in the same manner.

"And if you'll tell me the name of the seven-mile liar that said that I—"

"Well," answered the Kid, "I dunno that I'll tell you even now. Even if what he said was true, it don't make so much matter. I know how it is when a fellow comes in off a long trail and puts a few slugs of redeye between wind and water. It makes him feel strong. He thinks that he can carry half the world on his upper deck—and all the time the poor fool is simply sinking."

At this comparison, Champ Dixon broadly grinned.

"I wouldn't mind telling you," said he, "that a fellow come to me and said that he'd heard you say that Dixon was a worn-out old man and that it was about time that somebody had ought to brush him off the trail, and that you wouldn't much mind the job."

"Did I say that?" asked the Kid of himself.

He stared at a white, translucent cloud in the zenith, but got no answer whatsoever from it.

"I'll tell you how it is, Champ," said he. "A man says a lot of foolish things that he doesn't remember. But if I were sober and in my right head, I'd never say such a thing. I know that I've never felt such a way about you."

"You haven't?" barked Champ Dixon.

"No."

There was a pause, during which the pair of them stared earnestly at one another.

"Look here," said Dixon. "They say that you don't lie."

"Yes," said the Kid. "It's true that I don't lie."

"Then I'm to believe that you never were out after me, Kid?"

"That's right. I never was."

Champ Dixon suddenly sprang to his feet.

"Then I'm gunna let light into a couple of grand liars!" he said. "Kid, I've thought that you been after me for a year. Here's my hand, and a weight off of my mind, too!"

8

A Great Business

When they had shaken hands, Dixon acted like a man who is breathing a different air. "The dirty dog that told me—" he began.

"Don't tell me his name," said the Kid. He raised his hand and shook his head firmly. "I'll tell you, Champ, that a man has enough trouble in the world without asking for it."

"But what about a man that goes around telling lies about you?"

"Suppose that I started out to kill every man who is telling lies about me, old-timer?"

"Aye, that's true. But the sneaking—"

"Of course. Well, I'll tell you, Dixon, a fellow who hasn't any permanent home address is pretty likely to have stories told about him, a good deal. You can't expect to steal eggs and pass the plate, Dixon."

Champ Dixon chuckled.

"Morrison was telling me that you was this way," he observed. "I couldn't hardly believe it, until I set right here and hear you talk! You act, Kid, as though the people that set fast inside of towns was all good and that the fellows on the road was all bad."

The Kid shrugged his shoulders.

"Why, they're a flock of throat-cutting hypocrites, and you oughta know it!" exclaimed Champ. "Out here on the open road—look how it is! You and me have put a year's trouble straight in a coupla seconds."

"That may be true," said the Kid.

"Besides, most of the fellows that are ridin' long and sleepin' short, they have been drove out of society by the meanness of other men, and not because they wanted to go wrong."

"I've heard a lot about that," said the Kid. "I don't believe much in it."

"I'll tell you my own case," said the other. "I was doin' fine. I had as slick a little ranch as you ever seen. I was follerin' the letter of the law. It was down on the Pecos—it was away off down there. It was a good little old ranch, I'm telling you."

His hard, bright, overwise eyes softened. He dreamed about the happier past for an instant.

"I get me a wife, and the cows are running fine and fat, and everything is what I want it to be, and then along comes Pi Jefford and wants my land, and I won't sell it, and so he gets hold of that long-drawn-out skunk, that Dick Origen, and paid him a reward too for rustling every head of stock that I had on my place. I go bust, the bank gets my ground. Pi Jefford gets the place from the bank, and my wife, she figures that it's a dead waste of time for her to stick with a fellow as down and out as me. All inside of a week I was flat on my face. Why? Because I'd done something wrong? No, but because there was a great crook that pretended to go straight, and that lived inside of the law, and he wanted me out of the way. Well, the world owed me something after that, by my way of figuring, so I've gone and taken it."

The Kid nodded.

He made himself a cigarette, and smoked it with thoughtful care.

"Look here, Champ," he said.

"Aye? What is it?"

"Well, it's this way," the Kid continued. "You liked your life back there on the ranch?"

"That was life, Kid. Making things grow, and—"

"And round-up was a great time?"

"The best times that I ever saw!"

"Champ, I don't think that you mean it. I'd like to make you remember the time that you blew the safe of the First National in Carnedas, according to the story that Bill Jackson told me of that night."

"I remember that night."

Soft laughter brooded upon the lips and the throat of Dixon.

"That was a night, old son!"

"Did you ever have such a good night on the old ranch?"

Champ started to speak, changed his mind, and stared fixedly in front of him.

"Did you ever have so much fun in any twenty days and nights on your ranch," persisted the Kid.

Still Champ did not answer, and the Kid, apparently taking this silence as a confession, went on:

"There was no cruel sheriff that drove me out on the road, Champ. Nobody ever cheated or gypped or short-changed, robbed or beat me in any way."

"Hard times can rub through men's patience," declared poor Champ.

"Hard times didn't bother me, either," said the Kid. "I had enough money. My family is a good family. I could walk on Persian rugs and drink tea at four thirty every afternoon and sun myself with the pearls and paste of the opera boxes at night. But that stuff didn't appeal to me. There's too much dressing up and not enough places to go."

Champ regarded his friend with tightened lips and tightened eyes.

"Where can you go out here except from sunstroke into chilblains? What have you got here except a raw neck and an aching back, and dirt, dirt and more dirt? By heck, sometimes I almost think, Kid, that I'd chuck it all for the sake of living next door to a tin bathtub and a good supply of hot water all the time. This is a hard life."

"Yeah," said the Kid. "It's a hard life for those who don't like it. But let them have their soft rugs and deep beds and smart talk. I prefer to shoot my meat, cook it, and eat it. They get the pleasure of being together. I get the pleasure of being alone. They learn how other people live and imitate them. I learn how horses and wild cats live, and imitate them. They're inside the laws. I'm outside the laws. I'm above the laws, Champ. I kick the law in the face, because it doesn't walk on my level."

He yawned and stretched his arms.

"That sounds pretty fat-headed," said he. "Well, I don't mean it that way. I only mean to tell you that I've never gone home since the day I left, and I'll never go home if I live to be a thousand. I've cut myself away from 'em. I've buried my old name. And I'm free as a lark, old son!"

He laughed as he said that, the purest joy in life welling and bubbling in his throat, so that Champ grinned and nodded in return.

"You're all out by yourself, Kid," he remarked. "I've heard it before, and I believe it, now. You haven't even thrown in the sunsets, and the mountain air, and such stuff. I was afraid that you were going to be poetic."

"I knew you were," said the Kid, "and so I went soft on that pedal."

"Where've you been?"

"I've been down south with Juan Gil, the Portuguese in Yucatan. Very hot. Even gold melts down there."

He yawned again.

"You got some, I hope?"

"Yeah, I got some. I loaded a pack mule with what I got."

"Of gold?"

"Yeah. It was everything that Juan Gil had taken out of an old mine down there. Good, patient sort of boy, Juan is!"

"You caught him out?"

"One night he tried to knife me. You see, he thought I wouldn't be needed any more."

"What did you do to him?"

"Well, I pulled down the heads of two saplings and tied him to them. When they jumped up into the air again, they didn't pull him in two but they stretched him a good deal. I left him up there close to the sky, and took away his mules and the gold. Juan cried a good deal to see me go. But he was taken down that day with nothing worse than a few bones broken."

"You don't seem to be traveling very heavy now."

"It's a long way from Yucatan," said the Kid. "You wouldn't have me go all the way without stopping?"

"No. I bet you even threw roses on the desert, eh?"

"I threw a few," said the Kid, complacently. "Even Old Mexico City blushed a couple of times on account of me. And that's a habit that I thought the old town had forgotten a couple of hundred years ago. What have you been doing?"

"I've been selling some mining stock," said Champ Dixon. "It goes pretty well, too, if I can get far enough east. But lately the blamed sheriffs and their deputies have been pretty thick. So I've started in on a new game."

"What's that?"

"Jumping water rights."

"That's nothing new."

"Not new. All the better for that. It's a game that's been tried out and practiced until a fellow can learn all of its dodges."

"Like it?"

"Why not? It's exciting."

"What do you do?"

"Look around through the ranches, and find out the ones that have shaky titles. Why, most of them have, for that matter. They've got their land from the Indians, first of all, or from some old Spanish grant, perhaps, or a Mexican under a law that never was a law, or from some old-timer who never had any claim to the ground in the first place. We look around, Shay and me, and we pick out the likely ranches, and then jump in and claim and start to homestead on the best water on the ranch. Take most of those places back there where the big Milman ranch is, there's not more than one good stream to the ranch. You grab that creek, and they've gotta buy water rights from neighbors, if they can, and drive the cows a darn long march to get a drink; or else they cannot wait to go to the law, but they can shoot it out with you. Maybe they drop you, and then they have a chance to be hung for murder. Maybe they're dropped. And then it's a case of the poor homesteader defending his rights."

As the beauty of this business came home to Champ Dixon, he chuckled through his teeth again, and drew in a long breath.

"If they go to the law, Shay has got one of the slickest lawyers that you ever seen, and a lot of crooks that knows how to make evidence. Shay has got men that could remember the length of Noah's whiskers. They'll swear to anything. So if the trial comes off one chance in two, we win anyway. And the poor sucker of a rancher has to pay through the nose, and we live on the fat. Why, old son, it's the very kind of a life for you!"

Suddenly he stopped, and grew red. For he saw that the Kid was watching him intently, and without a smile.

9
A Suggestion

"A GOOD KIND of a life," said the Kid, "if a fellow takes to it."

"Why," said the other, more enthusiastically than ever, "it's the best kind of a life that I know about."

"And Shay is your boss?"

"Yeah, Shay is my boss."

"What sort of a fellow d'you find Shay?"

"The best kind. He's been around in the world, and knows something that you don't learn out of books."

"Square?"

"He pays up."

"The right sort, eh?"

"The right sort for me. He's no time waster. But he keeps you busy and he pays you for your time."

The Kid nodded.

"You like him pretty well for a boss, then?"

"I like him? I'll tell a man that I like him. I've drawn down thousands from Shay, Kid."

"Well," said the Kid, "there's only one thing I ever had against him."

"What's that?"

"Once he pulled out of Los Angeles bound for Arizona—packing out with a pair of horses, a pair of mules and an old-timer by name of Pete Coleman along with him. They had a bad time of it, I suppose. Anyway, on the other side of the desert, there was no more than one mule and your friend Shay. Old Coleman, two horses, and a mule, had disappeared on the trip. Well, I want to know what happened to Coleman, and I want to hear it from Shay's own lip."

"Come in to Dry Creek with me and ask him. They probably met up with a stack of trouble on the way. There's nothing that Shay wouldn't do to get you with him, Kid. He knows a man, and a man's worth!"

"Does he?" said the Kid. "Well, I've already stopped off at Dry Creek, and Shay wasn't interested in seeing me. He left his house. In fact, he climbed out of a top-story window and turned himself into a cat to get to the ground."

The other stared fixedly. His eyes gradually turned from surprise to a hard understanding.

"Did you go gunning for Shay?" he asked suddenly.

"Gunning?" said the Kid. "I never go gunning for anybody. But I wanted to ask Shay that question. He had business outside the house, though, it appeared."

"You hate Shay?"

"Not a bit. I only want to ask him a question."

"Why didn't you stay in Dry Creek?"

"Would you like to go to sleep inside the den of a wild cat?"

The other nodded.

"Well," he said, "you've missed a fine chance, Kid. If I was you, I'd go back to Dry Creek and see Shay under a white flag and make friends. Nobody is gunna get on in this part of the world unless he's a friend of Shay's."

"There's only that question," said the Kid. "When you see him, you ask him, will you? I'd give a lot to find out."

"You think that Shay double-crossed him?"

"Double-crossed him?" said the Kid, gently. "Why, man, Coleman was sixty years old. Who would double-cross a man that old?"

The other watched his face cautiously, and seemed to perceive a tone of iron in that last remark.

"I dunno anything about it," he said shortly. "Was Coleman a great friend of yours?"

"Coleman? Oh, not particularly. I just barely knew him. He took me in when I was hungry, once, and again he showed me the way out when I was in a tight hole, and another time he saved my life when I was cornered by a gang. Outside of that, he didn't have any claim on me."

Dixon frowned, and then stood up.

"I guess I know what you mean," said he. "If I should find out about Coleman—I'll let you know."

"Thanks," said the Kid, showing his teeth as he smiled. "I take that kindly from you, Champ."

"I'll tell you one other thing, Kid," burst out Dixon. "If you want to wear your scalp long, don't stay in this country unless you've made it up with Shay."

"He has everything under his thumb, has he?"

"He has everything under his thumb, and that's a fact."

"I'm glad to know that," said the Kid, "and I hope that we'll be friendly. You tell him something from me, will you?"

"Of course I will, when I see him."

The Kid looked up at him with the same smile.

"Tell him that unless I hear from him soon I'm going to have to drop in on him in a hurry and open him up to learn the truth about Coleman."

"Open him up?" asked Dixon, starting.

"Yes," said the Kid. "If I can't hear it from his mouth, I might find it in his heart, or his liver. And if I fail—he'll make good dog food, anyway. That's all I'd like to have you tell him from me, old-timer."

Dixon, during the last part of this speech, had been backing away from the Kid, frowning. Now, without a word, he turned to his horses, saddled one, and was about to climb into the saddle, when he paused, fumbling at the saddle straps.

The Kid was watching closely, though from the corner of his eye, while he saddled the mare. Then, glancing in the direction in which his companion was looking, he saw from the top of a distant hill the flicker of a light, as though the sun were glittering upon the face of a moving glass. Suddenly he found that Dixon was staring at him closely, critically.

"Yes," said the Kid, still smiling, "it looks as though your friend Shay had the country by the throat. There he is, winking at you across all those miles, old-timer. Wink back, when you get a chance, and tell him that I'm waiting for my answer."

Dixon, without answering, flung himself on the back of his horse. He seemed about to ride straight off, but changing his mind at the last moment, he returned to the Kid and leaned a little from the saddle.

"I'll tell you something," said he, "and it don't cost you nothin' to hear it. You're gunna be marked down in a pretty short while. Get out of this neck of the woods. I ain't got nothin' agin' you. I like you fine. But—I tell you to start movin', Kid!"

The latter watched him carefully.

"I believe you, old son," said he. "I'd better get moving, before you have to start on my trail. Is that it?"

"Put it any way you want to. You think that you know a lot, Kid. You don't know nothin'. You give Shay the run today and think you're the top dog. Why, that don't mean nothin'. He don't fight because he's proud. He fights because he wants your blood. And he'd sooner use hired hands than his own. Kid, watch yourself. So long. I've said a pile too much, already!"

He jerked his horse around and made off at once along the trail toward Dry Creek, while the Kid looked after him with a certain combination of pity, contempt and kindness. Then he mounted and went in the opposite direction, riding slowly, with a thoughtful cant to his head.

10

Handmade Shoe

FOR NOT MORE than a half mile did the Kid keep along the trail, and then, so seriously did he take the friendly warning of Champ Dixon, that he turned aside and cut through the open country, winding up and down through the ravines and over the hills patiently. There was a great deal to occupy his mind during this ride, and chiefly the figure of Champ Dixon.

That man had been famous in story and legend and fact for many a day. But now, like many another legend of the Far West, the Kid had met it, mastered it, put it behind him. It did not seem to him a thing entirely of rags and tatters. It was merely the boiling down of a great, great giant into a quite ordinary man.

And yet he could see the other side of the chance, as well.

As, for instance, if the mare had not spotted the approach of Dixon in the distance, and that red Indian of a man had found the Kid before the Kid found him. Then, there was a little doubt. Dixon would have increased his fame endlessly by a good, well-aimed bull's-eye, the center of the target being the forehead of the Kid. That was the sort of a man Dixon was. He lived for glory. And, beyond question, he had needed nothing but an audience, this day, to force him to take the most hopeless chances and fight out the battle against the Kid and all the odds of circumstance.

A comfortable warmth was in the heart of the Kid, as he thought of this.

The next instant the mare limped, and he dropped down from the saddle instantly to see what was wrong.

He found the trouble in a moment. She had cast a shoe.

This made him shake his head. For the terrain over which they were traveling was very bad, constant outcroppings of rock making the way dangerous for a shoeless horse. Even the regular trail was bad enough, but the cross-country work much worse.

From his saddlebag, with a buckskin string and a flat, thick piece of leather, he improvised rapidly, a sort of moccasin, and mounting again, he rode on through the broken sea of hills.

He went more carefully now, however, and studying the landmarks before him, he presently turned down a ravine that pointed to the left of his way. He wound the bend of this in the dusk of the day, while the sun was still rosy on the upper mountains, but here in the heart of the narrow valley the twilight was already so deep that he could see the faint shining of a light before him, dull as the evening star just after the sun is down.

Toward this he went, the mare picking her way adroitly. She seemed to realize as well as her master that that naked foot might be a cause of trouble in the future.

As he came near the house, he heard a clattering of hoofbeats, and looking up the hill, he saw a couple of riders coming over the crest, horses and men outlined like black, strangely moving cardboard figures against the red of the western sky.

This made him rein up, but, as he studied the horsemen, he made out that only one was a man. The other form was certainly no more than a small boy.

The Kid went on, more at ease, and now he could see the flat shine of the pool beside the cabin, the dim image of the tree at its verge, the straggling march of the shrubbery up the slope, and the little squat cabin itself, looking too small for human habitation.

It grew a little on nearer approach. He saw the woodshed, and the little corral. But the whole place had an air not of habitation so much as an accidental touch of human life in the midst of the wilderness. Men who lived here remained not for what they won from the soil, but for the freedom which they breathed in from the ground. They might be either thoroughly fine fellows, beyond price, or rascals not worth their salt.

When the Kid was close he called out: "Trainor! Trainor!"

A loud voice whooped instantly in answer: "Who's there?"

"A friend!"

"Come on in, friend!"

The swinging light of a lantern appeared outside of the door of the shack, and into the uncertain circle of this light rode the Kid.

He found that the lantern was held by a big bearded fellow with shoulders wide enough to have lifted the whole house behind him, it seemed. He was not more than thirty, but he looked older. Frost in winter and burning sun in summer put their mark on the skin of a man, and all the beards in the world cannot mask the pain of labor which appears in the eyes.

"I nearly forgot where your place was, Bud," said the Kid.

At his voice, Trainor lifted the lantern high—and then almost dropped it.

"It's the Kid!" he exclaimed.

"Shut up!" cautioned the latter, swinging down from the saddle, nevertheless, and grasping the hand of the other.

"It's all right," said Trainor. "There ain't nobody here but pa and ma and my kid cousin, that I've just fetched out from Dry Creek. Davey's been talkin' about nothin' but you. He's the kid that you give the ride to in Dry Creek. Here, Davey. Here's a surprise for you!"

Davey came, hurrying. And as he rushed into the lantern light, and blinked at the face and form of the Kid, his eyes opened and his mouth also.

"By golly," said Davey. "It's the Kid. Hello, Kid. You ain't forgot me, have you?"

"I haven't forgotten you," said the Kid. "I don't forget your kind, old-timer, to the end of my days. Bud, I've lost a shoe off this mare somewhere on the way across."

"On the trail?"

"No. I would have gone back for it, if I had. Have you anything in the way of shoes around here?"

"I've got some that the rust has been gnawin' at for a long time. You take a look. Hey, Davey. You fetch out that bunch of shoes that's hangin' agin' the wall of the shed. I got a kind of a forge, Kid, besides. You come to the right place."

"Aye," said the Kid. "I remembered that forge when I was five or six miles away. It's a forewitted fellow who has a forge on his place, Bud."

The latter accepted the compliment with a grunt.

"The old man done the thinkin' about that. He got it in the days when he had an idea that he was gunna be a cattle king. He started with more tools than cattle. He drawed the plans for his ranch house before he staked out his claim, and he wanted to start buildin' a mill before he put up a cabin!"

"A mill for what?" asked the Kid.

"For what? Why, to grind all of the wheat into flour."

"What wheat, Bud?"

"Why, ain't you rode up through the fields of it. Thousands of acres, over in yonder. Irrigated, too, from the dam up there in the middle of the ravine. And the mill runnin' with the overflow water. You must of seen all of them things! Or maybe they're just an idea that the old man had. Forewitted is what the old man is, and was. Me, personal, I'd rather have the cows and the wheat than the wits. I'd do my thinkin' behindhand, if I had something to think about. C'mon in, Kid, and rest yourself."

"No," said the Kid, "I'm making a long march. Here's Davey with the shoes."

The dozen or so shoes were cast down in the dust in the circle of the lantern light, and from the lot, the Kid instantly picked out two. At his word, the mare lifted her foot, the moccasin was removed, and the old, rusty shoes were measured against it. One of them came near fitting.

"There you are," said Bud. "That shoe's made for her."

"That's a rough cast for her," answered the Kid. "She's a tailor-made lady, the Hawk. She won't have any of these quick-fits, old son. Where's that forge?"

There were chickens roosting on the forge, but they were scattered, squawking loudly, the dust was puffed from the old, tattered bellows, and the charcoal raked together, while they lighted the shavings above the draft.

The family came out to see the famous wanderer at work as a

blacksmith. Old Mr. Trainor stood by, offering advice. Young Davey worked the bellows. Bud held the lantern in the right place, and his mother came out with dough on her hands and flour on her nose to give the Kid a withered smile and the promise of a hearty meal.

Old Mr. Trainor could not keep his hands away from the work. As he saw the fire glow and heard the light cracking of it at work, with the upward curling of the fumes, he began to spit on his hands and shake his head. And as he did so, he picked up an eight-pound hammer. He looked like a sheep, a shaggy, long-haired, tangled, unclean sheep of the west coast of Scotland. For he was bearded almost to the forehead, and from the tangle, as through a mist, his eyes looked out with an uncanny brightness.

"I'll hold and strike. You can tap if you will, man," said he.

He took charge of the business completely, while his big son snarled at him viciously: "Leave it be, will ya? The Kid knows his own mind about the makin' of that shoe!"

"A fitted shoe is a right good shoe," said the old man, enthusiastically. "I'll fit that shoe to the breadth of a hair."

"And you'll be all the night about it," declared the son.

"Better a late start than a never ending," said the father.

"There he goes with his blamed proverbs," said the other. "There'll be no stoppin' him now, Kid, unless you take the hammer out of his hand!"

The Kid, however, said nothing at all, but looked at the old man with a singular fascination, as though he saw a story in his bushy face.

In the meantime, old Trainor fell to shaping the shoe. He worked fairly slowly, to be sure, but with the utmost nicety. And even when the critical Kid declared that all was well and that the shoe would do perfectly, still the old fellow labored, with sweat running brightly down his nose and his eyes agleam.

"A thing half done is a game not won," said he. "If there's only one window in the house unlocked the devil may fly through it as easy as if the whole place was open."

"Hark at him," said the son. "Now he's well started, and there'll be no stopping of him, as I told you before. That's why we've gone to pot out here. He never could finish the first thing to his own content, and so he never got through to the end of anything."

The old man, shaping the shoe with many light, delicate

blows, and drawing out a small nose calk in the front of the bend, on either side, regarded his work with a most judicious eye. Now and then, holding the shoe on a cold chisel, he stooped above the foot of the mare and she, nervously aware of every movement, would raise her leg to show the hoof. Over it, making the shoe hover closely, he strained his eyes.

"Oh," said old Trainor, "I'll tell you what, Kid, it takes a wise man to learn from a fool, and that's what my son would never do. I been a failure and a great failure. I've kept his ma and him cooped up in a shed all their lives. Well, I ain't proud of it. I'm ashamed. But I've ate honest bread, and——"

"Shut up, will you?" shouted the son, savagely, so that Davey winced with fear at the bellows, where he watched all with great eyes.

The Kid waved his hand, for he saw that this last interpolation was to save his own feelings.

"It's all right," said he. "The whole world knows that I've been a thief. You don't hurt my feelings, Dad."

At this, old Trainor stepped from the anvil a short pace and dropped a hand upon the shoulder of the other.

"Good lad!" said he. "As if I would ever harm you, even with talk. But then, there's a thing that's harder to watch than a sword or nitroglycerin. It cuts and it tears—a tongue does!"

He struck himself lightly across the mouth with the back of his hand, and then shook his head as he turned back to the fitting of the shoe.

"Polite, you are," said Trainor to his father. "Always thinkin' about the right thing to make folks comfortable."

"I've spoke of the wrong that I've done him," said the other patiently. "What more can I do, son?"

"Keep your face shut, is what you can do!" thundered the other.

At this, the Kid lifted his brows, and suddenly looked down again, as though he saw that the business of his were done.

And old Trainor, bending over the hoof of the mare for the last time, began to trim it to a smooth, flat surface, using the knife gingerly, as though he were afraid that blood would follow the least touch that went too deep.

"Aye," said he. "Shut my mouth and be still. Listen to them that have made money, that ride fine hosses and wear fine clothes. Listen to them that have a big purse and something in it. They can talk, but old Trainor is not a long step ahead of a beggar. And therefore, he has no right. Let him talk to the prairie dogs and the squirrels, and the hens in the yard, but not man talk to men—not man talk to men!"

His mutterings did not force him to neglect his work, however, and finally he nailed on the shoe, cutting and clinching the nails with as much care as he had shown through all the rest of the work.

"A good handy blacksmith would of shod a hoss all around in the time you've took to fix one foot," said the son, growling as usual.

Then the Kid interrupted.

"He wouldn't have done a job to suit me," said he. "Not if he'd gone a bit faster. She's worthy of good shoes to stand in, is the Hawk. I'm thanking you, Dad."

Dad Trainor smiled suddenly on him, like a light shining through a fog.

"Aye," said he, "for them that has diamonds won't set them in brass. You understand, son! It ain't every hand that can move as fast as the eye can jump, and faster. But patience climbs the highest hill and—"

"And finds it bare at the top!" broke in the angry son. "I'm tired of hearin' such rot!"

He left the shed suddenly and strode off into the night in the direction of the house.

11
Callers

YOUNG DAVEY, leaving the bellows, remarked: "It sure fits her to a turn. That's what I'm gunna be when I grow up. I'm gunna make things. I'm gunna be a blacksmith."

"Don't go makin' no mistake," said Dad Trainor. "Hands that are strong enough to work in iron ain't strong enough to work with people. Don't you aim to work with iron. Aim to work with men. They're what need the bendin'. They're what it pays to shape. Heat 'em and temper 'em. Hammer 'em and form 'em. If you break one of 'em, here and there, it don't make no difference. Throw the pieces outside the shop. Leave 'em there to be tramped in the dirt by everybody that goes by. Go on with your hammerin' and shapin'. If you break two for every one that you shape for yourself, you're a mighty successful man. You'll have money in the bank. Pretty soon, folks that hated you for meanness will be glorifyin' you for strength. They'll take their hats off and when they shake hands, their palms will be turned up. Be a man-handler, not a blacksmith, Davey!"

The cold irony of this speech caused the Kid to look attentively and somewhat sadly on the old man, but before any of them could speak again, a horse neighed loudly somewhere near by.

The Kid sprang from the shed to listen.

But the sound had died down instantly. It was full night, now, and the stars thickly stippled the sky, setting out the black, heavy forms of the hills and more dimly, of the mountains beyond. He turned his head a little from side to side, trying to locate the sound, but it was not clear enough in his mind.

"Here, girl!" he called softly.

The mare instantly stepped from the shed to his side, and there he watched her as she lifted her head high and stared straight across the ravine.

"It was over there," said the Kid thoughtfully, nodding in the direction at which the mare was still looking what would you say, Dad," he added to the old man. "Was that neigh in the ravine or up on the bluff, there?"

"It was up there," said Dad Trainor.

"Nope, it was down in the ravine," broke in Davey instantly. "I heard the echo break."

"I think I did, too," said the Kid.

"It was off of the bluff," said Dad insistently. "Sure you'd hear some echo, but not loud, and bangin' back and forth from side to side of the ravine, like it would 'a', if the critter had been down on the floor. A noise like that, it's like a whangin' in a dish pan, I tell you."

"Any stray horses around here?" asked the Kid, his ear canted a little, his eyes still struggling with the darkness.

"Yeah. Pretty often some of the Milman stock, it straggles

here across the badlands. Most likely was one of them out there on the rim of the valley."

"Yeah. I've seen 'em there a lot," said Davey.

"Milman lands run this far?"

"Pretty nigh," said Dad Trainor. "He's been buyin' up and buyin' up all the time. Them that have enough money is like stones rollin' downhill. The longer they live, the faster they go. He's gunna own most of the countryside around here, before long. They's trouble ahead for him!"

"Because he is so rich?"

"A rich man with a pretty daughter is like a gent smeared with honey, when they's wasps flyin' in the air, on a hot August afternoon. Pretty soon he's gunna get stung bad, I can tell you! Stung right to the bone, so's he'll ache good and plenty."

"I've seen her," said the Kid, looking aimlessly across the night.

He seemed to begin to forget the alarm which he had been feeling the moment before.

"Scout out there and see if there's anything moving," he said to Davey. "Get close to the ground, and look at the sky line, will you?"

"Sure!" said Davey, delighted, and he bounded away.

"What are you suspicionin' about?" asked Dad Trainor suddenly.

"Oh, I don't know," answered the Kid. "You never know. In a way, I'm the honey that attracts a kind of wasp, too. The humming of them, Dad, is a thing that has waked me up in the night, a good many times."

"If you got any doubts," said Dad Trainor, "you wouldn't be sendin' out a wee kid like that one, would you? Kind of half town raised, too! If I could have him out here all the time, his eyes and ears would sharpen up, maybe."

"They're sharp enough," said the Kid, easily. "If so much as a partridge whirs within a mile of him, he'll hear it and he'll see it. I'll trust Davey. He knows how to look at a man in the day, and he'll know how to look for a man in the night. My bet is on Davey."

"Well, he's a good lad," said Dad Trainor. "Bright and quick, and I gotta say that town livin' ain't made his fists soft. The tannin' that he give to little Harry Michaels one-two year back, it was a beauty. He handed Harry a ten-pound handicap and a lickin' that was worth watchin'. But still, if they's any doubt about what's out there in the dark of the valley—"

"There's always doubt, Dad," said the younger man. "But if a fellow has nightmares by day as well as by night, what's the use of living at all, I say."

"Aye, and a true thing that is," said Dad. "Them that takes chances and changes hosses is them that makes the round trip through life, and the rest of us, we just travel along one road and never see nothin'—but dust!"

He shook his head violently, and led the way on toward the house. They only stopped outside to give the mare a nose bag of barley, and then they went into the little shack where Ma Trainor greeted them with a smile and a face shining with the steam of cookery. She declared that she had some sour-milk biscuits in that oven that would warm the heart of any man in the world. In the meantime the stove enriched the air with a multitude of vapors, while the Kid went over to lift lids, sniff contents, and discuss the properest ways of seasoning and baking in a Dutch oven. In these matters, Mrs. Trainor was a mint of information.

"Where you been keepin' yourself, Kid?" she said.

"A little bit of all around," said he. "But mostly south. What What have you been thinking since I last saw you?"

She accepted the question with a smile.

"Mostly tasting the first part of my life over again," said she. "That's what you do when you get my age, Kid. Them biscuits oughta be ready now. Kick that dog off that chair and sit down. Where's them other two?"

There was only one small lamp, the chimney slightly yellowed with smoke, and when this was placed on the table and the glass still further obscured with the steam of the food, it gave the room new dimensions, and a sort of gloomy dignity. In the corner, the ladder which led to the garret now climbed quite out of sight. As the food was piled on the table, which sagged a little to one side even under this light weight, the missing two now came in.

"I met Bud," said Davey, "and he told me that he'd already scouted around."

"Yeah," said Bud, rather gloomily. "When I heard that hoss nicker, I just took a look around, but it ain't nothin' but one of the Milman cayuses up there on the bluff. Them Milmans, it ain't no wonder that they lose a lot of stock by rustlers. They go and shove their hosses and cows right down your throat, sort of."

"A loose horse, eh?" asked the Kid.

"Yeah, a loose horse."

"I'm glad to know that. I thought that one hadn't whinnied himself out at the finish."

"Can you tell when a hoss has had his fill up of neighin'?" demanded Bud, somewhat sulkily.

"Pretty close," replied the Kid. "There's something about the way that he tunes up at the start that can tell you whether he's going to wheeze, snort, cough, or squeal at the finish."

"Well, I never could read the mind of a hoss that close," said Bud. "Throw me a coupla them biscuits, will ya?"

The Kid, silently, passed the plate, and while Bud helped himself, the eye of the Kid lingered for a moment, thoughtfully, upon the gloomy face. He shifted his glance, then, over his shoulder toward the door and seemed for an instant uneasy, but in a moment shrugged his shoulders and settled himself to his meal.

He had begun a little story of Yucatan in which the very steam of the jungle of that southland appeared, when, into the doorway behind him, stepped two men, silent as shadows. The Kid had his back fairly turned, but something made him stiffen as though he actually had seen the naked guns in their hands, leveled upon him.

But, little Davey, who hardly had been able to shift his eyes from his hero, up to this moment, now slowly rose like a ghost from his stool.

"Jiminy!" he breathed.

"Jus' take it quiet," said a voice from the doorway.

"Aye, take it slow and easy, Kid," said the second man. "And give a jury a chance at you!"

12

Notched Gun

The Kid rested his elbows upon the edge of the table.

"You wouldn't object if I was to stretch my arms—so long as I stretched 'em up?" he asked.

"Leave 'em be. Leave 'em still. We know you, Kid. It ain't where your hands are that counts. It's the way that you can move 'em. Watch him now!"

"Heck! Ain't I watchin' till my eyes ache?" said the other. "Go up and fan him for his armory. I'll keep him covered."

Old Dad Trainor had recovered from his stupor and had risen again.

"What's the meanin' of this, boys?" he demanded.

"Why," said the Kid, "it's just two old friends of mine dropped in for a little call. It's Sam Deacon and Lefty Morgan. How's everything, Deacon?"

"Right now," said Deacon, "it's pretty good. I reckon I can tell how good things is with you, though."

"You, Morgan and Deacon," said Dad Trainor. "What kind of jamboree d'you reckon that this here is, anyway? You ain't gunna do nothin' to the Kid, in my house!"

"Ain't we?" asked Morgan.

He had come well into the dull circle of the light, showing a death's-head, all bones, scantly covered with a tight-drawn parchment skin. His teeth were so prominent that the pale lips constantly grinned back from them, and they flashed brightly in even that dull illumination.

"Watch that old fool," said Morgan.

"You handle the Kid, then," said Deacon.

He had come up to his partner's shoulder, a great contrast to the other. He was one of those little, heavy-shouldered men with legs so bowed that they waddled like ducks in walking. He looked like a sailor. There was something free-swinging, frank, and easy about his bearing, and about his face.

"Here, Bud," said the other, "ain't you gunna keep the old man in hand?"

"Yeah," said Bud, rising in turn, "I'm gunna keep him in hand, all right."

He turned a grim face upon his father.

"You set down and don't make no fool or yourself, no more," said he.

Old Dad looked as though he had been struck with a heavy fist.

"You ain't with 'em, Bud," said he. "You can't be with 'em, ain' the Kid—ain' any guest right in our own house. There ain't no Trainor so dog-gone low as all of that! Bud, Bud, look me in the eye and tell me that I got the wrong steer about you, just now!"

"Aw, shut up and set down," commanded the big son. "Use your eyes. You ain't a hoss that's gotta keep neighin' till you've lost your wind—the way the Kid was sayin'!"

"Was it your horse that neighed, Deacon?" asked the Kid.

"What made you guess that?" said the Deacon, curiously.

"The last time I saw you, you were riding a piebald speed-burner, with the nerves of a sick woman and the look of a fool. That's the sort of a horse that doesn't know the right time for making a noise. You had to pinch his nose, didn't you?"

"I about pulled the nose off of him," agreed Deacon. "He's a fool, that gelding, but he sure can hump himself along. Fan him, Lefty. And fan him good!"

Lefty, nothing backward in this work, went carefully through the clothes of the Kid, searching his pockets and patting him all over to discover weapons.

Old Dad Trainor, in the meantime, had slumped down into his chair and remained with a leaden, hanging head.

To him, the Kid now addressed himself.

"Why, Dad," he declared, "these are hard times. You can't expect a man to turn down a chance to pick up a few thousand as easily as this. How much is your split, Bud?"

"None of your damn business," answered Bud.

"Oh, Bud, Bud!" said his mother.

Suddenly he shouted, white and crimson: "Leave me be, will ya? The two of ya leave me be! You kep' me out here all these years takin' care of you, didn't you? You never give me no chance to make anything decently, did ya? Now shut your faces and leave me be, while I make some money on my own account. I wanted a start, and I've got it."

His mother, looking like one who sees a ghost, stared straight before her, pressing her folded hands first against her mouth, and then against her breast.

"Take it easy," urged the Kid. "I'll be out of this mess, perhaps, before long. And I'll never come after Bud, if that's what you worry about. Bud's human, that's all, and he's been hungry for a long time!"

Dad Trainor lifted his head and looked with hollow eyes at the Kid, but he said nothing; and Ma Trainor, also, was mute.

In the meantime, as the weapons were produced from the person of the Kid, various comments were made upon them.

First of all, out came a sleek Colt of the old single-action model from a spring holster beneath his left armpit.

"I never could see no reason for packin' a gun there," declared Morgan. "It ain't gonna fool nobody nor make them think that you ain't loaded for bear. What's the good of buryin' your gat under your coat, that way?"

"Because it's the fastest place," said the Kid. "A gun comes up slower than it falls down. I jump an empty hand for that gun, and the weight of the gun itself helps the gun down and out."

"I don't see it," persisted Lefty Morgan.

"All right. I'll show you. Just hand me the old gat—"

"Easy, sonny, easy!" said Lefty Morgan, continuing the search. "I'm mighty young, and I'm mighty tender, but you can't see through me that quick. I've heard about the way you move, and I've *seen* it too."

"Look at it," said Sam Deacon, his voice lowered to a profound admiration. "Will you look at it now? Ain't it a bird? Them sights slicked off so smooth and polished up. There ain't no friction about that there Colt, sonny."

"How long," demanded Lefty, "did it take you to learn to fan a gat with one hand and hit something?"

"I used to work every Sunday in our back yard," said the Kid gently. "After I came home from Sunday school, I used to take off my little jacket and turn up the starched cuffs of my shirt, and I used to take a gun in my little hand and amuse myself, boys."

"Yeah," said Lefty, "and every week day, too, and twice on Christmas. Say, Kid, what was you? A juggler in a circus, once? Where'd you get them hands of yours?"

The Kid spread the taper fingers upon the edge of the table.

"Every night," said he, "I used to wash them with violet soap, boys, and then give them a good massaging with a pure cold cream, and then I put on kid gloves when I went to bed. You've no idea how that sort of treatment helps them."

Morgan, now facing the Kid from the far side of the table, with a ready gun balanced on the table's edge, grinned widely.

"Yeah," said he. "I reckon that you've used cold cream. Well, you don't have to confess to us. The jury'll be what will want to hear you talk."

"Always wanted to make a speech to a jury," said the Kid.

"Lookit!" broke out Deacon, examining the handles of the weapon they had taken from the Kid. "They's eleven notches in this gat, boys! Eleven dead men wrote their names here, eh?"

They looked at the Kid almost with terror, and yet with triumph, also. The discovery made their triumph all the sweeter.

"Not notches that I filed," said the Kid. "No, no, don't you attribute those marks to me, old fellows. That gun belonged to poor Jig Yates."

"Hey, you don't mean that this was the Jigger's own gun?"

"Yes, his own gun. You're looking at history, my lads!"

"Jigger Yate's own gun! How'd you get it from him?"

"He left it to me when he died," said the Kid sadly. "A great, game chap was Jigger."

"Game? As a bantam!" exclaimed Lefty Morgan eagerly. "There was a man. And I didn't know that he died. Who bumped him off? I mean, what crowd bumped him off?"

"Aye," said Deacon, "no one man was likely to take his checks all in a heap. Who done it?"

"Young chap that had a turn of luck," said the Kid smoothly. "Yes, the Jigger is dead. He loved that gun, though!"

"Where did he die? What was the young feller's name?" asked Lefty Morgan, his mouth wide open.

"Away down in Yucatan he came to his last day," said the Kid sadly. "He had a gun smoking in each hand, too. But that's a great mistake. If he'd trusted all of his attention to this one gat, he would have been better off. Too many irons in the fire, you might say, and so he slipped and went down."

"Shot in front?"

"Just between the eyes," said the Kid, nodding. "Just exactly between the eyes."

Bud Trainor had been silent. Now he slowly lifted an arm and pointed at the Kid.

"You done it yourself!" said he.

"I?" said the Kid, apparently surprised. "You amaze me, Bud. I don't hunt the land sharks that swim as fast as Jigger Yates did. Not I!"

But here the three exchanged glances. And they nodded to one another.

"Well," said Deacon, "I sure hope that you live out the year after you dropped Jig Yates. That's all that I hope."

"I'm not likely to," said the Kid.

"Ain't you? Why do you say that?"

"I see things in the future," said the Kid, and yawned a little.

"Whatcha see?" asked Deacon.

"I see Deacon and Morgan riding across the hills with a third man between them, his feet tied into his stirrups, and his hands tied behind his back. His face is dark to me. No, he comes closer. Yes, it's myself, as I suspected, and the horse is the Hawk."

"The devil you say," said Deacon. "Then what happens in this foresight of yours."

"Why, a thing that makes me very sorry for myself, old boy. A desperate idea comes to that prisoner. He makes a sudden move to escape. His two guards are forced much against their will to shoot him full of holes!"

"Why, they wouldn't dare!" shouted Davey, in a shrill, and tremulous voice.

"We wouldn't have to," said Deacon darkly. "We wouldn't have to because you wouldn't be such a fool, and the judge and the jury will take care of you, old son!"

"There's not a court in the world that has a claim against me —north of the Rio Grande," said the Kid, gently. "No, not one."

"You mean to say that you ain't wanted anywhere in the country?"

"Not in a single place," declared the Kid. "Oh, there might

be one or two old charges of disturbing the peace. But every-thing is self-defense and sweetness and light, as far as I'm concerned, boys!"

"It's a lie!" said Deacon; "and we know it's a lie, and we're takin' you because you're wanted, and we're gunna get the reward for you. We're actin' for the law, not for ourselves!"

"Of course, you're not acting for yourselves," answered the Kid. "A pair of big, clean-hearted American boys like you two —you wouldn't act for yourselves. It's just to mop up the criminal element and make the country safe for the poor shots. I understand you perfectly. Even if there's no charge against me."

"We've heard enough of this gabble," said Morgan. "Let's get him on the way."

"Drop me where there are a lot of big stones," said the Kid lightly. "You've no idea how I hate the thought of wolves playing sexton to me!"

"You think that we're gonna murder you, do you?" asked Deacon.

"Aye, aye, aye!" cried out old Dad Trainor suddenly. "There's nothin' but murder in your face, right now. Murder, and my guest, and as good as in my house. Heaven forgive me!"

He wrapped his arms around his old head, tortured by his impotence.

13
Branding Iron

"WE'LL BE STARTING along," said Deacon. "Are you ready, Kid?"

"Of course I am," said the Kid, cheerfully.

"Go on with 'em," exclaimed old Mrs. Trainor suddenly, to her son. "Roll up your blankets, and get along with 'em, and never come back here!"

"Ma, ma!" muttered her husband. "What are you sayin' to our own boy?"

"I'm sayin' the truth as I sees it. I never want to see his face ag'in. I've throwed him out of my heart and life. I'm throwin' away the misery and the care and the love that I've given him. I'm throwin' away the one thing that we've given to the world, Dad. But we ain't gonna have him set at our table with blood on him!"

The nerves of the Kid were of the nature of chilled steel, but even he was startled by this unexpected outbreak from the old woman. Her husband gaped at her as a spirit from another world. And both Deacon and Morgan almost forgot to watch their captive as they stared at Ma Trainor.

Bud, turning pale and purple in patches, growled out: "What kinda fool talk is all this? Dad, are you gunna set there and listen to ma talkin' like this?"

"All my life," said Dad Trainor, "I've done nothin' but listen to your ma, when it come to a pinch, and I'm pretty old to change my habits. She's told you to go, and if I was you, I'd git!"

"Here's mother love for you!" said Bud Trainor, desperate with anger and disgrace.

"I ain't no mother of yours!" cried the poor old woman. "There ain't no Trainor blood in you. Even a sneakin' copperfaced Injun wouldn't do such a thing. Him that has had his feet under our table, you've sold him. Heaven forgive you, for I ain't never gonna!"

"Aye," said old Dad Trainor, grimly. "It'll be you and me, alone, ma, like it was in the beginning. Bud, you roll your blankets, and git along with you."

"I'll go the way that I stand," said Bud Trainor. "I don't want nothin' from you. If you throw me over, I throw you—"

He paused, at the end of that sentence, and his wild eye rolled about over the faces in the room.

He saw little Davey, his face utterly white with horror and with loathing. He saw his companions in crime, Deacon and Morgan, watching him with a certain pity, perhaps, but with a more profound contempt and disgust. Finally, he saw the Kid, the betrayed man, regarding him not with hatred, but as if from a height looking down on lesser souls.

And the last words died out of the lips of Bud Trainor. His

great shoulders—they were even more massive than those of the Kid—twitched convulsively.

"What was I gonna do?" he said huskily. "What was I gonna do when I was ground down and beat and never had no chance? Is two thousand bucks something that I could afford to throw away like it was a paper of pins? I ask you that. Ma, d'you hear me?"

"If they was two thousand pounds of diamonds, I'd feel the way that I do now. Yo're gonna be a thing that'll be talked of for years. You ain't gonna be called Bud Trainor. You're gonna be called a sneak and a dog that sold his friends' lives from under his own roof. And me——"

Here her strength, which had sustained her marvelously for a moment, gave way utterly, and she dropped into a chair and began to sob in a stifled way.

Her husband stepped to her side, and put his arm around her bowed shoulders.

"Like the beginning," he said, "we got each other, and we'll get through, somehow, to the end of things!"

It was too much for Deacon and Morgan.

"We're movin' out of here," said Lefty. "Here, boys. Gimme a start. Kid, you hold out your hands behind the small of your back, will you? Hold 'em out and put the wrists close together——"

"Sure," said the Kid.

Now little Davey, startled out of his horrified stare at Bud Trainor, turned toward the other actors, sweeping his glance across the convulsed face of the traitor.

What Davey saw was the cord, ready in the hands of Morgan to tie the wrists of the captive. An inspiration came to Davey. He was standing with the lamp just before him, and rather close to his side of the table. That table was low, and Davey, leaning over, blew out the lamp with a single puff.

There were stars outside, burning brightly. And there was even a scattering of reddish streaks of light from the stove itself, where the fire shone through certain gaping cracks. However, the extinguishing of the smoky lamp acted like double darkness in which surprise was the chiefest element.

Two guns instantly spoke like two thunderstrokes on the heels of one another. Pungent scent of burned gun-powder stung the nostrils of all in the cabin.

There was a tumbling of wrestling bodies, curses, and then a wild scream of pain and terror.

Through the doorway, dimly silhouetted against the stars, leaped a man who was throwing out his arms before him, and still yelling as he fled.

Then Davey, who had put out the lamp, lighted it again.

It revealed an odd scene.

In the doorway stood the Kid, with a rifle all ready in his capable hands. He was looking after the fugitive, who now departed with a rapid pattering of hoofs, putting his horse at a dead gallop. But the Kid did not open fire. Instead, he lowered the weapon and turned back into the room, as though he cared too little about the matter to shoot down the fleeing rider.

In the room itself, old Ma Trainor was cowering into a corner. Her husband stood in front of her, with a short-handled axe gripped in both hands, and a wild light in his eyes. There was a faint hint of red on the edge of the heavy blade. An explanation, perhaps, of the shriek of terror which had filled the cabin the moment or two before this.

But, most interesting of all, in the corner of the room where two men had been struggling, one of them was now rendered helpless. That was Sam Deacon, and he who had pinned him down was none other than Bud Trainor!

"Thanks, Bud," said the Kid. "It's all right, now. Let him get up after you've taken his guns away."

The guns were promptly taken away, and the two got to their feet.

The thin, white face of Deacon was covered with a ghastly smile, his habitual expression, which he deepened now in order to show that he was not at all afraid.

But afraid he was, most ghastly afraid, and this smile of his only accented his terror.

He looked at Bud and snarled from the side of his mouth:

"You double-crossin', sneakin', dirty, hound!"

And Bud winced, and made no reply. He hung his head, doggedly, until his small mother ran to him out of the corner of the room and cast her meager arms around him.

"Oh, Buddy, Buddy darlin'!" she sobbed against his breast. "My own boy, my brave boy. Oh, thank Heaven, thank Heaven!"

He cradled her in his arms, and he turned to the wall for fear that the others might see what was happening upon that grim face of his. His father gripped his arm with a brown old hand and said not a word, but it was plain that the ties which held that family together had been riveted with something stronger than steel, in the last moment.

The Kid, in the meantime, sat down in the chair and drew a breath.

"Well," he said frankly, "I thought that I was a goner, that time."

Then he nodded toward Davey.

"You're a cool kid," said he. "I can thank you first, Davey. And, Bud, something more than cancels out, too. He lost two thousand and put up a fight, besides. And this Deacon is a wild cat. I know all about him. Aren't you, Deacon?"

The smile with which he asked this last question turned the pallor of Deacon from yellow-white to green-white. He blinked. But resolutely he maintained his smile.

"Well, what's the game?" said Deacon, lightly.

"Sit down and make yourself a cigarette," said the Kid. "There's no hurry. We'll just have a friendly little chat. That's all."

"About what?" asked Deacon.

"Oh, about old times. And new ones, too. I want to know who hired the pair of you for this job, Deacon."

"Yeah? You wanta know?" said Deacon. "You ain't expecting me to talk, Kid, are you?"

"Yes," drawled the Kid. "You'll talk, all right."

Sam Deacon shrugged his lean shoulders. His eyes flickered aside toward the door. Then they returned to the face of the Kid, who was lighting a cigarette. Almost desperately, Deacon followed that example.

"You'll talk," said the Kid. "You'll tell me everything."

"I'll not say a word," declared Deacon, and pinched his lips together with an effort.

"Deacon," said the Kid, "don't you think that you ought to pay something for your life?"

"I'm no double-crossing cur!" said Deacon, looking bitterly at Bud Trainor.

"All right," said the Kid. "You don't double-cross. You simply murder, eh? Well, Davey, take a lid off of that stove and freshen the fire and put the poker in under the lid, will you?"

Davey, without a word, did as he was told.

And Deacon watched him, curiously. Sweat began to gather on his forehead.

But the silence continued, through which the Kid was smoking quietly.

At length he said: "Bud, will you take your mother and father outside of the house? Davey, you'd better go along, too. What's going to happen now won't be pretty to watch. You'd better get out of earshot. There may be a little noise in here."

"Kid," said Deacon huskily, "whatcha got on your mind?"

"When that poker's hot," said the Kid, "it ought to make a good running iron. That's all I mean."

Deacon got up slowly from his chair.

"You ain't serious, Kid," he gasped.

"No, only joking," said the Kid, "if you intend to talk."

Deacon rubbed a hand violently across his face.

"Aye," said he. "You'll do what you say! There ain't nothin' but a devil inside you. Kid, whatcha wanta know?"

14

A Compact

THE KID, at this, smiled in the most amiable manner.

"I want to find out about the whole idea," he said. "Who sent you, why you were sent, and how much money was promised."

"Send out this crowd," said Deacon glumly. "If I gotta tell, there ain't any reason why I should tell anybody besides you."

"They'll go out," admitted the Kid. "That is, Davey and the old folks will. But not Bud."

"Not Bud?" almost shouted the other. "What has that sneak got in the way of a right to hear?"

"Why," said the Kid, "Bud and I are partners, old son. You ought to know that, by now."

"Partners? A fine partner he promised to be to you," said Deacon.

Already the others were leaving the cabin, though reluctantly, but Bud lingered near the door.

"You mean that you want me to stay here?" he asked incredulously of the Kid.

"Of course I do," said the latter.

"And why? Why?" shouted Deacon, infuriated until he trembled. "Here's the gent that sold you, and then changed his mind and double-crossed me and Morgan. Why should he stay?"

"You thought that he'd sold me," said the Kid. "No, no, Deacon. Bud Trainor's not the sort of a fellow to ever do that. He's not the type for it, at all. Bud is in partnership with me, and when you tried to buy him, he simply led you into the middle of the trap."

"By heck!" cried Deacon. "Is that it? Is that why you were so cool, all the time? You knew that you had something up your sleeve?"

"Of course I did," answered the Kid, genially. "You never had a chance against Bud and me, because all the while Bud was waiting for my signal before he jumped you from behind."

Bud Trainor, listening near the door, dropped his head a little, so that the bewilderment in his face might not be too openly apparent to Deacon.

The latter twisted from side to side, in the agony of his humiliation—not humiliation because he had attempted to take advantage of the Kid and failed, but shame, because he seemed to have been tricked and trapped.

"Have I gone and been a fool?" he asked bitterly.

"You've been a fool, Deacon," said the Kid gently. "You might have known that Bud Trainor isn't the double-crossing kind."

Deacon turned aside and glared at Trainor.

The latter, lifting his head, gave to the Kid an odd look and a faintly twisted smile, as though there were some deep consideration between them. But he said nothing.

"I see it!" said Deacon. "Bud was simply drawing us on!"

"How about the news that you have for us, Deacon?"

"Say it over again, what you want to know?"

"Who sent you?"

"Why, Jack Harbridge up in the Mogollons is the feller. He wants to get even with you for the game you trimmed him in, two-three year back."

"Harbridge?"

"Yes."

"That poker game still sticks in his crop, eh?"

"It sure does."

"He tried to crook me, that game, and I only stacked the deck with two crimps in it. He found the first crimp, but he banged into the second one. Well, it's Harbridge, is it?"

"Aye, it's Harbridge."

"I'm glad to know that. What was the price?"

"Ten thousand flat."

"That's worth while. I'm glad that Jack puts that high a price on me. Where did you see Jack last?"

"Up there in the hills. About two weeks back."

"You been drawing a long bow at me, eh?"

"It was worth time."

"It wouldn't take that long to get down here."

"We didn't know where you were, for a while. And then we wanted a little practice with our guns. We expected a hard job ahead of us. And if I'd plugged you when I came through that door—"

He paused, his teeth showing, but not in a smile.

"You wouldn't do that, Deacon," said the Kid. "Bud, see if that poker's hot enough now, will you? I want it white hot."

Bud went toward the stove.

"What's the idea?" asked Deacon, growing whiter than he had been.

"I have to burn the truth out of you," said the Kid. "I don't want lies from you, Deacon."

"I'm telling you the honest truth."

"Then I'll have to burn honester truth out of you. How about the poker?"

"It's pretty nigh ready to melt," said Bud, lifting the lid from the roaring, glowing stove.

"It ought to be ready for the work, then," said the Kid. "Bring it here, will you?"

Bud, accordingly, first wrapped a rag around his hand and then withdrew the poker from the fire. The end of it was white hot, and snapped out little bright sparkles. It seemed, indeed, as though the tough iron had been melting, and was forming a liquid drop at the point.

"You wouldn't dare," said Deacon, in a gasp. "I've told you—"

The Kid smiled.

"You're a rat, Deacon," said he. "You're a low rat and you always were a rat. I'll have the truth out of you or I'll mark you so's the boys will be able to read your face like a book, a block away!"

"Put back that thing!" groaned Deacon.

"Put it back, Bud," said the Kid.

Bud, almost unwillingly, obeyed.

"Now, who sent you, man?"

"Shay," said Deacon.

He dropped into a chair.

He was almost fainting, and his head fell back, his body shook convulsively.

"I thought so," said the Kid. "Shay has a sort of reason for wanting me. Shay offered ten thousand, did he?"

"Aye, he did."

"I'm glad to know it. I'm glad to know that he has that much spare cash. Why didn't you bring Dixon along?"

This startled Deacon erect in the chair again.

"Who told you that?" he cried.

"About Dixon, you mean?"

"Yes, about Dixon. What sneaking crook has been spilling news on us all?"

"I can guess, Deacon," said the Kid. "I know that he's with Shay, and that this sort of a job is just about his size."

"He wouldn't horn in," said Deacon, bewildered by the answer. "He said that his luck was bad, today, so far as you went. I dunno why he said that, but he's a superstitious kind— and by Heaven, they's something in his superstition, too. I've seen what luck a man can have with you today, Kid!"

He glowered as he spoke.

"That's about all," said the Kid. "I don't need you any longer."

Deacon stood up.

"It's to be a bullet in the back, I reckon?" said he.

"Did I ever shoot a man through the back?" asked the Kid.

"You're one to learn, though. You mean that I'm free to go?"

"I told you that I'd turn you loose, for the sake of the news that you could give me."

"You mean it, Kid?"

"I mean it. Get out, Deacon."

Deacon went slowly to the door. There he paused and turned, at last. "I dunno that I make you out, Kid," said he. "You must have underground wires all over the world. What made you know that Harbridge wasn't behind this? He hates you enough, and he's got the money to hire men."

"Harbridge generally does his own killing," said the Kid. "And after all, it was only a guess, Deacon. Just a bluff, but it seems to have worked."

The face of Deacon wrinkled with hatred and with anger.

"I ain't fit to wear long trousers," said he. "I been bluffed all the way through. You got anything else to say?"

"Yes," said the Kid, "I have a little message for Shay. Will you take it to him, word for word?"

"Aye."

"Tell him that one of these days I'll call when I can find him at home and not in a hurry to leave. Tell him another thing. If any of his rats come here to make trouble for the Trainors, Dad and Ma, I mean, I'll never sleep on the trail until it takes me to them. And I'll never rest till I've got Shay. Tell him if he so much as breathes on their windowpane, I'll burn him alive with —a song and dance. I'll hire Indians to do a good job on him. That goes for the old folks. As for Bud, of course, he takes his chance with me. The open season is on for Bud and me, as far as Shay is concerned. That goes without saying. Now get out of here, Deacon, and the next time you see me, don't stop to ask questions. Fill your hand, even if it's in church!"

Deacon gave him one backward, glowering look, then glided through the door, and a moment afterward, they heard the sound of his horse, as it departed at a dogtrot across the valley.

It left the two inside free to face one another.

"Kid," said Bud Trainor huskily, "I dunno that I got much to say to you."

"You can thank me for putting a lot of bad men on your trail, Bud," said the other.

"Them?" said Bud. He smiled, and waved his hand. "I'll take my chances with them! But you, Kid—what made you do it?"

"Do what?"

"Talk as though—as though I was your partner?"

"Well, Bud, are you happy here at home?"

"Here? I'd rather be in prison."

"The open trail is not a prison. Why not come along—as my partner?"

"I'd rather than anything on—. But hold on. You know what I am, Kid. I ain't worthy of—"

"Hush up," said the Kid, smiling. "I'll take my chances. Shall we shake on it?"

Bud Trainor suddenly bowed his head. He fumbled vaguely before him, but the strong right hand of the Kid found his, and closed like gentle iron upon it. The compact was sealed.

15
Land Sharks

TWO DAYS after this, "Spot" Gregory of the Milman ranch daubed his rope on a tough Roman-nosed broncho in the corral, and started out to teach the brute manners. That big-headed mustang bounced up and down between the sky and the hard ground until Spot's teeth were loose in his head. After ten minutes the gelding decided that its luck was out, and settled down to a good, steady lope going along with pricking ears, quite good-naturedly.

This sign did not altogether deceive Spot Gregory. He knew all about horses, and pricking ears are apt to mean forethought as much as good nature; so when a mustang thinks ahead, it is likely to think of trouble.

Therefore, the foreman of the Milman ranch was not at all surprised when, on climbing over the hills toward Hurry Creek, on the first down slope, the Roman-nose began to pitch once more.

It is ten times as hard for a horse to pitch on a down slope as on the level—but if it manages the feat, it is a hundred times harder for the rider to stick in the saddle. Spot Gregory, nearly flipped out of place in the first ten seconds, settled down to give that broncho a busting that would last him the rest of his days, but in the midst of accomplishing the good work, scratching the pony fore-and-aft and flogging it thoroughly with the cruel quirt, he became aware of an odd condition in the valley before him.

For the edges of Hurry Creek were rimmed and lined with cattle which were not going down to drink, but remained up on the hills, red-eyed with thirst.

Spot Gregory rubbed his eyes and looked again.

Hurry Creek was to the Milman ranch what the heart's blood is to the human body. In the whole length and breadth of the big place, there was not a drop of water except for the creek. Sometimes during periods of heavy rain, little rivulets formed in the hollows, but they were not worth thinking about. There was any quantity of the finest grass on the ranch. The woodlands were a small fortune, also. But of water, there was only this one vein.

It was enough!

When Milman's old father came here, long years before, he had had wit enough to pick out the place with forethought and locate with care.

All through its upper course, Hurry Creek went shouting and raving through a high-walled canyon. On still days the noise of its anger drifted far away to the ranch house, like a faint prophecy of trouble. At a certain point, leaving the canyon, it spread out suddenly through an almost level tract of rolling land, and then dropped into the opposite hills through another high-sided trench. Cows could not get up or down the walls of either the higher or the lower ravine, but they did not need to. The Milman ranch was in outline like a huge dumb-bell. The narrow grip was where the waters of Hurry Creek ran from canyon to canyon across the rolling ground. The huge knobs were the wide-spreading acres, thousands upon thousands, which formed what they called the western and the eastern ranches. And, from the farthest corners of the two districts, the cattle would march into the creek for water.

The younger ones usually went in every day. The older stock often remained away two or three days in the best grazing at the edges of the far hill and then would come at a trot or a lope the long distance to the stream. There, standing belly-deep, they drank and drank to repletion. They waded back to shore and browsed a little on the short grasses which were always eaten close. Then they would drink again, and begin a leisurely trip back to the chosen eating places.

But on this morning the thirsty legions did not go down to drink. Some were lying down on the upper edges of the valley. Some wandered back and forth uneasily. A few milled and lowed frantically close by the water's edge. Sometimes, singly or in groups, they made dashes for the bright promise of the water, but they were always turned away by certain riders who careened up and down either bank of the stream, whirling lariats, shouting, running the cows off to a distance, where the animals turned in despair and looked hopelessly back toward the creek.

There were enough men to ride herd in this arduous manner both east and west of the creek. On the eastern side, moreover, farthest from Spot at this moment, appeared several wagons. Smoke rose from a camp fire, here, and one of the wagons, being partially unloaded, showed on the ground a heap of what looked like thick coils of newly burnished silver.

Spot could guess its true nature; it was barbed wire!

In the brush beside the water, other men were cutting stakes of a sufficient length, and beginning at the mouth of the northern canyon, on each side of it, two small groups were setting up the posts and stringing the wires upon them. Anger darkened the eyes of Spot Gregory until the whole scene disappeared before him in a swirl of black. He blinked and looked again, half hoping that the vision would disappear like a bad dream.

It did not disappear. It grew more and more vivid.

The early sun, now breaking through its veil of morning mist, made the whole view clearer to him. The men, little with distance, toiled on unceasingly. Behind them, on the new-made fences, the barbed wire gleamed like spider threads, bright with dew, and up and down the open bank of the creek, the watchful riders wheeled and flashed upon their active horses.

He tried to count all heads, and numbered sixteen, besides those who might be out of sight around the wagons, or who perhaps were otherwise concealed from him.

How they had come in was plainly to be seen. The tracks of the wagons stretched away toward the south, on the eastern side of the creek. No doubt they had worked the heavily laden wagons up through the high hills to a place of advantage, and when they were ready, they had simply driven down in the middle of the night. Now they were busy in pushing ahead their lines of battle, for a battle certainly would be fought for the possession of those streaks of barbed wire.

Grinding his teeth, he calculated chances.

He had under him a number of good men on that ranch. They could ride like fiends, and when it came to shooting, they were more than average. He could rake together as many fighting men as were present in the hollow, there, beneath him. He could recruit still other hands in the neighborhood.

But even if he had forty or fifty men to throw against the strangers, what would that accomplish?

Men who were willing to jump claims knew beforehand the resistance they were likely to encounter, and they were sure to come well prepared. If they were not great in numbers, they would be great in ability. Not a soul among the crowd down there, as Spot Gregory shrewdly guessed, but was a thorough ruffian, a man-killer, or ambitious to kill men. Every one of them had proved his desperate character, or he would not now be present. They were hand-picked villains who probably had lived by the guns for years, hunting down their fellow men as more respectable hunters might chase bears or wolves.

So Gregory felt a rising sense of helplessness.

He was on the verge of swinging his horse about and rushing for the ranch house, to let his employer know the disaster which had befallen them. The water claim of the Milman ranch had been jumped, and that would be tidings to make Milman turn green with passion.

However, Milman was too much the honorable man to meet murder with murder. Bare-handed aggression he had plenty of courage to meet, but if there was the ghost of a legal form lined up against him, he would be certain to wait for the law to show him the way.

The law!

How could the law act in time to save the thousands of the Milman cattle from death by water famine?

In the meantime, it was better to go down and look this trouble in the face. So he cantered the nervous mustang down the easy slope toward the men who, on this side of the river, were toiling to run the fence line. There were four of them so employed, two cutting post holes, stamping out the earth with cutters, or drilling it with augers. The second pair set up the posts and tamped them in place, or stretched the wire.

The posts were poor, twisted ones, and the wire was but loosely strung—two meager strands of it. Plainly the boundary was not to be strong, unless gunpowder could strengthen it enough!

In the background, there was a fifth man, who rode slowly back and forth, keeping an eye on the fence builders, and again on those hands who warded back the thirsting cows as they descended from the hills. To this fellow of apparent authority, Spot Gregory advanced, with a wave of his hand, which the other came forward willingly to meet.

They met one another close to the fence makers, and the latter stopped work gladly to watch the interview.

As for the rider, Gregory found him to be the true Western type, spare in flesh, but looking tough as whip leather. A magnificent forehead rose above the lean, brown face.

"Hello!" said Spot Gregory. "You're Champ Dixon, ain't you?"

"That's me," said Dixon, pleasantly. "I've met you, somewheres. Gregory. Is that your name?"

"Yeah. That's my name. What in hell-fire are you up to here, Dixon?"

"Oh, just picking up a right smart little piece of ground for me and my partner."

"Who's your partner?"

"Billy Shay."

"Shay!" exclaimed Spot angrily. "That—"

The other raised his gloved hand.

"Easy, Gregory!" he warned.

And Spot Gregory set his teeth with a stifled groan.

He had expected the worst, and yet this was a little too bad even for his expectations. The snakelike cunning of Shay and the deadly hand of Dixon to back him up made the combination hard to defeat.

For his own part, he was a mere child before such a practiced assassin as Champ Dixon.

"Dixon," said he. "How're you gonna back this up in the law courts? Or is it only a way to blackmail poor Milman out of money to water his cattle, for a few days?"

"Money for watering his cows?" said the other genially. "Well, old son, the fact is that we wouldn't plunge like this except for a big thing. We've looked into Milman's title to his whole ranch, and it ain't worth a whoop! So we've took over the piece that we want!"

16
Storm Clouds

WHEN DISCRETION and judgment were considered; Spot Gregory seemed to possess both. He looked Dixon in the eye. He even allowed himself time to glance to the side, and to observe the broad grins upon the faces of the four men who were looking on, leaning on the posts of the fence.

"Well," said he, "if you was to hunt around to pick out a piece of ground that would do you less good, and more harm to Milman, I dunno that you could of picked better than this."

"No, sir," said Champ Dixon, "I dunno that we could. I looked over this here layout personal, a while back, and that's what I figgered myself."

"Tell me, Dixon," said the foreman of the ranch, "what made you boys have it in for Milman? What's he ever done agin' you, or any of you?"

Champ Dixon, at this unimpassioned appeal, was forced to scratch his head with such earnestness that he pushed his hat far back.

"What's he done agin' us?" he echoed, while he gathered his thoughts.

"Yeah. That's what I'm askin'."

"Well," said Champ, with a twinkle in his eye, "I'll tell you about that. Out here in the Far West, where they's still a frontier, as the books put it, and out here where the hair grows long, they ain't much law nor not much respect for the other feller's rights, is they?"

"Well, in a way I reckon that there ain't," said Spot Gregory.

75

"And I reckon that worryin' about how the law goes through pretty nigh bites you folks to the bone!"

Champ Dixon permitted himself a broad grin.

"Well," said he, "maybe that's a way of puttin' it. The way that it seems to me, a whole lot of gents, they step into this here country, out here, and they says to themselves that the country's so big that they got a right to pick out the parts of it that they want for themselves. So they sashays in and they picks out what they want and they don't pay nothin' much for it, and they settles down onto it, and they says that because they're here, there ain't any reason why they should ever have to budge. Now, sir, some of us, we take a look around and we say that the pigs that is the fattest might be the pigs that is the most profitable to drive to market, if you foller what I mean?"

"Yeah, I sort of foller your drift," answered Spot Gregory. "And so you want to budge the old landholders?"

"You might say that!" remarked Champ Dixon. "What I mean is that here is the Milmans set down on the land and gettin' hog-fat, and how? What title they got to this land, I ask you?"

"Why, I dunno that anybody has asked that question for a long time," said Gregory. "Everybody that I know has took it for granted that the Milmans own the Milman land."

"Yeah," said Dixon. "They's a lot of incurious folks in this neck of the woods. But supposin' that I ask you, how did the Milmans get this here land. D'you know?"

"Why, they bought it from the Injuns."

"And who sold it to them?"

"I dunno that I know that."

"I'll tell you. It was Little Crow, was his name. He was a tolerable sizeable man, in his day, and a big war chief. And he had a pile of scalps to his credit. He's got a war suit all trimmed up with scalp locks. He's got more than one suit. If he goes on a Comanche trail, he can put on a suit dressed up with Comanche hair. And if he tackles a white war party, he's got a suit tricked up with white folks' hair. Some tolerable long and golden hair, in the lot. And he's a great fighter, this here Little Crow. When it comes to the finish, it takes booze and three whites to take the scalp of that infant, what I mean to tell you.

"Well, sir, along comes old Daddy Milman, before this here boy of his ever see the light, and he reckons that he'll take up land here. And he picks up the spot that'll suit him the best.

And then he finds out that it's Injun land. And he says, what Injun shall he buy it from, him wantin' to be all straight and honorable. And so he picks on the big war chief and grand scalp-getter, Little Crow, that had counted so many coups that he gets the arm ache every time that there come along a grand feast and lyin' party among the tribe.

"So he goes to Little Crow and he says, what do you want? And whatcha think that Little Crow wants?"

"I dunno," said Spot Gregory, "that I ever heard."

"Most folks ain't. But it's been our business to find out. What he wants is six rifles, all in prime shape, and a hundred rounds of ammunition for each of 'em, and two dozen hosses—because that's about as high as he can count—and one whole keg of thirty-six gallons of fire water."

"That's what he wanted for this ranch?"

"Aye," said Champ Dixon, "and he thought that he was gettin' a whale of a big bargain, and that he could step in and run out the whites with the guns that he had got from them whenever he had a mind. So he makes the bargain, and old Milman, he counts out the goods, and he goes better than his bargain, and he makes that set of rifles the finest that can be got, and he chucks in an extra lot of ammunition, and he makes them hosses an even thirty, and the best that money can get or ropes steal off the range. And that fire water he makes, it's the pure stuff, because he don't make it alcohol, prune juice, and water, but he makes it straight alcohol, and on the night of that sale, and payment, they is three braves that plumb die of joy, and a couple of squaws they change husbands, and they is five sets of hair lifted inside of the next week or so, because the whole bunch goes on the warpath. But anyway, the Injuns is happy, and Milman is happy. He's got a coupla million dollars' worth of land, and the Injuns, they has got one grand jag.

"After a while, they start in tryin' to get paid over again."

"Blackmail?" said Spot Gregory.

"You can call it that," admitted the other. "Anyway, they try to collect some more of that thousand proof fire water, but they find that in behind old Milman there has sneaked another man, by name of Uncle Sam, and when the Injuns climb onto their war ponies, old Uncle Sam, he hits out of the dark, and pops 'em in the nose and knocks 'em off again. You foller that?"

"I foller all of that," said Spot Gregory, looking with the

corner of his eye at a tangle of fifty thirsting cows who were trying to rush to the water, but in vain.

"Now along comes Billy Shay and me," continued the narrator, "and we get to lookin' over the lay of the land, and we get to seein' how much law and order they is around here, and how good a claim a lot of these cattle kings has got to their land, and the first thing that we find out is that most of them ain't got none at all. And that old Milman, he sure made a grand mistake, and I'll tell you why.

"Little Crow, he was a great chief, and all that, and he had cut off enough hair to plant a forty-acre field, but the trouble was that he wasn't the main chief of that tribe, and that he had no more right to sell off a part of the land than I have to sell Broadway and Beekman Street. No, sir, he didn't have no right at all. And before there was a sale, there should of been a grand palaver, and all the chiefs there, and specially New Monday, which was really the head of the tribe, though he hadn't taken a scalp for thirty years he was that old.

"When we heard that, we went around and we found out that the Injuns still had a right to this land, if the sale by Little Crow was wrong and we find out that the real head of the tribe today is Happy Monday—he's a descendant of New Monday. So we go to see Happy Monday, and he's sick in one eye and can't see very good out of the other, and we get Happy Monday to sell us this here bit of land for three hosses and three hogsheads of alcohol, which is dirt cheap. But it's hard to educate redskins up to high prices. And we get that sale made, and we come down here and move onto the land that's rightfully ours. And if Milman, he don't believe that we got the right, he can go to the law and get licked—or he can try gunpowder—and get licked."

Spot Gregory bit his lip.

"That's a mighty movin' story," said he. "Maybe you'll tell me what you'd sell out this bit of land for?"

Champ Dixon looked around him with an obvious complacency.

"They's a thing that you might of noted," said he. "That we got the water rights of this here ranch in our pants pockets."

"I've noted that the cows is stickin' out their tongues and bawlin' for somethin' more than air," said he.

"Well, sir," said Champ Dixon, licking his lips, "it occurs to me and Billy Shay that it would be a dog-gone outright shame to sell this here crop of water, that never needs to be planted and that comes to hundreds of millions of tons a year—it would be a dog-gone shame to sell it for less'n a coupla hundred thousand dollars."

Spot Gregory looked blandly around him at the flowing stream and at the running water.

"You want two hundred thousand?" said he.

"That's the price, old son."

"And how much you charge for all of the fine sunshine and the air that the cows will be breathin'?"

"Billy and me is downright generous," said the other, "and we throw that in as a kind of bounty to sweeten the deal."

"Yeah, it sweetens it, all right," said Spot Gregory. "Now, just supposin' that we wanted a time to think this deal over— that Milman wanted time, I mean?"

"Take all the time that you want," said the other. "Only I hope that your cows won't be dyin' like flies in the meantime."

"And suppose that we wanted to water 'em while we was thinkin'?"

"I never heard of a cow needin' water to think on," said Dixon grimly. "And you can tell Milman that for me, too."

"I'll tell him," agreed the other. "Now, then, suppose that we wanted to water them cows, how much would you charge a head?"

"We're reasonable," said Champ Dixon. "It sure does grieve us a lot to think of cows goin' thirsty. So we're willin' to let you water them cows for two dollars a head."

"Two dollars?" shouted the foreman. "We might as well haul beer up here and water 'em with that!"

"Well," said the other thoughtfully, "I never figgered on that. But maybe it would do as good!"

"Gregory hastily pulled out his plug of tobacco and bit off a liberal corner.

"Is that a go?" said he.

"'Yeah, that's a go."

"No changin'?"

"No."

"Tell me, Champ—ain't that Two-gun Porter, and Missouri Slim, and the Haley brothers, over yonder?"

"Yeah, you're right."

"And the rest of your bunch match up? Well," said Gregory, "I got an idea that more'n money is gonna be paid for this land. And the color of it is gonna be red."

He did not pause to say adieu, but turned the head of his horse and rode away.

17
Bad News

WHEN THE FOREMAN was over the ridge, he turned loose that stubborn broncho, and made him run for his life, with a jab of the spurs or a cut of the quirt every fifty yards or so.

He made that poor mustang hold to the one gait until it had reached the ranch house, and then Spot Gregory threw the reins and jumped from a horse that did not need to be tied. It stood like a lamb, while Spot ran on into the house.

It was just such a house as a thousand other ranchers in the West had built before Milman, and would build after him. It was a long strung-out place in the midst of what had once been a flourishing grove, but the nearest trees had been cut away for firewood, regardless of shady comfort in the middle of the summer. All the ground around the house was stamped bare by the horses which were often tied up in great lines to the hitching racks. Through the naked dust, a dozen or so of chickens scratched and went about thrusting their heads before them at every step.

A heavy wind of a few years before had threatened to knock down the kitchen wing like a stack of cards, and this had been secured with a great pair of plough chains, taken up taut with a tourniquet. This chain was the only ornament that appeared on that unpainted barn of a house. It leaned all askew. It was plainly no more than a shelter, with little pretension of being a comfortable house. Yet the Milman hospitality was famous for two hundred miles.

Into this house ran Spot, entering through the kitchen door, which he kicked open in the face of the Chinese cook. The latter sat down violently upon the floor and the armful of baking tins which he was carrying went clattering to the farthest corners. He looked surprised, but not offended. He was prepared for anything up to murder from these wild white men.

"Where's the boss?" shouted Spot.

"No savvy," said the cook, blinking.

"I'm in here, Spot," said Milman from the dining room.

Gregory strode to the door. He was too excited and angry to remember to take off his hat. He stood there towering in the doorway, scowling as though it was Milman whom he hated.

It was still fairly early in the morning, though late for a ranch breakfast, but Milman had adopted easier ways of living, since his fortune had become so secure in the past few years. The ranch was a gold mine, and the vein of it promised to last forever.

Opposite the rancher sat his daughter, and Mrs. Milman who looked small and frail at the end of the table. She was one of those delicate and thin-faced women who seem to be half with the angels all the time; as a matter of fact, she always knew the price of beef on the hoof to an eighth of a cent.

"What's loose, Spot?" asked Milman.

"Hell's loose," said Gregory shortly. "Plumb hell, is what is loose!"

Then he remembered the ladies and by way of apology, he took off his hat.

"Go on," said Milman.

Gregory pointed with a long arm.

"Champ Dixon, he's jumped the water rights. He's camped with about twenty men and he's runnin' a fence on both sides of Hurry Creek."

Georgia Milman jumped to her feet.

"The scoundrel!" said she.

Her father pushed back his chair with an exclamation at the same moment, but Mrs. Milman looked up to the ceiling with narrowed eyes, and did not stir.

"They're keeping the cows away from the water?" demanded Milman.

"That's what they're doin'."

"I'll get—I'll send to Dry Creek, and we'll have the law out here to take their scalps. That murdering Dixon, is it?"

"Champ Dixon."

"Did you see him?"

"I talked to him."

"Does he know that we can have the sheriff—"

"He says that it's all legal. That your title from Little Crow ain't worth a scrap and that he's got the real title, now, from another buck in the tribe."

"They're going to use the law. Is that what you mean?" asked Milman shortly.

"That's what they say. Billy Shay is behind the deal. Him and his crooked lawyers, I suppose."

"Shay, too!" exclaimed Milman. "I'll—I'll—"

He stopped.

Perspiration began to pour down his face, though the morning was cold enough.

"Oh, Dad," said Georgia, "what can we do?"

"We gotta pay two dollars a head for water rights," said the foreman, writhing in mighty rage at the mere thought.

Milman turned purple, but still his expression was that of a dazed man.

Said Mrs. Milman suddenly: "There's only one thing to do, my dear."

"What can we do?" said her husband.

"We can drive them from the water by force."

"Not that crowd," declared the foreman. "I know 'em too dog-gone well. I saw the face of a lot of 'em, and I knew 'em out of the old days. They're a hand-picked bunch of yeggs. Every one of them is a gunman with a record. And there's Champ Dixon at the head of 'em! You know Dixon."

"I know all about Dixon," said Mrs. Milman. "But—we've got to get the cows to the water. We have neighbors. We'll have to send to them all. The Wagners and the Peters and the Birch families will never in the world say no to us."

"They'll never budge agin' a fellow like Dixon," prohpesied the foreman. "They all know his record. We need State troops. Besides, Dixon is claimin' the law. The Peters and the rest would ride with us agin' plain rustlers, or such. But not agin' Dixon and the chance of the law, besides."

"He's right," said Milman. dropping his head a little.

He looked like a beaten man Silence came into the room like a fifth person and laid a cold hand on every heart.

Then Mrs. Milman went on in her gentle voice: "The cows will soon be dying, my dear."

Her husband looked wildly up at her and then away through the window. At that very moment a calf began to bawl from the feeding corral where the weaklings were kept.

"We can run the pump night and day—" he began.

"That well runs dry with very little pumping at this time of year," said his wife.

"We could dig—"

"You know how deep we have to dig in order to get water, and through what rock. The cows will be dead, my dear. Every animal on the place, except the few that we can water from the mill—and precious few that will be."

"You've heard Spot Gregory talk," said her husband. "He knows these people and what they can do. God help me!"

He was suddenly in a blank despair.

Said Mrs. Milman: "Georgia!"

"Yes, mother."

"Take a horse and ride to the Chet Wagner house. Tell Chet what has happened. Ask him if he'll come over here and help us fight. Remind him, if you have to, how we helped him through that bad winter, two years ago."

"I hate to go begging to Chet," said the girl. "He—"

"Are you going to let your pride stand between you and bankruptcy?" asked her mother coldly. "Chet is a good lad. He'll never say no to you."

Georgia looked desperately at her father for help.

"No, no, Georgia," said he. "I won't allow you to use your influence when you—"

"Georgia might fetch in the Wagners," admitted Spot, thoughtfully. "And I might be able to raise the Birch outfit. Tom Birch always was a pretty good friend of mine. I dunno about the Peters. They're a pretty hard lot. We can try 'em, though. But I tell you what, we ain't got the kind of men ridin' this range that can stand up to such a bunch as Dixon's crew. However, it's better to make a try and slip than not to try at all. It's the ghost of the law that he has behind him that's gonna hold back everybody. It's just robbery, I know. But you'd have to pay him two hundred thousand dollars for a quit claim!"

There was a faint cry from Milman.

Then he exclaimed: "Well, if the worst has come to the worst, two hundred thousand will have to be paid—and then we'll fight him in the courts and get the money back!"

"Get back water from the desert!" said Mrs. Milman, her voice much gentler than her words. "Are you going to quit and surrender, my dear?"

"Look the thing in the face!" exclaimed her husband. "What else can I do? The cows—"

"I'd rather," said Elinore Milman, "see every cow and horse on the ranch dead of thirst than to allow crooks to beat you in this manner. Get the money back from them in the courts? Why, ten minutes after you paid the cash down, they'd have scattered to the four winds. Get the money back, indeed!"

This grave speech had such weight that Milman suddenly threw his hands above his head.

"I'll get our boys together and lead 'em down!" he cried. "Spot, send out a call to—"

"No," said the foreman with unexpected firmness.

"Are you going to quit on me, too, Spot?" asked Milman sadly.

"I'll do my share of range ridin'," said Spot, "and I'll keep care of the herd, and I'll do my share of fightin', too. But I'll never go against the mob that I saw down there by the river until we've got the odds on our side. I've only got the ordinary share of sand. I ain't got enough to want to throw myself away. Why, Milman, there's single men down there that would eat any three men we've got, and eat 'em before breakfast."

"You see, Elinore?" said the rancher to his wife, in despair.

"Well," she said in her usual gentle calm, "go ahead and see what neighbors we can get to join us. If they haven't turned up by five or six this evening, I'll take a gun and see what I myself can do with the desperadoes."

18

A Volunteer

THEY LOOKED at her in amazement.

Her cheek had not reddened, her voice had not altered or her eye brightened. She was as gently calm as ever, but suddenly they knew that she was steel. All three stood like children before her.

She explained to her husband: "I've put a good deal of my life into this ranch and its affairs, my dear. If I have to die for the sake of it, I'll die without a whimper. But in the meantime, let's find out what our friends will do. Georgia, ride to see Chet Wagner. You try the Birch family. I'll go to the Peters myself."

"You'll do nothing of the kind," broke in Milman. "*You* ride about begging? I'll go myself. And you stay here!"

She nodded at once.

"Of course, I'll do what you wish, my dear," said she.

But when the other three left the room, they all realized something they had never guessed before—that little Elinore Milman was the real controlling force in that ranch. Her own husband had not dreamed how true it was, but looking dizzily back through the years, he could now realize that a hundred times her voice, like a hand upon his shoulder, like a hand at his back, had pushed him along the way she chose, and given him courage for great attempts.

There was something mysterious—this utter manliness of resolution in a woman—and to the mystery they trusted a good deal. If her body were small, her soul was so great that it seemed to all three of them an overwhelming thing.

They took horses at once and cut across country in varying directions.

There were a few squatters here and there who might have been picked up more quickly, but Milman's outfit, for many good reasons, was not on speaking terms with the squatters. The nearest big ranches were the only ones likely to be able to send forth men in sufficient numbers. Chet Wagner, in particular, was as brave as a lion, though Georgia blushed when she thought of appealing to him for help.

However, she set her teeth and went grimly on her way. She had a good fast half-bred gelding under her, and the horse worked well this morning. Her spirits rose. The keen morning wind of that gallop cut into her face and blew away her doubts and sense of shame. After all, what was shameful in asking the help of a man who once had asked her to marry him?

She thought back to her mother, rather bewildered by that quiet exhibition of strength, and yet she could tell herself that many a time before she had found the steel under that silken glove.

Her heart rose higher. Every rock was flashing with dew, and the grass sparkled. Midsummer would have been thrice as trying, but at this season the dew alone would enable those hardy range cattle to last quite a time. In the meanwhile, they could find some way. If the neighbors could not or would not help with guns, they might help with wise counsel. The familiar face of the big blue mountains was a comfort to her, also. They had looked down on her through so many happy days that it seemed impossible that they now should see her in despair.

All would come out well, she told herself. There was too great a crop of chivalry and manhood in the West for the Milmans to be abandoned in their time of need.

Then, as the horse trotted to the top of a low hill which looked down upon a wide, pleasant hollow, she reined it in suddenly with a leap of the heart. For over the opposite knoll swept a big mule deer with its long ears laid back with the speed of its running. It floated down the hillside with the peculiar, bounding gait of its species, and the girl, watching and wondering, listened for the cry of dogs behind it, or the howl of the wolf running on the trail.

There was no such outcry, but an instant later over the same hilltop darted a rider on a black horse which had a strange vest of shining white over the breast and the lower part of the throat.

Instantly she recognized the markings which had given the Duck Hawk its name. And she saw the rider skillfully jockeying the fleet mare down the slope.

It lost ground. Nothing that lives and runs on four feet can keep up with a mule deer over sharp ups and downs. As though it had wings, the deer smote the ground and rose, and settled, and floated forward again with apparent lack of effort.

But in the flat of the hollow it was a different matter. The Hawk, stretched out in a straight line, came like the wind, and the frightened deer, with the shadow of a swinging rope whipping across it, vainly strove to dodge.

That instant the rope started out and the deer, snagged around both forefeet, tumbled head over heels.

It was fast to rise, but not fast enough.

Out of the saddle whipped the rider, and the hunting knife flashed across the tender throat of the deer as it threw up its head to rise. Then, stepping in, the Kid gave the poor beast the *coup de grâce*.

It was over in an instant.

But Georgia Milman found herself laughing with excitement.

Here was a man who ran down his venison on horseback! And suddenly she thought of the wild Indians of the old days. Such feats must have been accomplished by their most famous riders, now and then, a thing for the hunter to boast of to the end of his days!

But there would be no boasting from the Kid.

Before she started her horse down the slope, she saw his knife expertly at work in cutting up the quarry—speed and business were combined with a rare efficiency.

And it seemed to the girl that it was as though she had seen a hawk drop out of the sky. Now it tore the prey which it had struck down, and presently it would be winging away across the hills.

She jogged the gelding down the hill, but had not gone far before the Hawk jerked up her head and whinnied softly. The Kid, at this, stood up from his butchering and watched the newcomer. He raised his hat and waved it to her while she was still at a little distance.

"There'll be venison steaks around here in another half hour, Miss Milman," said he. "Hop off and wangle the fire, while I get the cuts off."

She shook her head, still smiling down at the red-handed killer and his kill.

"Do you do that often?" she asked him. "Do you run down your meat like that very often?"

"It keeps the Hawk on edge," said he. "Nothing like a good brush through rough country to tune up a horse."

"And nothing like a run after a mule deer to get you a broken neck," she observed.

He nodded, but there was no seriousness in his face.

"Well, rifles make a lot of noise," said he, "and ammunition costs a lot and weighs a lot. This is the Hawk's fourteenth deer, if you'll believe it."

The girl looked critically at the mare. She was breathing hard, but her head was up, her eye was bright, and it was patent that she was still full of running.

"I'd believe almost anything about her."

Her face darkened suddenly.

"Are you with those people back at Hurry Creek?" she asked him. "Are you out here hunting for that crew?"

"What crew?" said the Kid. "Who's at Hurry Creek? I thought that ran out on your land?"

"You're not one of them," she nodded, with a sigh of relief. "No, if you were with them, of course, you'd be the top man, and not Champ Dixon."

"Oh Dixon's there, is he? What's his game?"

"Jumping my father's water rights."

The Kid squinted at the skyline, as if he hunted for a thought.

"That's the only water on your place, isn't it?"

"That's the only water," nodded the girl. "They're herding the cows back from the creek and putting up a line fence on each side."

"Dixon and Shay," nodded the Kid.

"How do you guess at Shay, too?"

"I've heard that they're working together. Dixon turns the rabbit, and Shay eats it. They make a pretty neat pair, working together."

"There's another man coming," she said, pointing to a horseman who had just bobbed into sight in the far distance, in the same direction from which the Kid had come on his hunt.

"That's my partner," said the Kid, without looking.

"But you never have partners," said the girl.

"I've changed my ways," he declared briefly. "Are you going to dynamite Dixon and his men? How many has he?"

"Something more than fifteen. About twenty, I think."

"That'll take some blasting. I know the kind of fellow he'd pick for company on a job like that."

"He's got 'em," said the girl. "Well, I'll drift along. I've still got a stretch ahead of me."

"If I can be any help," said the Kid suddenly, "give me a call."

She jerked in the reins so quickly and so hard that the gelding reared, and then landed prancing.

She paid no attention to this. She sat the saddle like a man, conscious of strength, and unafraid.

"What do you mean by that?" she asked. "Help us against Dixon and his lot?"

"If there's to be a game," said the Kid lightly, "I might as well sit in for a hand or two."

She stared at him.

"Would you do that just for the fun of it?" she asked him.

"You see how it is," said the Kid. "That would give us an

excuse to camp in one spot until we'd cleaned up this venison. Otherwise, a lot of it will go to waste."

She, watching him curiously, could not help asking: "Is there anything in the world that could make you take care of your neck?"

"I carry a thousand dollars' insurance," said the Kid. "You can't expect a man to do more than that."

She laughed heartily, and said:

"D'you seriously mean that you'll help us?"

"I'll shake on it," said the Kid, extending his hand.

She moved her own, then jerked it away.

"No," she said, shaking her head. "I don't think I have a right to tie you down to a promise. But if you'll go back there to the ranch house and tell Mother that you're a little interested, she'll think you're an angel newly out of heaven!"

19

Two Reasons

WHEN Mrs. Milman had finished her second promenade between the house and the woods, walking with a quick, eager step, she was no closer to a solution of the problem than before. She knew that the ranch was confronted by the most imminent danger of destruction. And the place meant something more than dollars to her. Sometimes her mind turned quickly toward her husband, now far off trying to bring guns to help them, but her confidence in her spouse was not great. He was made of too mild a metal to cut through to the heart of such a problem as this.

And for her own part?

She measured out her way with the same brisk steps, her head high, using a long stick for a cane like one of those dainty great ladies of the old century who had played at dairy maids in the woods of the Trianon.

She had completed her second round when, pausing by the verge of the woods, she watched two horsemen coming up the slope, one on a sorrel and one on a black with a white breast. Men and horses were about of a size, she decided, but the black had a way of going that made his rider appear small and light. He danced up that hill as though a mere form of paper were in the saddle on his back. Somewhere before she felt that she had seen that horse.

She was an expert in horses, but she was a still greater expert in men, and that rider of the black horse had a way of holding up his head that pleased her. It was, in short, like her own, though this did not come into her mind.

The pair of strangers were well up to the top of the rise, and coming in between the wood shed and the feeding corral before she recognized the Kid, and her heart leaped. For she was, as has been said, a connoisseur of men. Besides, she could remember how that single man had entered the house of Billy Shay, and how fugitives had begun to appear at its doors and windows, as though thrust out by an explosion.

Suppose such a man were applied to the affair down there at the creek.

But no! He was far more apt to be in the employ of Champ Dixon, that wily cutthroat.

She waved her stick as they came closer and the Kid, seeing her, turned instantly in her direction. Lightly as a dancer, the Duck Hawk came on, flicking the dust behind her. Then the Kid swung down to the ground and took off his hat. Bud Trainor, behind him, and a little to the side, did the same thing.

"Are you Mrs. Milman?" said the Kid.

"Yes," said she. "Have you seen me before?"

"I simply guessed," said he. "I was looking for the lady of the house. This is my friend, Bud Trainor."

Here Bud mumbled something, downfaced, for Elinore Milman was several cuts above the people of his familiar world.

"And I'm called the Kid, by most people."

I saw you calling on Mr. Shay in Dry Creek," said she.

"Oh, yes. An old friend of mine," said the Kid.

"You'll let me call you something beside 'Kid,' I hope," said she.

"My real name," he answered, "is Reginald Beckwith-Hollis, with a hyphen. That's why people call me the Kid. The real name takes up so much time."

She permitted her eyes to smile, and the Kid grinned gayly back at her.

"Are you just passing through, Mr. Beckwith-Hollis?" she asked him.

"I was just passing through," said the Kid. "But something stopped me."

"Champ Dixon and his boys at Hurry Creek?" she asked.

"No," said the Kid. "I'm not playing this hand with them." She sighed with relief.

"I met your daughter," said he.

Mrs. Milman gripped her stick a little harder and looked more closely at that handsome, boyish, careless face.

"Ah, you met Georgia?" said she.

"Yes. She was signing up recruits, and we joined. She sent us here to report to you."

"Georgia is a good recruiting agent, then," said she. "What terms did she offer?"

"We didn't talk of that," said the Kid. "What d'you suggest?"

She looked away from him across the hills, and noted the steady drift of cattle heading toward Hurry Creek. Before long, all the cattle on the place would be gathered in vast, milling throngs which would stamp the turf to dust near the water, and that dust would quicken the pangs of thirst. She could visualize hundreds, thousands lying down to die under the hot sun. And how hot it was. It burned through the shoulders of her dress. It scorched her hand through the thin glove which she was wearing.

Then she made up her mind.

"The minute that the Dixon gang is driven off—to stay," said she, "you'll get a check for ten thousand dollars. You can split that with Mr. Trainor any way you see fit."

Bud Trainor glanced up as though the heavens had opened. But the Kid, still smiling a little, shook his head.

"We're only here for a short job," said he. "We'll work for two dollars a day—and keep, if that's agreeable to you?"

She stared at him.

"You don't want money Mr.—Beckwith-Hollis?"

"Certain kinds, I can get along without."

She turned suddenly upon Bud Trainor.

"And what about you?" she asked.

Bud started eagerly to reply. He had heard a fortune named. He had seen his start in life presented as on a golden salver. But then he remembered in what company he was traveling. He cast a sidelong look at the Kid and muttered: "The Kid does my thinking for me on this trip."

Mrs. Milman confronted the Kid again.

"I don't understand you," she said bluntly. "Of course, it's generous. But to drive out the Dixon outfit will mean risking your life! Is there something else that you want?"

The Kid smiled upon her with his utmost geniality.

"I'll tell you how it is," said he. "A man doesn't like to make money outside of his regular trade. That's the way with me, I suppose."

"And what is your regular trade?" said she.

"It has several branches," he answered her. "You might call me a miner. I use a pack of cards for powder when I'm breaking ground."

"You mean that you're a gambler?"

"Yes. That's my main line."

"And that leaves you—scruples"—she hesitated for words—"about making money in this way?"

"Yes," said he. "I have scruples. Behind Dixon is Billy Shay. And Billy Shay took a friend of mine into camp, one day. He started on a trip with my partner. He finished the trip alone, and the other fellow never was heard of. You see, this job of yours is my job, as well, because Shay's on the other side of fence from you."

"Does that go for your friend, too?"

She nodded toward Trainor.

"We're thrown in together," said the Kid. "All for one and one for all. Is that all clear, now?"

She paused again.

"It's not clear at all," said she, "but if you want to have it this way, heaven knows how glad I am to have you helping us. Have you any plans?"

"Not a plan in the world."

"You don't know how you're going to begin?"

"Why, I suppose that we ought to wait to see how the recruits turn in from the ranches around here."

"Do you think that they'll come in?" she asked.

"What do you think?"

"I believe they won't."

"I agree with you."

"Why do you?"

"Because Dixon seems to have a bit of law behind him. And the only way to save your cows is going to be to forget that such a thing as law exists."

The smile died from his eyes. He looked at her as straight as a ruled line; and she looked back, her color gradually ebbing from her face.

"Bud," said the Kid, "suppose that you take the hosses and give 'em a swallow of water over there at the trough."

Bud nodded, and taking the horses by the bridles, he led them away.

"Thank you," said Mrs. Milman. "I wanted to talk to you alone."

The Kid nodded. "I thought so," said he.

He was as grave as before, waiting.

"Don't you think," said she, "that we'll get on a lot better if we talk frankly to one another."

"Don't you think," said the Kid, "that there's nobody in the world that any one in it can talk frankly to?"

"Husbands and wives, even, and parents and children?" she suggested.

"Well," said the Kid, his old smile glimmering at her, "don't you have to be polite to your husband?"

"I suppose so. What of that?"

"That's not frankness. And with children—you have to be hard on 'em when you want to be soft; and you have to shake your head when you want to smile. Is that frankness?"

She looked at him with a new interest.

"You seem to know about such things," said she.

"Oh, I know what everybody knows. I've had bunkies who were willing to die for me, but never one that I could talk frankly to."

She nodded.

"This matter about the law—"

"The law would probably save you," said the Kid. "But your cows would be dead before that."

"Then we have to be law breakers in order to save the cows?"

"That's it. Are you willing?"

She looked again across the hills. Steadily the cattle were marching across them toward the distant water. And the color flared suddenly back into her face.

"I know that we're right," she said, "even if we're outside the law."

She waited. Then she broke out: "You can't be frank, but I'd like to know if you're doing this only because you hate Dixon and Shay."

He also hesitated a moment, and then he looked her straight in the eyes again, an intolerable brightness in his glance.

"No," said he, "I'm not!"

20

A Challenge

THE FIRST THOUGHT of a mother is for her child. And though she knew that Georgia had hardly more than laid eyes upon this man, suddenly Mrs. Milman was thinking of the girl. So strongly, so vividly the thought struck home in her that the name bubbled to her lips. And she had to make an effort to keep from speaking it.

For, above all, there was in this straight look of the Kid a confession of a dangerous purpose that shook her to the ground.

It frankly told her that what he wanted was something more than she would give, and the bright face of Georgia rose smiling across her mind like a sweet vision.

"You won't tell me the other reason, I suppose?" she said.

"Mrs. Milman," said the Kid, "you see how it is. I'm a gambler, and you can't expect me to play with my cards face up on the table."

She sighed a little, and then nodded.

"I'd better ride down to the creek," said the Kid, "and look over these fellows and the lay of the land. I'll be back in a couple of hours. By that time, we'll have the recruits in camp, I suppose?"

She could not speak, and merely made a little gesture, but she was worried to the heart. She watched him striding off toward the horses with a darkened brow. She had met strong men

before this, but she never had met men who were both strong
and free, and the Kid seemed to her as free as a bird. Studying
him, she thought that she could understand why he was called
"the Kid," and simply that. In his step, in the carriage of his
head, there was something inexplicably and eternally young. He
was the very spirit of youth. And, adding up his qualities as they
occurred to her, she thought of youth as a thing swift, cruel,
careless, and without precedent or law to bind it. So much the
more natural that upon youth, this youth, she should be depend-
ing in the great time of stress. Through the Kid they might be
able to drive the transgressors from their land and save the
cattle. What other danger would they be taking in exchange for
it?

She sighed.

But, after all, there seemed nothing else to do about the
matter. It might be that her shrewd suspicion was right, and
that the Kid was here primarily to distinguish himself in such a
manner that he would be forced most favorably upon the attention of Georgia. It might be that she was entirely wrong, and
that he had no such hope in his mind. In any case, she would
have to be a gambler, and with her cards also hidden, she would
have to play out this game against the professional, which he
confessed himself to be.

When she had come to this conclusion, she started back
toward the house, her head a little bowed, and the shadow of it,
made large by the wide brim of her hat, falling always before
her, so that she was stepping continually into the edge of it.

The Kid, in the meantime, had joined Bud Trainor at the
watering trough, and found him tracing designs in the dust,
while the horses drank. He noted carefully that the cinches had
not been loosened, and this he did himself, letting them sag
down.

"What's that for?" asked Bud Trainor.

"Well," said the Kid, "how would you like to come in dry
and have to drink with your belt sunk into the middle of you?"

"Why, a hoss can stand that," said Bud, curiously.

"A horse can stand it, all right," said the Kid. "But I'll tell
you what, Bud, these horses are more than horses to us; they're
to us what wings are to birds. They're life and death to us.
We've got to keep them fit."

Bud regarded him strangely.

"I see," said he. "They've finished drinking now, I guess."

"Don't hurry 'em," said the Kid. "They'll take a sip or two later on. Have a cigarette and we'll watch 'em digest their drinks."

"You'd think it was whisky, to hear you," grinned Bud.

"Better than whisky, to them," said the Kid. "Are you sorry about that play I made, over there?"

"You mean about the ten thousand?"

"Yes."

"No, I'm not sorry."

"You're sure?"

"I'm sure. But what about this job with Dixon and his hired thugs? You ain't bit off more'n you can chew?"

"I dunno," said the Kid, carelessly. "We can have a try at it."

Trainor swallowed hard, and then nodded.

"All right," said he.

"Does it seem like a crazy thing to you, Bud?"

"I'm not thinking," said Bud hastily. "You're the boss and the lead hand in what we do. I'll follow on."

The glance of the Kid dwelt upon him, gravely.

"Tell me," broke out Bud Trainor. "Whatever made you wanta have me along with you? What made you finally decide to take me along from my house?"

"I'll tell you. By my way of thinking, murder's not the worst crime in the world."

"I know," said Trainor. "I tried a worse one, back there. I tried a lot worse one. What of that? Did that make you think that I could turn straight, and stay straight?"

"I think you can," said the Kid. "You needed more rein than you'd been having. I'm going to give you the rein. You may break your neck—or you may have a good time out of it. I don't know."

The other sighed, faintly.

"Which way now?" said he.

"Down to Hurry Creek."

Bud, without a word, stepped forward to pull up the cinches.

"Let 'em hang for a while," said the Kid. "Give 'em a chance after drinking, and they'll run ten times as well for you later. And likely we may have to come back from the creek a lot faster than we went down to it."

Bud, without a word, stepped forward a little as though these marching instructions irritated him, but he went on at the side of his companion, as they led the horses forward across the grass.

The Kid, finishing his cigarette, seemed in high spirits. And, as they went over the top of a hill, he even made a dancing catch step or two. Bud watched these maneuvers askance. But it seemed that his friend had nothing better to do, as he sauntered along, than dance like this, and to look cheerfully up the stream of little white clouds which the wind was hurrying across the sky, sometimes compacting them into solid puffs, very like the smoke blown circling from the mouths of cannon, and sometimes stretching them out to translucent fleece.

They walked for a good half hour through the heat of the sun, Bud stumbling now and then in his high-heeled boots. At last, the Kid gave the signal, and pulling up their cinches again, they mounted. Bud's gelding came up strong and hard against the bit, and he grinned aside to the Kid.

"You know hosses!" he confessed.

The Kid said nothing. He merely smiled. And suddenly Trainor felt that he had been let into the intimacy of the wisest and strongest man in the world. He himself was older; but he felt that all the knowledge he had was as nothing compared with the information lodged in the brain of his confederate.

So they jogged easily along, swinging into a mild canter over the level, but always walking the horses up and down the grades.

"Shoulders!" the Kid explained. "You have to watch their shoulders more than diamonds!"

At last they drew toward Hurry Creek, and on a hill before them, they saw a horseman waiting, on guard, with a rifle balanced across the pommel of his saddle. Moveless he watched them as they came up the last slope.

The Kid, from a short distance, waved his gloved hand.

"You know that gent?" asked Trainor.

"It's Tom Slocum."

"Is that the Slocum that killed the Lester boys?"

"That's the one. He's done other things, too. Oh, this must be a hand-picked crew that Champ Dixon has with him!"

As they came closer, Tom Slocum was revealed as a mild-appearing man with pale, sad blue eyes and a pair of old-fashioned saber-shaped mustaches, which drooped past the corners of his mouth as far as his chin. The wind was blowing the long tips of them.

"Why, hello, Tom," said the Kid.

"Hello, Kid," said Tom Slocum, starting in his saddle. "You come up to the right place, Kid," he went on as they came closer. "We got a need for you here, old son. Is that Bud Trainor? We can use you too, Bud."

"What's the wages on this job?" asked the Kid.

"Twenty bucks a day, and found, and good found," said Slocum. "Look yonder!"

They were at the top of the rise, now, and could see Hurry Creek, and the working men, and the glistening strands of the wire fence stretching almost to the end of either side of the gap between the canyon mouths. The gesture of Slocum indicated the camp wagons in the center of the farther shore, with horses tethered around them. In the midst was a tent, above which smoke curled lazily into the sunny air.

"Nothin' but the fat, in there," said Slocum, licking his lips at the thought. "Anything from fresh bread to marmalade. And no questions asked. Steaks three times a day, smothered in onions. You live like in a restaurant and nothin' to pay. Nothin' to do but to bluff out the shorthorns on this here ranch, Kid. And twenty bucks a day for sittin' pretty. Come along down, and I'll show you to Champ Dixon, because he's the boss. He might sweeten your pay, Kid, if he's got any sense. He's sweetened mine!"

"Who else have you got down there?"

"Boone Tucker, and Hollis, and Dolly Smith, and Graham, and Three-finger Murphy, and Canuck Joe, and Silvertip Oliver, and Doc Cannon, and——"

"Do they all stand up to that level?" asked the Kid, thoughtfully.

"Sure they do. Come down and meet 'em, will you?"

"I'm on the other side of the fence," said the Kid, running his eyes casually over the prospect. "I'm on the other side, and I'll stay there."

Slocum, instinctively, reined back his horse with a jerk.

"What kind of a game is this?" he demanded.

"A straight game," said the Kid. "You might slide down the hill and ask if any of those boys are feeling restless. If they are, come back with any of 'em, and we might have a little party up here, the four of us. Judge Colt, and plenty of ground to fall on. What say, Tom?"

21
Watching

THE REPUTATION of Tom Slocum was very high among those who knew. It was increased now by his bearing toward the Kid. For he seemed interested in only one thing, and that was the hard, square angle of the end of the Kid's chin.

"Tell me, Kid," said Slocum. "You're anxious for a pair of us to come up here and have it out with you—with guns?"

"I'm not anxious, Tom," the Kid hastened to inform him. "But you boys are on one side of the fence, and I'm on the other. If you want a little action to stir up the game, come along and have it. That's all that I mean."

"Come on down with me," suggested Tom Slocum, "and pick out the fellow you want to make number two with me."

"I won't come down, Tom," replied the Kid. "You've given me enough names. Plenty enough to suit me. Any one of them will do. I wouldn't cramp your style, Tom, by telling you who was to play partners with you."

Slocum turned burning eyes from the Kid to Bud Trainor.

"You're number two in this party, are you?" asked Slocum.

And Bud, with a nod, waved his hand toward the Kid, as much as to say that he had been elected by that formidable youth for whatever work lay ahead.

"I'll go down and find out what the boys say," declared Slocum. "Just wait up here, will you?"

"We'll be here," said the Kid, and Slocum, turning his horse, jogged quietly off down the slope.

But Trainor kept an anxious eye fixed on his companion.

Nervously Bud passed his hand under his coat to the new spring holster which was attached under the pit of his left arm. He had adopted this contrivance at the suggestion of the Kid, but still it seemed strange to him. He had practiced until the Kid declared that his time on a draw was less than it had been when pulling from the hip. Still, he was uncertain. Next, he slipped his hand down along the stock of the Winchester which, in its long holster, ran down between his right leg and the saddle. But the Kid did not seem to see these uneasy movements of his companion.

He was too busy, it appeared, in watching the motions of the crowd of cattle which milled on the slope. Some of them lay down, their heads sinking low as though they were already far spent. These, doubtless, were the ones which had come in from a great distance, half dead with thirst and on fire with eagerness for water. Every hour they spent was bringing them closer to death. Others, again, were mixing in swirls and tangles. Some of them ran with their heads high. Others swung their horns right and left, red-eyed with the burning famine, eager to fight. And brigades of these, from time to time, surged ahead toward the fence line, where they crowded close, lifting their heads above the top strand and pressing their throats and breasts against the cruel barbs. There they hung, until the riders swept down the line and flogged them away with whips. Even whips were not enough, now and again. They had to fire blank cartridges into the faces of the poor beasts, which then milled slowly away to a short distance. The same scene was duplicated on the farther side of Hurry Creek by equal numbers of the animals.

Over the fence, a little away from the spot where "Dolly" Smith had jumped his horse across, another rider now sprinted his mount toward Dolly.

The latter turned in his saddle, reining in to meet this danger from behind.

"Now watch Champ Dixon work," said the Kid, laughing softly. "It'll be worth while. He is a champ, when it comes to a job like this."

"Smith oughta break him in two," said Bud Trainor, "if Dixon means fighting. Smith has got twenty pounds on him!"

"Twenty pounds of man, and Champ is all wild cat. You see?"

Champ Dixon leaped out of his saddle like a panther, and plunging through the air, he tackled Smith and hurled him to the ground like a stone. They rolled over and over, raising a dust, but then Dixon stood up, and Dolly Smith remained in a heap on the ground.

"He's broken his neck!" said Bud Trainor, in horror. "I saw his head bend back as he hit—he's busted his neck—"

"That won't bother Champ Dixon any," said the Kid. "He's broken necks before this. Look at the strength in his hands."

For Champ Dixon, leaning, picked up the fallen man like a child and literally threw him across the empty saddle of Dolly's horse, which had come back to sniff at its fallen master.

A shout went up from the Dixon men. It roared dimly up the slope, mingled with the continual voices of Hurry Creek.

"Gents like to see a thing like that," said Bud Trainor. "They'll eat out of the hollow of Dixon's hand, after this, but how could you of knowed how all of this would happen, Kid?"

"Oh, I know Dixon. He's a fox, as well as a panther. Do you think that he'd let any pair of the boys come up here to fight it out? Not at all! If they were dropped, you and I could grab one of them and ride him back to the ranch house in a rush. Then we could claim that he and his partner had come out and attacked us. Malice prepense!"

"What's that?" asked Trainor.

"Trouble that's been planned ahead. On the strength of that, we probably could get the sheriff out here from Dry Creek to slap an injunction on Dixon and Shay, and spoil their whole show. That's what I wanted—to get that crook Dixon to offer to take a first hold. Then we could have thrown him hard enough to snap his back. No, no, Bud. He's taking Dolly back to camp, but Dolly won't ever forgive him, and a lot of other boys will feel the same way. We've split that crowd into two sections. We've cracked the solid formation, anyway! If Dixon could only gather us in and make sure of our scalps, he'd strike soon enough. But he'll take no chances!"

Dixon, with his reclaimed puncher, now entered the fenced enclosure along the creek through the narrow gate which had been left there, and another shout went up from the mob.

"Those are the ones who are willing to lick his boots," said the Kid. "The others will hate them for it. Slow poison will work as sure as a quick one, sometimes. I'm going to start hoping!"

A group of twenty or thirty cows, which had begun to mill aimlessly, suddenly broke and headed straight for the two of them. The Kid shouted a warning, and the Duck Hawk, as if with a sudden stroke of wings, floated well to the side of the charge. But Bud Trainor's less electric animal barely got aside, switching its tail across the savage horns of the flanking cow.

This mad charge went thundering on over the hill and wasted itself on nothingness. But all the animals on the slope began to toss their heads, and their eyes were red with anger.

"They'll settle down, pretty soon," said the Kid. "They'll settle down and get groggy. Before long, they'll be too weak to stand. Oh, thirst kills 'em almost like bullets."

"Aye," said Bud Trainor. "I remember once when I was making a drive with Ned Powell and Pete Lawlor, up the old Santa Fe, we found two water holes dry, one after another, and there were nine hundred head beginning to sag at the knees—"

"Let it go!" groaned the Kid. "I don't want to hear about it. It makes me sick, Bud. It makes my heart grip and turn over. Child murder—that's what it is!"

"It's a low business," agreed Bud.

But he looked at his companion with wonder.

"After all, Kid," he could not help saying, "they ain't your cows!"

"What difference does that make?" asked the Kid, turning on him almost fiercely. "They're helpless, aren't they? And the curs who'll take advantage of a helpless cow, or a helpless woman, or a helpless man, for that matter—"

He stopped in the midst of his tirade, and seemed ashamed of himself. But he was so worked up by his emotion that the Duck Hawk partook of the excitement, and began to prance lightly up and down, her fetlock joints almost touching the ground, so supple was their play.

"Hold on, Kid," said Bud Trainor. "What's the meaning of the three of 'em, over yonder?"

He pointed out three riders who had left the gate and headed to the right, northward, pointing toward the rim of the hills.

The Kid took keen note of them. Then he turned sharply about in the saddle.

"I thought so—the old fox!" said he. And he chuckled.

"What is it?" asked Bud.

"See those four who are sneaking off through that gap where the fence isn't finished? They're heading south, but they aim to swing around and join hands with that bunch which is moving north, and then they'll have us in a net!"

He laughed, and calling to Bud not to press his horse too much, they cantered back across the hills toward the ranch house. They had barely topped the second rise of the hills, when they could see the two groups of riders, both to the right and the left, spurring their horses wildly forward, jockeying them and leaning into the wind of the gallop like so many Indians.

22
The Chase

"BEAR RIGHT! Bear right!" called the Kid at that instant.

And Bud Trainor, his heart in his mouth, but his confidence in his wise young leader unshaken, did as he was told.

Then a new pulse of fear came to him.

It was plain that the Duck Hawk could drift away from this pursuit as easily as her namesake leaves a flight of sparrows behind, or shoots across the sky to overtake the lowlier fishhawk, as it rises laden from a stream or a lake. For the mare ran with her head turned a little, taking stock of the galloping horsemen to her right, and then to her left. She could dart away to safety at any moment.

But that was not true of the gelding which Bud Trainor himself bestrode. Already they made a good long march on that day, and although the careful watering seemed to have put vigor back into the body of the horse, still the edge was taken from its early foot. It could not sprint with some of the enemy mounts.

Above all, there to the right and north of them, a tall gray, flashing like silver and marked with darkness on the head and all four legs, was leading the others. Now it stretched away further and further, eating up the ground. Bud Trainor, watching this magnificent animal at work, groaned deeply. He could see that there was no escape for him from such a speedster.

Why were they bearing north? Toward the south, surely, and away from that silver racer was their only chance of any escape! Seven men and seven guns would soon be opening against them!

Then, amazed, he heard the Kid's voice, calling: "Easy, Bud, easy does it!"

He looked across.

Aye, the Kid was smiling, almost laughing. Not at Trainor, not at the enemy, but for the sheer joy of the excitement.

Trainor blinked. No matter what the Kid said about maneuvers to get the law on their side, he simply had gone out and put their heads in the lion's mouth, and now the jaws of the lion were closing! Well enough for him, on his lightning-fast mare— but what of his companion!

The next instant, Trainor was ashamed of the thought. Whatever else might be true about the Kid, he was not one to abandon a comrade in a pinch. But still, what was the meaning of his present laughter? And why tell him to ride more slowly?

Yes, the Duck Hawk herself was being drawn in.

"What's the matter with you?" shouted Trainor, in a sudden frenzy. "Don't you see that they're takin' us in the holler of their hands?"

"They won't take us in the hollow of their hands," answered the Kid, calmly. "You think they're riding the finest stuff in the world, but they're not. That tired gelding of yours could give a beating to most of 'em, for that matter! Believe me, old son, when I say that easy does it. They've started behind us, and they've made up ground too fast. Look there!"

Trainor, staring toward the northern trio, saw the rearmost of them suddenly stumble and almost go down.

"That's the pace that tells and the pace that kills," said the Kid. "Only, that silver devil in the lead. What horse is that? What man is that? I ought to know the name of anybody who can ride like that—and keep such a horse for the riding!"

Bud Trainor, only dimly encouraged by the stumbling of one horse—which now seemed to be running again as strongly as ever, though half a dozen lengths farther to the rear—stared ahead at that silver beauty, and then a picture flashed suddenly across his mind of a thing he had seen the year before. A rodeo, a wild crew of hard-riding punchers, of leather-handed bull-doggers, of straight shots and hard drinkers. And in the midst of all the splendid riding, one brilliant figure standing out—a silver horse which flicked the cleverest riders out of the saddle as a child snaps wet watermelon seeds from between forefinger and thumb. Such a horse—a silver beauty! And defying them, making a game of the contest, laughing at all those skilled buckaroos!

Then, out of nowhere, a slender young man appeared, with a dark and handsome face. A very quietly dressed youth was this, who spoke very politely, and used good grammar. He wanted to ride that silver tiger, and people half laughed at him and half pitied him. But ride it he did. Rode it to a stagger, and bought it afterwards, and departed quietly, as he had come. Then, afterwards, a murmur had gone around. That murmur was ringing in his ears, now, and he shouted.

"Kid, Kid! D'you know who that is? I tell you, it's as bad a one as ever was made! It's Chip Graham! It's Chip Graham! I seen him win that hoss at the Bunting Rodeo a year back—"

"Oh, that's Chip Graham, is it?" said the Kid, nodding, the brightness never failing in his face. "That's Chip, is it?"

"I'll swear that's Chip. Bear south, Kid. We better bear south. We never can get away from that devil of a Chip Graham. And that hoss of his—you see—it's faster'n the Duck Hawk, I guess!"

"Keep your hat on," replied the Kid.

He began to measure distances.

"Listen to me, partner. I'm going to leave you for a minute. You hear me?"

Bud Trainor blanched, but he did not answer.

"I'm going to leave you," persisted the Kid, "but not for good. This is a fine lot of hard-riding boys that we've met up with today. And I'm a fool!" he added with a sudden bitterness. "I never should have brought you this close to them on a tired horse. I'm a fool! I'm too used to Duck Hawk. And she never says no!"

He scanned the group of pursuers to the south, and those to the north. Those to the left were riding still like so many jockeys, and so were the men in the north. But the latter had, already, one mount which was being hopelessly distanced. The horse which had stumbled had been steadily losing ground. Now it stumbled again, and again, and at last it pulled up, apparently dead lame.

The second of the trio to the right had lost a great distance, also, but still he was almost abreast of the fugitive. The rider of the silver charger was now far in front—so far that he was beginning to swing a little to the south, and so the holding net would soon be completed! Very fine horsemanship, indeed, but Bud Trainor could not admire it any more than he admired the death which it was spelling for him and the Kid.

And a great, generous impulse suddenly swelled his throat, and he found himself shouting furiously:

"Go on, Kid! You go on and save yourself. Don't you mind me. Cut loose with the Duck Hawk and—lemme see if she can outrun that silver devil, yonder!"

For answer, the Kid looked straight at him, a single second. And yet that look almost paid Bud for death itself.

"Keep your gelding at this pace," said the Kid critically. "He has a pair of lungs and a set of legs that won't let him down. Don't get rattled and attempt to sprint. Go straight on—and keep edging north! I'm going out ahead to do what I can. But I won't leave you, Bud. Not unless gunpowder sends me on the way."

And he was gone.

Bud Trainor, staring after his comrade, saw the mare for the first time settle to her work, and he could hardly believe his eyes. She seemed to lower toward the ground as her stride lengthened. There was no appreciable increase of effort, so far as he could see, no bobbing of the head, no bumping at the hips. But straight and smooth she blew away from him, two feet for every one his own mount was traveling.

Almost immediately the pursuers were aware of this new maneuver. Bud could see them frantically flogging their horses. He saw the rider of the silver beauty turn and look back, and then go to the whip in turn. But it was of no avail. Either the mare was the much faster animal, or else the silver flash had been burned up too fast by an early sprint. For now the Hawk gained with wonderful ease.

Chip Graham, if it were he, now turned, metal winked at his head. And the sound of the gun shot came dimly flying back to the ears of Bud Trainor.

He looked, holding his breath, but the Kid had not fallen, had not winced. He rode on, flattened close to the neck of the mare, weaving a little in his course. Was that to baffle the marksmanship of the leader, or was it to take advantage of the best going?

To right and left, then, Bud Trainor measured the positions of the pursuers. For all of their whipping, they did not seem to be gaining perceptibly. Yes, they were crawling ahead a little, but not much. They were crawling ahead so far that his own gelding, to be sure, could hardly be expected to escape from their speed, unless the Kid performed some miracle.

But might he not?

Miracles, to those strong young hands, seemed everyday matters!

Still the long, rating gallop of the Hawk continued, devouring distance, and then the inevitable happened.

Chip Graham, if it were he, suddenly wheeled his silver horse around. A man cannot shoot straight from a galloping horse. Above all, he cannot shoot to the rear. And now the Kid was in close range. So around came the silver horse, and as it turned, the rider opened fire again.

This time there was an answer. Bud Trainor saw the flash of the weapon in the hand of his comrade, saw the muzzle of it jerk suddenly upward. And the other, spreading out his hands before him, leaned slowly from the saddle, and then slid to the ground!

Dead?

He lay still where he had fallen, while the Kid, sweeping on, caught the silver stallion by the reins and, completing a small circle, headed straight back for Trainor in the rear!

Then, at last, Bud understood, and his heart leaped in him. He looked again to the right, to the left, and now he saw still more frantic efforts on the part of the pursuers.

Let them try!

He asked the gelding for its last speed, now, and he gave it with a strong heart. A moment more, and the Kid had turned before him, holding the silver stallion on his left side, and well out.

A circus trick to change mounts at full gallop, but Bud Trainor had spent all his life among saddles, and stirrups, and bare backs, for that matter. Shifting his left foot to his right stirrup, he waited for the proper moment, and then swung out. His left hand missed the pommel and caught the flashing mane. But his right hand gripped true, and in another moment, he was on such an animal as he never had backed before.

ALL THE RUNNING which it had put behind its long legs had not in the least broken the spirit of the silver stallion. As it felt the weight of a new rider mount its back, it swerved and pitched so that Bud Trainor nearly fell on his face on the ground which. was spinning past beneath him. But he found both stirrups in a moment, and the grip of his strong knees established him in place. He had the reins thrown to him by his friend, next, and with a new animal beneath him, Trainor was riding for his life.

And yet not that, either!

For a sudden change had come over the tactics of the Kid. Instead of spurring wildly ahead, he glanced around him and surveyed his antagonists with a new eye.

He had ridden out to get a horse of safer speed for his comrade, but now that that was done, the need for flight somehow or another did not seem so pressing.

Four men were swinging up toward them from the southeast. One rider was hard-galloping out of the northeast. And the two, the Kid and Bud Trainor, were the focal point at which the five men were aiming.

Suddenly he pulled his horse to a trot, to a walk, and Bud Trainor, wondering, followed that example, while his discarded gelding, badly spent, but still gallant, came lumbering past at a winded gallop.

"We'll have a look at those fellows if they want to press us," said the Kid, as he stared toward the group of four to the south.

"Give it to two, Kid! That's no safe gamble!" said Bud.

"Not safe. There's no fun in a safe gamble," declared the Kid. "Who'd want to tackle a dead-sure thing, and an odds-on bet? A hundred bucks to win one, say? No, no, Bud. Here's a chance to take some of the starch out of these fellows. They came out seven strong, these hand-picked beauties of Champ Dixon, these hothouse flowers, these orchids, you might say. Well, one of them is out of it with a broken-down horse. And there's another who won't be dangerous for a while. And as for the other five—why, let's play tag with 'em!"

As he spoke, he snatched the Winchester from its saddle scabbard, and, whipping it to his shoulder so fast that the barrel flashed in the brilliant sunshine like a sword blade, he took a shot at the last remnant of the northward-riding contingent of the enemy.

This man, who had ridden very well on a strong little piebald mustang which simply could not match strides with the longer legs of the silver stallion and the mare, was coming in gallantly now, bent far forward.

But as the rifle exploded suddenly in the hand of the Kid, this champion's hat blew off, as though a gust of wind had snatched it.

The Kid, looking after him, laughed loudly for, indeed, it was a funny sight.

For the other, jerking the piebald mustang about as fast as he could, was spurring to the rear at full speed. He had not dreamed, apparently, that he had come into such good shooting range.

"Kid," gasped Bud Trainor, "I knew that you was good with a Colt, but I didn't know that you could do it with a rifle, too! Why, all you gotta do is to wish a bullet on its way!"

But the Kid merely laughed.

"That was luck, Bud," said he. "I'm no giant with a rifle, take it from me. I'm a tramp, compared to some of these old hunters. But now and then good luck comes to the fellow who wants it most. Now watch those fellows give us leeway!"

Plenty of room, in fact, all the five pursuers now appeared willing to give to the two fugitives.

Those who were coming up hand over hand out of the southeast now jerked their horses about and scattered to either side, frantic to spread out so that they might not offer one large, united target to such a rifleman as the Kid appeared to be.

Then, from a distance, they resumed a cautious approach once more. They began to open fire.

Every now and then one would halt his horse and fire. Several times the rider on the piebald actually dismounted, threw himself on the ground, and fired from a rest.

It was plain that he had been angered by the bullet hole in his best sombrero!

But these shots were falling wild. The distance was great. And now the two who were withdrawing came to the place where Chip Graham sat up, clutching at a red spot over his left breast.

He was dusty. He had received a scratch across the forehead in falling to the ground, but in spite of his wounds, his fall, he looked up at them with such an eye that Bud Trainor shuddered profoundly.

"You're Chip Graham, are you?" asked the Kid.

Chip, in place of answering, turned a solemn eye upon the silver stallion, and then he raised his glance to the face of Bud.

"You're Trainor, are you?" said Chip. "And you're the Kid, of course?"

His fine, dark eyes dwelt malevolently upon the pair of them.

"How badly are you cut up?" asked the Kid.

"I'm shot just inside of the shoulder," said Chip, with utmost calm. "It's nothing bad. Three weeks. Unless the shoulder's stiffened up for good."

"We'll take you on where you'll get medical treatment," said the Kid. "We'll take you on to the ranch house, Chip. Bud, get down and give him a hand up on your old gelding, while I take a look at the rest of these fellows."

He began to ride in a little circle, while the five who had been following gradually rode at high speed around a great circumference. Plainly they were planning to thrust themselves between the fugitives and the ranch house, and hoping to find such good cover that they would be able to get fairly close to the deadly marksman, the Kid.

Bud Trainor saw this, and he called out: "Listen to me, Kid! If we take Chip along, they'll fight like devils to get him away from us. He's one of their best men, and they won't give him up without making a scrap of it. It would disgrace them! Leave Chip lie here, and we'll go on safely, I reckon."

"Get him up into the saddle," returned the Kid shortly. "I

know what I'm about in this game, Bud. Get him up. Chip, stand up!"

"I'll not move!" said Chip sullenly. "If you really want me, you can carry me!"

At this, Bud looked blankly toward his companion, and he was in time to see a startling change in the face of the Kid. It seemed as though his brow swelled with black blood, and his eyes glared like the eyes of a beast. His nostrils were expanded, and his lips pinched in.

"Carry you? Carry you?" cried the Kid. "I'll carry you!"

He swerved the mare back and, leaning a little from the saddle, he cut young Chip Graham across the body once and again with the lash of his quirt.

"Get up and into that saddle," commanded the Kid.

Chip Graham uttered no sound, but looked up at the Kid with the incredible malice of a ferret. His lips parted. His teeth showed. He seemed to be smiling at some exquisitely secret jest. And Bud Trainor, in spite of himself, rubbed a hand across his eyes to shut out the ugly vision.

The Kid, having already delivered the whip strokes, whirled away again on the mare to resume his survey of the enemy, but Chip did not wait for a second flogging.

He rose, unassisted, and, while his left arm dangled, and the blood flowed down from within his wristband and trickled across the back of his hand, he gripped the pommel with the right hand, and swung himself lightly into place on the gelding.

"I'll tie up your shoulder," suggested Bud Trainor.

"Ask him if he'll let you," answered Chip through his teeth.

There was an odd dryness in the throat of Bud Trainor. He had felt, in his day, that he was as rough and as tough as most. He had been proud of the way in which he had flung himself at the raw-handed mankillers in his father's house, the evening when he had saved the Kid. But now, compared with the nature of the Kid himself and Chip Graham, Bud felt like a child in a savage wilderness on a wild night. He seemed to be pressed upon from two sides.

However, he did not ask permission from the Kid. In his saddlebag he had bandages and an antiseptic. He cut away the sleeve, and cleaned and tied up the wound as well as he could. Lightly as Chip Graham had spoken of it, it was a grisly thing to see. It explained a part of the singular green pallor which was on the face of that proud young man, now. But the chief part of that color was, no doubt, owing to the infernal passion which was consuming him.

Somewhere in the future—perhaps before the end of this very day—he would have his chance at the Kid again, and that second time one of them would surely die.

Like a grim prophet, Bud Trainor was aware of these things. But, the wound being dressed, he now found the Kid impatiently waiting, as he called out:

"Are you going to put him into a cradle, Bud? Get him along here. And if he holds back, give him another taste of the same sort of quirting. It's all that he understands. Some dogs come to heel when you speak, but some of them have to be flogged into shape! And as far as I'm concerned this baby-murdering cur, he is in the second category!"

By "baby-murdering," Bud knew that the Kid was referring to the starving of the dumb cattle. But this explanation probably was not so clear to Chip Graham. However, he said nothing at all, and they rode on, side by side, approaching they knew not what danger might await them.

For Champ Dixon's men had already disappeared behind a rather high rise of ground in the direction of the ranch house.

"By gosh!" broke out Bud Trainor. "Suppose that they've gone off to rush the ranch house, now that the fightin's begun?"

"They're not likely to," said the Kid. "They've no orders to that, and Dixon's a man who keeps people strictly to his orders. Is that right, Chip?"

Chip sneered, and said nothing.

"He's proud, Bud," said the Kid. "Look at his proud, handsome, enduring face. He won't speak. He scorns speaking. And all he wants is a slice of my heart and another off my liver to toast and feed to the dogs. But I tell you, Chip, when the time comes that you can pull a gun and manage it again, free and easy, I'll come across the continent to get at you, and I'll finish the job that I started today, you hell-cat, you sneaking rat of a baby murderer!"

His face was convulsed as before, and Bud Trainor, who had endured enough already, cried out:

"Kid, he's a guest, you might say. Watcha mean by talkin' to him like that?"

The Kid whirled in the saddle. He seemed as if he would leap at his friend. But he mastered himself at once, and loosening

the rein, made the mare bound forward and away from the
other two.

24
The Law

WHETHER DIXON'S men found no proper cover, or perhaps
changed their minds about pressing matters with the myster-
iously good marksmanship of the Kid against them, at any rate,
they did not appear again to trouble Trainor and the captive
beside him. But they went on comfortably, with sometimes a
glimpse of the Kid on a ridge before them.

Whatever bad temper he might have been in when he left
them, he was ahead, now, scouting out the lay of the land. Only
when they were in sight of the ranch house did he appear once
more, riding suddenly out at them from a thick copse of poplars.

He waved his hand toward the house.

"Take this boy in with you, Bud," said he. "If everything is
all right over there, I'll come on in when you give me a signal."

"What could be wrong?" asked Bud Trainor, amazed.

"Well, I've told you before. The Dixon men might be lying
there. I don't think they will, though, or I wouldn't ask you to
go in alone. But I don't like fixed quarters, where people can
look for me. See if everything is all right. I'll have my glass
turned on the house. If you'll come out and wave a hand in a
big circle, I'll come in."

So Bud Trainor rode on in with his companion.

It was the full heat of the middle day, now. The effect of
the waves of reflection was to make the ground tremble like
water before them, and the very shape of the old ranch house
was distorted, the roof sometimes dissolving, so that it seemed
quivering with blue flames.

This heat was hard enough even on a sound man like Train-
or, but it turned the wounded captive white with suffering and
distress. When they reached the house, Bud had to help him

down from the saddle, and through the door into the dining room, where he slumped down on a couch.

Mrs. Milman and Georgia came hurriedly to help.

"I'm all right," said the white-faced Chip. "I dunno what's the matter with me, cracking like this. Gimme a drink of water, and I'll be fine as silk in a few minutes."

Georgia took charge. She made him stretch out on the couch, and arranged a pillow under his head. At her command, Bud Trainor pulled off the boots. The shirt was opened at Chip's throat, and his head raised so that he could take a swallow of water.

His face, however, began to assume a more amd more set expression of suffering, and, avoiding their faces, he stared fixedly up to the ceiling.

Mrs. Milman dressed the wound with care, putting on a pad of the softest lint, and she declared, after manipulating the arm a little, that there was no danger at all. No bones had been crushed by the bullet in its passage. There had not been enough loss of blood to make serious trouble.

"Are you still in great pain?" asked Georgia, leaning above him.

He drew his eyes from the ceiling to her face, and flicked them hastily back again.

"Poor fellow!" said Georgia. "Poor chap! Won't you tell me what's the trouble—where the pain is the worst? We might try a cold pack, Mother. He's in a fever!"

"Aw, I'm all right!" declared Chip in a husky murmur.

Here Bud Trainor touched the arms of the two women and drew them to the farther side of the room.

"Leave him be," he suggested. "You dunno what's the matter with him, but I do."

"What is it?"

"He's one of Dixon's crowd that's been trying to throttle your ranch."

"Well, I guessed that."

"But to see you treatin' him so like a white man, it's sort of hard on his nerves."

"What do you mean?"

"It cuts him up a good deal. He don't deserve to be treated no better than a dog, and he knows it."

The women exchanged glances.

"How was he hurt?" asked Mrs. Milman.

"And where is the Kid?" broke in Georgia. "Oh, good heavens, Mother. He's got to be warned away if he's coming back here!"

"He's not coming back in a hurry," answered Bud Trainor. "He's taking his time and waiting for a signal to call him."

They went into the next room.

"What's happened?" they asked of Bud.

"Why, the Kid went out explorin'. He wanted to lead Dixon into makin' an attack on us, and then he thought that the law could be pretty useful to you all. You could put an injunction on 'em—kick 'em off the land by process of law, or something like that. Anyway, you could switch the law on 'em and get it around to our side of the fence."

"And so? You mean that he went out there, and dared the lot of them?" demanded Georgia.

"Aye, that's what he sure enough done."

"But that's——"

"Aye, that's crazy. But he done it. They tried to sneak some men out on both sides of the fence and slip around us. Oh, they wanted the Kid's scalp pretty bad, all right. We come back flying. The Hawk, she could wing away from 'em any time, but my gelding didn't have enough foot for that sort of work. They gained on us——"

"And the Kid wouldn't leave you?" cried Georgia, with a shining face.

Her mother looked sharply across at her, but said nothing.

"The Kid," said Bud Trainor, speaking slowly, and rather softly to keep the emotion out of his voice, "is the kind that's always better than anybody else, in a pinch. No, he wouldn't leave me, even when I told him to go."

"That's grand!" said Georgia.

There were tears of pleasure and excitement in her eyes. And again her mother saw them.

"It was grand, all right. And dangerous, too. This here Chip Graham, he was on that hoss of his, the Silver King. And the King stepped out pretty fast. He got ahead of us. He aimed to turn us or to hold us till the rest of the crowd came up. There was seven of them, all told. But then the Kid went out and dropped Graham, and got the King for me to ride. And when the rest of 'em came too close, he just up with his rifle and shot the hat off one of their heads!"

He laughed with a fierce pleasure.

"He didn't kill that man?" gasped Mrs. Milman.

"Him? Of course not," said Bud Trainor with an almost religious and devoted belief. "He could snuff a candle at about a thousand yards, I guess. But when we came back near to the house, he wouldn't come in with us. He thought there might be trouble waiting for him here."

"He's right! He's right," said Mrs. Milman. "Nothing but trouble for him here. My husband and Chet Wagner are in the front room with the sheriff and a deputy, right now. They've come out for the Kid; or Mr. Beckwith-Hollis, as he calls himself."

"Stuff!" said Georgia. "He was only joking."

Mrs. Milman shrugged her shoulders.

"I wouldn't try to read the mind of that young man," said her mother. "But what are we to do? The sheriff is here with a warrant for the arrest of the Kid, alias I don't know how many other names and nicknames, for breaking the peace, forcibly entering a house, attempted murder, and a good many other things. All because he drove Billy Shay—the scoundrel!—into the street!"

"Is that Sheriff Lew Walters? What kind of a man is he, then?" demanded Bud Trainor angrily.

"He doesn't like the business, but as he points out, he's a servant of the law," said Mrs. Milman.

She leaned a hand suddenly against the wall and supported herself there.

"It looks like a lost cause," said she. "The neighbors won't help us. Not till the law is clearly on our side. Georgia brought back poor Chet Wagner with her, and that's the only man who would come. The rest—oh, they're playing safe!"

"We can go in and try the sheriff," said Bud Trainor. "That was the idea of the Kid. He's safe enough out there. They'll never catch the Duck Hawk and the Kid, together. The Kid's idea was that if we could bring in one of 'em, it would be a proof that Dixon had started a fight on your ground. And that would be pretty hard for him and Shay to get out of. Let's go tell the sheriff what's happened!"

Mrs. Milman shook her head.

"We'll try, however," she said grimly.

And, as they started for the next room, Georgia murmured to Bud Trainor, "I wish I'd been there to see it!"

"Aye," sad Trainor. "It's all right to look back on. But it

wasn't so slick going through it. I ain't the same sort of steel that the Kid is made of. I was scared sick!"

She merely laughed.

"I know," said she. "It's a point of pride with you fellows to understate things. We'll see what the sheriff says."

In the front room, accordingly, they found Lew Walters and his deputy, who was a timid-looking young man, with a frightened eye and an apparent desire to squeeze himself through the wall and away from the presence of the two women. But they could guess that the sheriff would not have selected this youngster for dangerous business like this without a good cause. His big wrists and long fingers were suggestive of more strength than he showed otherwise.

Lew Walters met Trainor with a nod and a smile.

"How's your ma and pa?" he asked. "And how's yourself?"

"Everybody fair to middling," admitted Bud. "I'm out here tryin' to give a hand agin' the Dixon crew, sheriff. Now, how come that the law is agin' an honest man like Milman, and behind a crook like Dixon?"

The sheriff shrugged both shoulders and made a weary gesture with his hands.

"The law," said he, "is somethin' that I never been able to understand at all. No, sir, I can't foller the workin's of the law, young feller. All that I can do is to ride when the law tells me to ride, and to arrest what the law tells me to arrest. Heaven knows that I ain't willin' to side agin' my old friend Milman, but the law tells me to arrest the Kid, and that's why I'm here. Where is he, Bud?"

25

Mixed Answers

AT THIS DIRECT APPEAL, Bud looked around him. On the wall, by way of decoration, there were some elk heads, badly mounted, and therefore coming to pieces before their time. And, on the floor, there was the enormous pelt of a grizzly bear which Indians had cured, and which was therefore in an excellent state of preservation. From these adornments, or from the old-fashioned Kentucky rifle and powderhorn across the door, Bud received no ideas.

At last he grinned and waved his hand all around the horizon.

"Oh, he's out yonder," said Bud.

The sheriff grinned in turn.

"And in there," said Bud, "is one of Dixon's men that jumped us and tried to run us down when we went up to see the creek and what was happening there."

The sheriff got up from his chair.

"One of Dixon's men? How come he's here?"

"The Kid nudged him off of his hoss with a bullet. Chip Graham is his name."

"Hah!" exclaimed the sheriff. "That wo'thless Chip Graham? I've had room in my jail waitin' for him since—"

He clapped a hand over his mouth.

"I'm gettin' old, John," he said to Milman. "My tongue, it takes charge, and is always runnin' me downhill. Well, the Kid knocked Chip off of his hoss, did he? Off of the Silver King, d'you mean?"

"Aye."

"And then you took the hoss, I reckon?"

"Aye, to get away from the crowd that was follerin' us."

"Humph!" said the sheriff. "Now, to be honest, Bud, wasn't that crowd follerin' you because you had grabbed the hoss first?"

"Hey," exclaimed Bud Trainor. "Are you tryin' to make me into a hoss thief?"

"I'm not tryin' to make you into nothin'. All I know is that if the Kid was to see the Silver King, it'd wring his heart plumb to the backbone to let it get away from him before he'd give it a try under the saddle."

"I tell you—" exclaimed Bud Trainor.

"Never you mind your telling, Bud. Don't you go and talk yourself into jail, which is something that a lot of folks is fond of doin'. You say that the Dixon bunch tackled you and the Kid. You, maybe; but folks around these parts don't go tacklin' the Kid offhand, just for fun. Not by a long shot, they don't."

"We'd gone down and told them what side we were on," said Bud, growing hot and angry. "They just wanted to bag us and—"

"Here, here, Bud," answered the sheriff. "I want to be fair to everybody, but this here sounds kind of fishy. Who's your witnesses?"

"Why, the Kid, of course!" said Bud.

The sheriff grinned.

"All right," said he. "You bring the Kid in and I'll hear what he's got to say!"

Mrs. Milman exclaimed: "Aren't you taking sides unfairly, now, Sheriff Walters? You're willing to believe the Shay and Dixon crowd when they ask you to make an arrest; but you won't listen to our side of it?"

The sheriff smiled upon her almost tenderly.

"Mrs. Milman, ma'am," said he, "I wanta tell you that there ain't a man in the world that I respect no more than I respect John, here. And there ain't a lady that I'd rather please than you. But here I've got a warrant swore out all straight and proper for the arrest of the Kid, alias a lot of other names—but who the Kid is I know. I ain't sayin' that Shay and Dixon is my friends, or that I think much of 'em. But I know that the Kid busted into Shay's house. It may be that he didn't fire no shots. He was just havin' a little picnic of his own. It was his idea of a good time and a sort of a joke! On the other hand, you want me to believe the Kid. Well, the Kid for what I know of him is the slipperiest, hell-raisin'est youngster in the West. Here's Bud Trainor talkin', you say. But after a look at Bud, I know what's happened. He's found him a hero, and the Kid is that man. He'd go and jump off a cliff, if the Kid told him to. Wouldn't you, Bud?"

"You don't want to believe me," said Bud, "and I suppose that you don't have to! Maybe you could get the truth out of Chip, if you was to half try!"

"All right," said the sheriff. "That's another young gent that I know about, and you'll see how much he'll say!"

They all went into the room where poor Graham lay, patiently studying the ax work which had shaped the rafters that held up the ceiling of the room.

"Hello, Chip," said the sheriff.

"Why, hello, Walters," said the boy.

"Sorry to see you laid out like this," said the sheriff.

"Aw, I been needin' a rest," said Chip.

"I hear as how the Kid got the drop on you," said the sheriff.

"The Kid?"

"Aye. Wasn't it him?"

"You mean that give me this in the shoulder?"

"That's what I mean."

"I'll tell you what, sheriff," said the boy calmly, "I dunno who's been tellin' you that kind of bunk. But the way it happened was that I was cleanin' an old gun of mine——"

"Oh, I see," said the sheriff. "Just cleanin' an old gun, and it went off in your hands, eh?"

"Yes," said Chip, looking him in the eye.

"Why, I saw the Kid shoot you off your hoss!" exclaimed Trainor.

Graham stared calmly at him.

"It's been a tolerable hot day," said he. "Maybe you got your brain touched up with the sun, eh?"

"That gun exploded as close as that, and didn't leave no powder burns?" went on the sheriff, smiling faintly.

"Nary a one," said Chip, unmoved.

"Well," said Lew Walters, "I hope that you get well right quick—and then I reckon that you'll kick the handles right off of that old gun, Chip?"

"I reckon I will," said Chip.

They went back into the front room.

"You see how it is," said the sheriff. "He's not going to give the law a grip on the Kid. He wants the Kid free, so that *he* can handle him, when he gets back on his feet. Georgia, did you hear—where's Georgia?"

But Georgia was not there.

Mrs. Milman, with a faint exclamation, ran out of the room and called as she went, but no Georgia answered.

She went on, and hurrying out the kitchen door, she looked toward the hitching rack, where the Silver King had been standing.

He was no longer there, and Mrs. Milman suddenly clutched her breast with both hands. She looked, at that moment, as though she had lost something far more precious than all of the big Milman ranch and all of the cattle that grazed upon its grasses.

26
Past History

GEORGIA, in fact, had not waited to hear the end of the conversation.

Very shortly after Trainor attempted to argue with the sheriff, she could tell how matters were apt to drift, and the moment she was sure of that, she had left the house. The Silver King, standing high-headed at the rack, was too much of a temptation to be resisted. So she quickly shortened the stirrups and mounted.

After that, she scanned the rolling ground around the house.

Here and there were clumps of trees, bunches of high shrubbery, and even nests of rocks which would hide a man and a horse without any trouble. But she judged that the most likely place would be the larger growth of the woods to the north of the house, and toward them she rode.

In a moment she was passing under the drift of the brown shadows, sometimes in the blinding brightness of a patch of sunshine, and again in the thicker shadows where the trees grew high and dense.

Crossing a small opening in the forest, a blue jay screeched suddenly overhead in such a discordant note that she reined in the King sharply and looked up.

"A good day for lazying in the shade," said a voice behind her.

She jerked about in the saddle, and there was the Kid, sitting on a fallen log and whittling at a stick with a long, bright-bladed knife.

How had he come there?

It could not be that she had ridden straight past him! And yet he was so thoroughly covered by the shadows that the thing seemed possible. The beautiful head of the Hawk appeared dimly behind some small branches near her master.

"How did you get here?" she asked.

For was it not possible that he had been trailing her, the mare moving with catlike softness, and he had dismounted, even now, for the mere sake of surprising her?

"Ah, I just dropped in," said the Kid, rising to greet her. "How's things?"

She turned the King and faced him.

He was smiling a little, and he had raised his hat high, and then settled it slowly back on his head. He had the air of one who knows how to talk easily to women. That air, and his smile, troubled her a little; yet she felt that it was a foolish emotion.

"Things are pretty bad," said the girl. "I've heard a little about what you did with the Dixon crowd, though. And over at the house is the sheriff and a deputy, waiting for you."

"Let them wait and rest," answered the Kid. "It's a sort of sad thing, when you come to think of it, that a man at the sheriff's age should have to be riding, riding, riding all the time. Let him rest in the cool of the house for a while—and I'll rest out here. Why does he want me?"

He canted his head just a trifle to the side, and waited.

"He wants you for breaking into the Shay house, and for attempted murder—"

"In the Shay house?"

"Yes."

"I didn't fire a shot in there. It was the crowd already there that made the noise like a Fourth of July."

"What made you go in there?" asked the girl.

"Oh, I wanted to see Shay."

"You wanted to scare him, you mean."

"You think so? Well, if his nerves got a little jumpy, I wouldn't be sorry, as a matter of fact."

He added: "Is it only about the Shay business that he wants me?"

"That's all. What else would there be?"

"You never can tell," said the Kid, smiling again in that odd way which troubled her. "People sometimes rig up all sorts of foolish grudges, you understand."

"They persecute you, Kid, do they?"

"A lot," said he.

She laughed, and the Kid laughed with her.

"Sit down and rest your horse," said the Kid.

She hesitated, then slipped suddenly out of the saddle. But she did not sit down. With the reins over her arms, and the riding quirt tapping against her boots, she confronted him. She felt much smaller, now, as she stood upon the ground, facing him.

"You act a little nervous yourself," said the Kid.

"I am nervous," she answered.

"And why?"

"Look here," said she, "are you pretending that I ought to take you as if you were just—anybody?"

"No. Take me as if I were just the Kid."

"I don't want to call you that. What other name can I give you?"

"Reginald Beckwith-Holman is my real name," said he.

"Beckwith-Hollis you told my mother."

"Did I? Matter of fact, I have a hard time remembering names."

"It must be hard—having so many," she observed.

They waited through a pause.

"I wanted to ask you a question," she said.

"Go ahead."

"About what you will do now."

"I don't know. Dixon and his crew have dug themselves in. They have a regular fort down there at Hurry Creek."

"I know that they have. And there's nothing that can be done about them. They have the law on their side—until the case is tried!"

"Does the sheriff admit that?"

"Yes, he admits that. Poor Lew Walters! He wants to help us, but his hands are tied!"

"Of course they are," said the Kid.

"And you're in danger from the sheriff, if you stay near here."

"I'll stay, I think," said the Kid. "Walters is only joking. We've known each other such a long time, I don't think that he'd do me any harm."

"He'd shoot you down in a second!" she exclaimed. "You know it, too!"

"Good old Walters," said the Kid gently, and shifted the subject by saying: "Did you come out to send me away?"

"What right have I to send you away?" asked the girl. "Whatever hope we have is in you!"

"You do have a hope, eh?" said the Kid. "Thanks. That makes me feel a little better."

"I wish that you'd come out in the open," said the girl. "What really makes you take such wild chances as you took today? It's as if you despised life!"

"Not a bit," said he, "but I like life with a little seasoning in it. You can understand how that might be?"

She nodded.

Suddenly she had to pinch her lips together to keep from smiling.

"What's the real reason?" she asked him. "Only the adventure? Or mostly because you hate Dixon and all his crowd?"

"It's the cattle," said the Kid with a sudden gravity.

She shook her head.

"You don't believe that?" he asked her.

"Hardly!"

"Well, I'll tell you. When I was a little youngster, my father and mother started to move. We were poor people. Dirt poor. We had a few head of horses, and some cows, and a few head of beef. The land where we were living—"

"Was it out here in the West?"

"Well, it was not East," he answered evasively, frowning a little.

The girl flushed and bit her lip.

"Do go on," said she.

"We moved off the old land—there was nothing but a small shack on it—and then we started across the hills for a sort of promised land about which we'd heard a lot. We plugged along at a good rate. There was no hurry. We wanted to have our cattle in good condition when we came to the badlands, where we'd heard that the grass had been burned out, and that it was very hard to push through. So we slogged along very slowly, and enjoyed being on the road. Our first bad luck was a real smasher. Half a dozen rustlers came down on us one evening, and scooped up everything that we had in the way of livestock, except for the two milk cows. They took the horses, the mule, the burro, even; and the steers."

"The scoundrels!" said the girl. "The contemptible scoundrels! Did you ever learn who they were?"

"There were five of them," said the Kid dreamily, as though he were looking across the years and seeing that evening closely again. "Yes, I learned all of their names. A tough bunch. Very tough. I learned all of their names, however."

"How? But go on! What did you do, then?"

"My father was a hard man," said the Kid. "He'd lived a hard life. He had the pain of work in his eyes, if you know what I mean."

"Yes," she answered. "Of course I know."

"He'd been a farmer. And a scholar! But a farmer—frosty mornings, chilblains at nights, freezing behind the plow, roasting in the hayfield. He worked like a dog.

"Well, when we lost our stock, we were on the edge of the desert. My mother begged him to turn back, but he wouldn't do it. He wouldn't go back to the old life. He lightened the wagon of everything that we didn't absolutely need, and then he yoked up those two milk cows—and we went ahead!"

"Great heavens!" said the girl. "Across the desert? With cows!"

He paused. His face, losing its characteristic smile, became like iron.

"My mother was a very young woman to have had a boy of six. She was a jolly sort. She was straight, and had a good, sun-browned skin, and her eyes were always laughing. Like a dog that loves all the people all around him. You know?"

She nodded. She felt a breathless interest.

"She was rather tall," said the Kid, looking straight and hard at the girl. "She had blue eyes. They sparkled like sea water under the sun."

The straightness of his glance took her breath. She herself

was tall, her skin was brown, and she knew she had dark-blue eyes. Her mirror told her that there was life in them!

"Well," said the Kid, "after a couple of days, I got sick. Very sick. My mother began to worry. There was hell in the air!"

He looked up, as one suddenly struck to the heart by an irresistible pain.

"Yes," said the girl, barely whispering. "Yes?"

"The cows kept plugging along. I was sick, but my brain was all right. I mean, I knew everything that was happening around me. I watched those cows get thinner and thinner. The flesh melted off them like the tallow off candles. They turned into skeletons. It was a terrible thing to sit there on the wagon seat and watch them dying on their feet. It was a terrible thing to sit and watch it."

"Go on!" breathed the girl. "What happened?"

"One of them died. I remember her. She was big Spot, we used to call her. She was hard milking, and she was mean with her horns. But we got to love her on that march through the desert. She pulled two thirds of the load. Then she didn't get up one morning. She was dead.

"There we were, stuck in the sands. There wasn't very far to go, now, to get to the grasslands, and one night I heard my father begging my mother to go ahead and get to safety. He would wangle me through—me and the wagon.

"Well, after Spot died, there was no chance of that. Mother wouldn't leave. They made a pack of everything that they dared to carry along. They left the old wagon. They loaded me onto the back of the other cow. She was old Red. One horn had been broken off. The other one curled in and touched her between the eyes. She had eyes like a deer and a shape like a coal barge. You know the way cows are."

"Yes," said the girl.

"They loaded me and part of the pack on top of old Red. Well, she was pretty far gone. Her backbone stuck up like a ridge of rocks. I was pretty weak. They had to hold me on her. They didn't dare to tie me, because every minute they thought that she might drop. And I could feel her weaving under me. Staggering, and then going on. She was used to pain, I suppose. It never occurred to her to lie down and give up.

"We went on for two days. At night, I used to stand in front of her and rub her face, and she would curl out her long, dry tongue, and it felt like a rasp on my hand.

"The third day, she went down with a bump and a slump. She was stone dead.

"But she had done her part.

"Over to the north, we could see a green mist, and we knew that that was the grass country. The edge of it.

"My father took me in his arms. I was too weak to walk. We went across the rest of the desert and got to the grasslands, all right. My father and I did, I mean."

"Your mother——" said the girl, in horror.

"Oh, she came through, also," said the Kid. "But a good deal of her was left behind on that trail. She lasted through to the winter. I could see her dying from day to day. So could my father. After a while she stayed in her bed, and then died. The trail took too much out of her. She never could get rested again."

The girl placed her hands over her eyes.

At last she said: "And the men who did it? The cowards—the devils who stole your stock?"

"Well," said the Kid, "that's a funny thing. You know that a mule lasts a long time. Nine years later, when I was fifteen, I saw the mule that had been stolen, and naturally I was a little curious. I started following its back trail, and I looked up the five men, one by one."

"They were all alive?" she asked.

"Only one is alive now," said the Kid, and, lifting his head, he looked at her in such a way that the blood turned to ice water in her veins.

27
Strange Tales

To THINK of this matter calmly and from a distance, there was nothing strange in the fact that the Kid had just implied that he had killed four men, one after another. He had a reputation that attributed stranger and more terrible deeds than this to him. But to be there in the quiet of the woods alone with him was another matter. The friendliness in his blue eyes upset her. And then he seemed amazingly young. There was not a trace of a wrinkle about his eyes, and the only line in his face was a single incision at the side of his mouth which appeared, now and then, when the rest of his features were gravely composed, and gave him a look of smiling cynically to himself. Whatever cruelties and desperate actions he was guilty of, it seemed also manifest that he was as generous as cruel, as manly as fierce.

Then, suddenly, she asked him: "Did you kill all of those men?"

"I?" said the Kid.

He smiled at her.

"You don't think that I ought to ask you that," she agreed, "and I don't suppose that I should. You've never told a soul, I suppose?"

"No, I've never told a soul, and I never intend to."

She took her place on the log, she turned about on it to face him, and, resting an elbow on her knee and her chin in the cool, slender palm of her hand, she studied the Kid as he never had been studied before. He looked straight back at her, but it was not easy.

"Well," said she, "I don't lose anything by asking, I suppose."

"Are you asking me to tell you?"

"Yes, that's what I'm asking."

He still had in his hand the knife with which he had been whittling. That whittling, she now saw, was no real use of the edge of the steel, but a mere testing of it, while the whittler produced long, translucent shavings which fell as light as strips of paper to the ground, and slowly dried, and warped, and curled. Now he flicked the knife into the air. It whirled over and over in a solid wheel of silver that disappeared with a thud. The blade had driven down into the earth its full length, and the hilt had thumped heavily home.

"That's a weighted knife," said the girl.

"Yes. It's weighted."

He pulled it out and looked down the steel, which was hardly tarnished by the moisture of the ground. He began to wipe and polish the blade slowly and carefully.

"I asked about the four killings," said the girl. "You won't talk about it, Kid?"

At this, he laughed a little.

"Do you expect that I'll answer?"

"I sort of do expect you to," said she.

"Well, tell me why."

"Because I want to get to know you, and I hope that you'll want to get to know me."

The Kid started a little. He looked at her in amazement, and in bewilderment, and suddenly he seemed to her younger than ever before. There was actually a slight tinge of red in his cheeks, and at the sight of this color, she could have laughed, outright. But she swallowed her triumph with a fierce satisfaction.

In fact, he was taken quite off balance.

"That's fair enough," said the Kid. "Friends as much as you like. Do you have to know my story, first?"

"I'd like to, of course."

"Would you have to?" asked the Kid.

He smiled in the way he had, secretly, to himself, as though he were criticizing both himself and her, and wondering at the way he allowed himself to be drawn out.

"Yes," said the girl, calmly and firmly.

"Well," said he, "the newspapers have written me up a good deal, and what they leave out, you'll find almost anybody willing to fill in—on a good long winter evening when the fire's burning well and the pipes are drawing."

She nodded.

"I know that sort of talk," said she. "But I'm after facts."

"You'd make an exchange, I suppose?" said the Kid.

"Of course I will. I have some dark spots of my own to show."

He balanced the knife on the tip of a forefinger. It stood up as straight and steady as a candle flame upon a windless night.

"Well," she said. "I'm waiting to make the bargain. You ought to have me for a friend."

"Yes?" said he, in query, but very politely.

"Yes, because I'm straight."

He blinked a little, as though he had seen a sudden light.

Then he said: "Suppose that I tell you the story of the four men? Will you let me off with that chapter?"

"What am I to offer in exchange?"

"Nothing," said the Kid. "I've seen your story, and I don't need to hear it."

She blushed in her turn, but without lowering her eyes.

"The first man," said the Kid, striking at once into the middle of his story, "was a fellow named Turk Reming. He was a darkish man, with a mustache that he twisted so much that it curled forward instead of back. He had three wrinkles between his eyes, and he always seemed to be smiling like a devil. I found the Turk doing business as the chief boss, gunman, and professional bully of a big mining camp—a new strike up in Montana—"

"How old were you?" asked the girl.

"Well, the age doesn't matter," said he.

"You were fifteen," she insisted.

"I suppose I was."

He seemed irritated by this.

"I took my time with Turk. I wanted to take my time with all of 'em. My mother had died by slow torture. My father had died after forgetting how to smile for nine years. And Spot and old Red had died slow, too."

The girl jerked in a little, gasping breath, and then the Kid went on:

"I got a job digging and mucking around in the mine. It was about the last honest work that I did in my life!"

He looked at the girl, and she looked straight back at him, studious and noncommittal.

"While I was working, I spent the evenings and Sundays and all my wages burning up gunpowder. My father had raised me with a gun in my hand, and besides, I had a natural talent. People in that camp got to know me. They used to come out and watch me shoot, and laugh as I missed. Then there were competitions in the camp, pretty often. Shooting at marks of all kinds, you know. But I stayed away from them until I had my hand well in. Then I found a Saturday afternoon, when Turk was trying out his own hand, and showing up a lot of the boys. They were shooting at an ax slash on the breast of a tree. The tree was pretty well peppered, but Turk was the only one who had nicked the mark. So I took my turn, and snaked three bullets into that ax cut in quick time. That's not boasting," he added. "I'm only fair with a rifle, but I can hit nearly anything with a revolver—up to about twenty yards. This shooting attracted a good deal of attention, and when I'd landed the three slugs in the mark, I turned and smiled at Turk—I mean to say, I smiled so that the rest of the boys could see me. He got pretty hot. He tried to laugh the thing off, but the men stood around and watched, and waited. I thought that he'd pull a gun on me, but he didn't.

"After that, I still kept on in the camp for months. I haunted Turk. I haunted him so that he never knew when I'd show up. I stood around and smiled at him, with a sneer in my eyes; and I'd measure him up and down. The boys began to be interested. They waited for something to happen, and Turk knew they were waiting. He wanted to get rid of me, but his nerve was bad. He'd seen those three bullets go home. It had shaken him up a good deal. He lost a lot of prestige in the camp, right away, but he stayed on. They were a wild mob up there in those days, but Turk ruled them. He was tougher than the toughest. The more afraid of me he became—I mean, the more afraid of his idea of me—the harder he worked to make trouble with the others. In that month, he picked three fights that turned into shooting scrapes, and in those scrapes he sent four men to the hospital, and one of them died there. In the hospital tent, I mean. But every day Turk's face grew thinner, and his eyes more hollow. He wasn't sleeping much at night. One evening he rushed into the shack where I was sitting alone, and cursed me and told me that he'd come to finish me. He was shaking. He was crazy with drink and with anger and hysteria. So I laughed in his face. I told him that I didn't intend to fight him until there was a crowd to watch. I told him who I was then, and how the cows had died, and then my mother and my father. I told him that I was going to make him burn on a slow fire, and when I chose to challenge him, he'd take water, and take it before a crowd."

"Good heavens!" said the girl. "Did he draw his gun on you, then?"

"No. He turned as green as grass, and backed through the door. He looked as though he had been seeing a ghost. He ran off through the camp. I think he was more than half crazy with fear. Superstitious fear, you know. But the fellows that he started the fight with that night, they simply thought that he was crazy drunk. They shot him to pieces, and that was the end of Turk Reming. Do you want any more?

"Harry Dill was a fellow with a lot of German blood in him. And he had the sort of a face you often see among Germans— round and pink-cheeked, with the eyes and ears sticking out a good deal. He'd given up guns and taken to barkeeping. He had the most popular saloon in the town. Everybody drank there. He'd about put the two older places out of business. He knew everybody in town by a first name or a nickname. He had a house, he had a wife, he had a pair of children with round, red faces. His wife was a nice Dutch girl, with a freckled, stub nose. She was scrubbing and shining up her house and her children all day long. And she kept Harry as neat as a pin. That was the way he was fixed when I walked into his bar, one day. I beckoned him down to the end of the bar. He came down, still laughing at the last story he had been telling, and wiping the beer foam from his lips. He wheezed a little; he was shaking with good nature and fat.

"So I leaned across the bar and told him in a whisper who I was, and what I'd come for."

"Did you tell him that you'd come to kill him?"

"Yes. I told him that. But I told him that I hadn't yet figured out the best way to do it. I would take my time, and in the meantime, I'd come in and visit his place every day. It was hard on poor Harry. He couldn't be jolly when I was around. I used to sit in a dark corner, where I could hardly be seen, but Harry was always straining his eyes at that corner. He'd break off in the midst of his stories. When people told him jokes, he couldn't laugh. He simply croaked. He got absent-minded. And there's nothing that people hate more than an absent-minded bartender. Some of his old cronies still came around, but in three days, that bar was hardly attended at all. The cronies would tell him that he was sick, and ought to take liver pills, but that wasn't what was on Harry's mind.

"He knew that I was the trouble, and he made up his mind to get rid of me. So he sent a couple of boys around to call on me one evening. However, I was expecting visitors. I persuaded them to confess how much he'd paid them, and how much more he had promised. They wrote out separate confessions and signed them. Then they got out of town."

"How did you persuade them?" asked the girl. "You mean that they tried to murder you?"

"They came in through the window," said the Kid. "They came sneaking across the room toward the bed where I was supposed to be lying, and pretty soon they stepped on the matting. And I'd covered that matting with glue. In two seconds they were all stuck together; and then I lighted the lamp."

He chuckled. The girl, however, did not laugh. She merely nodded, her eyes narrowing.

"The next day," went on the Kid, "I strolled over to the bar and read those two confessions aloud to Harry Dill. He took it rather hard. He'd turned into fat and beer, in those ten years or so since he'd been a bold, bad horse thief and baby murderer. He got down on his knees, in fact. But I only told him that I was still busy figuring out the best way to get rid of him.

"This went on for another ten days. Harry Dill turned into a ghost. I used to go in there and find him standing alone, his head on his hands. He tried to talk to me. He used to cry and beg. On day his wife came to me. She didn't know what the trouble was, but she knew that I was it. She begged me to leave her Harry alone, he was so dear and good! I read her the two confessions, and she went off home with a new idea in her head. A little after that, Harry offered me a glass of beer in his saloon. I took it and poured some out for his dog, and the dog was dead in half an hour.

"That upset Harry some more. He was very fond of that dog! And, after I'd been two weeks in town, poor Harry shot himself one evening. He'd been having a little argument with his wife, the children testified."

"And the poor little youngsters!" cried the girl, her heart in her voice.

"Oh, they had a good mother and a fine fat uncle, who took them all in, and they were happy ever after. Do you want any more?"

She passed handkerchief across her forehead.

"I don't know," she said. "I didn't think that it was going to be like this."

"Is it going to make you feel a lot closer and more friendly?" he asked, with a faint and sardonic smile.

"It makes me shudder," she admitted, "but I'd like to hear some more. Do you mean that you drove every one of those men to suicide, or something like it?"

"If I had simply shot them down," said the boy, "would that have been punishment? Why should I get myself hanged for their sakes?"

"I suppose not," she answered. "Who was next?"

"The next was a sheriff," said the Kid. "I've had a good deal of experience with sheriffs, but, take them by the large, I've found them an honest lot—very! But there are exceptions. And Chicago Oliver was one of them. He wasn't calling himself Chicago Oliver any more, when I found him. No, he had a brand-new name, and it was a good one in the county where he was living. They swore by their sheriff; he was the greatest man catcher that they'd ever had. Of course he was, because he loved that sort of business. Particularly when he had the law to help him.

"I met the sheriff on the street one day. He'd just come up for reëlection. Every one knew that he'd get the job, but every one was campaigning for him and making speeches just to show him how much they appreciated his good work. Oliver was a solemn, sad-looking man, with eyes that were always traveling around, quietly anxious to pick up even the smallest crumb of admiration. I stopped him on the street and told him who I was.

"It seemed to upset him a good deal. In fact, I went off down the street and left him leaning on a fence post, trying the best he knew not to drop on the sidewalk.

"The next time I met him, he asked me what I wanted. He was running a lot of cows on a fine bit of range, and he could afford to pay high, but I had to tell him that money was no object to me. He explained that he had never wanted to strip us, that night so many years before, and that he'd resisted the idea, and that the others had forced him on. But I reminded him how he had told my mother that a girl with such a pretty face would never miss such a thing as a few steers and a mule or so. She carried a fortune with her, he had said.

"That stopped Oliver's explanation.

"There was a robbery in town a day later, and he tried to frame me. He made the arrest all right, but on the way to jail, with me in the middle of his posse, I began to tell some stories about Chicago Oliver, and, after I had told a few of them, the sheriff decided that he must have made a mistake. He asked me a few questions, and then he told his posse men that he was all wrong, and would have to let me go.

"The day before the election, I met him in a barroom, and in a corner of that place he sat down with me, and offered me everything that he owned in the world. He said that his good name meant more to him than anything. I told him that I understood his type preferred newspaper space to a place in heaven, but that I still was merely making up my mind what I'd do to him. The same evening, he gave up and headed south, and that county lost its sheriff. He simply left a note behind, saying that he had had to leave on account of his health. That was reasonably true, too, because he'd lost thirty pounds since I came to town. That was the finish of him!"

"Ah, that was one who didn't die!" said the girl.

"Die? Oh, yes! The crooks found out that his nerve was gone. They began to hunt him just as enthusiastically as he ever had hunted them in his palmy days. A half-breed got to him in Vera Cruz, one evening, and killed him with a knife. I didn't envy the half-breed, though. I never have liked to get my hands dirty."

And he laughed, suddenly, through his teeth. The girl, shocked by the sound, jumped up, but sat down again at once.

"Are you getting nervous?" asked the Kid.

"No," she gasped. "I can stand it, I think. There's only one more horror to hear, I suppose!"

"You look," said the Kid coldly, "as though you had been watching an operation on a dear friend."

She waved a hand and mutely invited him to continue.

"All right," he said. "I'll go ahead and show you what a Gila monster I really am. The next and the last of the four was Mickie Munroe. He was the only one of the lot who hadn't reformed—on the surface, at least. Mickie had been the youngest of those five baby killers. He was still not thirty when I came up to him. He was riding the range, for this outfit or that, most of the year. But when he ran short of funds—faro was his pet lay—Mickie did better things than punching cows. He still knew how to rustle. And with a running iron, Mickie was one of the best artists that I ever saw. The hide of a cow was to Mickie Munroe like the canvas of an artist.

"This Mickie, I'm telling you about, was a jolly, happy-go-lucky chap. He was always smiling. He was always the life of any party. Everybody liked him pretty well, except a few who had an idea about his cattle rustling, and a few others who had seen the ugly side of Mickie's face. I spent a good deal of time wondering what I could do to Mickie. Finally I hit on the right thing.

"There were two things that Mickie was crazy about, when I caught up with him. One was faro, and one was a Mexican girl who pretended to wait on the table in the hotel. But really she was just there to cover up the bad cooking and the high prices in that place. She was so infernally pretty that men were willing to eat shoe leather, if they had the pleasure of looking at her face while they chewed. She made the crook who owned that hotel a pretty well-to-do-man, and she broke about every heart in the country, until Mickie came over the edge of her horizon.

"Mickie was almost as good-looking as she was. He was as free and easy. And he had a way with the girls. Well, to cut the story short, they fell in love with one another, and Mickie forgot even faro, for a while. He was working like mad to make a stake, and as soon as that stake was made, he was going to marry the girl. Not that Carmelita bothered much about money. She said that she was willing to live in a tent, so long as it was with him. It was a strange thing to see 'em together. She was as hard as nails, and so was Mickie. They were both professional flirts, but they were mad about each other. Not so many people went to the hotel dining room, in those days, and the ones who did get inside had a melancholy time of it, watching the calf looks that went back and forth between the pair of 'em.

"However, I judged that Carmelita was able to change her mind, and in case she did, I thought that I'd try to put myself on the map, where she could see me. So I broke into some flowing Mexican duds—you know—gold, silver, even spangles, and lace at my wrists. I put on a new high sombrero, and a new Spanish name that took two minutes just to sign. Then I dropped into that town and let Carmelita know that I had arrived.

"She seemed to notice me right away, too. Girls are apt to like noisy colors, if they haven't been brought up well. Then some of the boys took offense at me and thought that I was more of a sissy than a high Spanish Don. They started to kick me out of town the day after I arrived. But the kicking business was right in my line, and by the time that afternoon ended, Carmelita was not only sure that I was beautiful, but that I was a warrior and a hero."

The Kid paused to roll a cigarette, and he lighted it with a reminiscent air.

"I'm talking a good deal about myself," he remarked.

"I've asked for it," said the girl, suddenly husky. "And what happened with Carmelita? Did you break her heart?"

"That kind of a heart doesn't break," said the Kid. "Not if you dropped it out of a tenth-story window. You could break India rubber as easily as you could break a heart like Carmelita's. But she was a lovely picture. And she danced in a way that made me dizzy. Now and then I had to catch hold of myself and give myself a shake, as it were, to keep from getting really off my balance about her.

"Well, Mickie Munroe was taking all of this very hard, I can tell you. In the first place, he went to the girl, and she told him that he gave her a headache when he shouted so loud. In the second place, he came to me. Mickie was a fighting man, but I had had so much luck that afternoon when they started to kick me out of the town that he didn't quite make up his mind to run me out on his own account. But he had a talk with me, and tried to convince me that I had no serious intentions so far as Carmelita was concerned. I told him that he was wrong. And then I told him some more about myself, and a bit about his own affairs that interested him a good deal.

"Mickie was up against a bad job.

"He wanted to cut my throat. He was sure that with me dead and gone, Carmelita would not remember me very long. And he was right. Carmelita's memory for men was merely a thread, a spider thread, you might say. Any wind was able to blow it away.

"When Mickie decided that he had to murder me, he went about it methodically.

"Now that he couldn't have Carmelita—at least, not right

away—of course he was madder for her than ever. I was three weeks in that town, waiting, and I give you my word that in that short time poor Mickie turned gray and grew thin, and appeared to be a tired, old man. I don't think that he ever slept more than ten minutes at a time all those weeks. He was like a scared cat; a wild cat, mind you.

"He tried me with poison, a little home-made bomb with a time fuse, a riot gun fired around the corner of a building, and a knife thrust in the dark. But he had no luck, though with that bomb he laid out four other men, and two of them nearly died.

"I let their friends into the secret as to who it was that had made the bomb, and then things began to hum for poor Mickie.

"He could only sneak into he town at night. He was hunted like a mad dog. Carmelita, when she saw him, laughed in his face and snapped her fingers, because she'd entirely made up her mind that he was a waste of time.

"Well, the end of it was a dull affair, in the talking. But really I think that Mickie suffered more than all the rest put together. There was enough decency in him, d'you see, really to love a woman. I'd say that his heart was broken, and that he died of that. One night I heard him moaning and sobbing like a baby under her window, and I heard her open that window and tell Mickie that if he didn't get away, she'd call me to go down and horsewhip him out of the town. And Mickie left. His spirit was gone, you understand? His nerve had broken down—"

"Like the others!" said the girl, her voice rasping.

"Yes," said the Kid thoughtfully, as he inhaled a deep breath of cigarette smoke. "The doctor said that it was an overdose of whisky—he'd emptied a whole bottle in a single evening—but I imagine that it was the broken heart that killed Mickie."

"And the girl? The Carmelita?" asked Georgia.

"She? Oh, I used to remember the names of her first two husbands, but I've forgotten them, now."

28
The Fifth Man

AFTER THIS fourth narrative had ended, Georgia got up from the log and hastily crossed the clearing. She walked back and forth for a moment, breathing deeply. And the Kid, watching her through half-closed eyes, continued to smoke, letting the cigarette fume between his fingers, most of the time, but now and then lifting it in leisurely fashion to his lips.

"You don't really care what I think?" she demanded stopping suddenly in front of him.

He seemed to rouse himself from a dream, starting violently.

"Care?" he echoed. "Of course I care."

"Ah, not a rap!" said she.

"More," answered the Kid, "than I care about the opinion of any other person in the world."

He said it so seriously that she stepped back a little. She put up her head, but her face was pale, and the color would not come back into it.

"I'm not Carmelita," said she.

"No," answered the Kid, with perfect calm. "I wouldn't dream of trying to flirt with you."

She watched him closely.

"I'm trying to get words together," she said.

"Take your time," said the Kid. "I know you're going to hit hard, but I'm ready to take the punch."

At last she said. "I've never heard, and I've never dreamed of anything like the four stories you've told me. I don't want to believe them. I won't believe them. You've made up four horrible things—the most horrible that you could conceive, and you've strung them together for the sake of giving me a shock!"

"My dear," said the Kid, "there's nothing but the gospel truth in what I've told you. Not a word but the exact truth."

Staring at him fixedly, she knew that he meant what he said.

"Then—" she cried out.

She stopped the words; and the Kid, with his faint smile, watched her and waited.

"You be the judge and the jury, now," said he. "You can find me guilty and hang me, too."

"Why have you told me all this?" she asked him, almost passionately.

"Because you asked me to," said the Kid.

"No," she replied firmly. "That's not it, I think. Merely asking wouldn't make you do it, I know!"

"I wanted you to know about me," said the Kid. "That's why I told you."

"You wanted me to know?" she cried.

"That's it."

"Will you tell me one thing more?"

"I probably will."

"Did you take a pleasure out of what you did to each of those four men?"

He answered instantly: "When I started with each one, I would have enjoyed feeding him into a fire, inch by inch. I would have enjoyed hearing him howl like a fiend. But before the end, I admit that I was sick of it, each time."

"Then why did you keep on?"

"Because each time the business was done so thoroughly that at the end it didn't matter what I put my hand to. The thing always got outside of my control. Turk Reming's reputation that he loved and was proud of was gone completely before he was killed. Harry Dill's business was ruined, and his happiness with it. Oliver's self-confidence which he'd always been able to trust like bed rock, was knocked to pieces under his feet. And finally, Mickie Munroe had turned into an old man. Toward the end I pitied each one of them. But I pitied them too late."

"Suppose," said the girl, "that you're judged, one day, just as you've judged them?"

He nodded frankly.

"I understand perfectly what you mean," said the Kid. He looked up to where a woodpecker was chiseling busily at the trunk of a tree, the rapping of his incredible beak making a purr like that of a riveter. Down fell a little thin shower of chips as the tree surgeon drilled for the grub.

"Some day I'll be judged," said the Kid. "It'll be a black day for me. Mind you, I haven't tried to excuse what I've done. And yet, if I had to do it over again, I'd do it. I'd go through the same steps in the same way."

"What would drive you?" asked the girl. "There's no real remorse in you for what you've done, then? What would drive you on? Pity for your mother's death?"

"No," said the Kid, after a moment of consideration. "Not that. She's in my mind, now and then, of course. So's my father, and the pain in his face. But what haunted me always was the memory of those two old milk cows swaying and heaving under the yoke, and finally dying for us. Well, not for us. It was the death of my mother; and my father would have been better dead, I suppose. But those poor beasts did their work for me. I used to think of them, I tell you, and the heat of that desert, and the way old Red wobbled and staggered under me—I used to think of that when I was working on those four in the final stages."

"And there'll be a fifth man?" said the girl.

"As sure as I'm alive to deal with him."

"It's Billy Shay!" she broke out suddenly.

"No," said he.

"You're not going to tell me, of course."

"I am, though. It's because I have to tell you that, that I told you all the rest that went before."

"Who is it, then?"

"His name is John Milman," said the Kid.

He rose as she rose. Then, with a quick step forward, he caught her under the arms, steadied her, and lowered her back to the log.

"I'm not going to faint!" she said through her teeth.

Her head fell. There was no trace of color in her face. "I won't cave in," she repeated fiercely, faintly.

In a rush, then, the blood came back to her, and her head seemed to clear.

"That's a ghastly way to joke!" she said to him.

He took his hands gingerly from her, as though still not sure that she was strong enough to sit upright, unsupported.

"If it were a joke, it would be ghastly," he admitted. "It's bad enough even when it's taken seriously."

"Are you trying to tell me," said the girl, "that my own father —my John Milman—my mother's husband—that he—was one of the five men that night?"

As she spoke, the wind changed, grew a little in force, and brought to them a vaguely melancholy sound from the horizon.

"Your father, your mother's husband, your John Milman, he was one of the five," said the Kid.

"You've heard it, but it's not true!" said the girl. "Why, it would have been after I was born—after we were settled down here—after—why, you think that you can make me believe that?"

"I think I can," said he. "I've made myself believe it."

"A hard job, that!" she said fiercely. "You wanted to believe. You've simply wanted to find subjects to torture, and you hardly cared who! But this time—" She altered her voice and exclaimed: "Will you tell me what makes you think it could possibly be he?"

"I'll tell you," said the Kid. "It was night, as I said. And I was sick, so that you'd think that I couldn't have seen very well. But the fact is that they were quite free and easy. The law was a pretty dull affair, those years ago. Blind, mostly, and no memory at all. So they didn't bother to wear masks, and they didn't trouble about turning away when they lighted cigarettes. I remember those faces, the way pictures slip into the brain of a sick child, and stay there for reference. I remember Turk Reming laughing and showing his white teeth, while he held a match to light the cigarette of another man—a middle-sized fellow, with a good forehead, and good features altogether. That one had a cleft chin, and halfway down the right side of his jaw there was a small, reddish spot, like the mark of a bullet, or a birthmark, perhaps—"

He stopped, and the girl, moistening her white lips, watched him. She was breathing hard. The laboring of her heart choked her.

"What are you going to do?" she asked.

"I don't know," said the Kid. "That's why I was glad to talk things over with you."

"You actually mean murder!" said the girl.

"Not with a gun," said the Kid. "They didn't use guns on my

father and mother, or on old Spot and Red. No, not with a gun."

"There's no other way that you can harm him!" said Georgia.

"Well, perhaps not," said the Kid seriously.

"You can air his past as much as you please, but you'll never ruin his reputation. He's spent too many years doing fine things. He's filled the whole range with his charities! I don't care what your methods of detestable blackmail are, you'll never be able to destroy him the way you did the cheap ruffians and fools!"

"There's a great deal in what you say, of course," said the Kid. "He seems to have gone pretty straight since that night. Oh, I've looked him over before, and I've always put if off, and put it off."

She grew, if possible, paler still. Faint, bluish shadows began to appear beneath her eyes.

"You mean that you've been watching him?"

"Oh, for years!" said the Kid. "He had the mule, you see. It was his house that I found the first of all."

She pressed her hands suddenly across her face, and jerked them down again.

The Kid, watching her, went on: "A gray mule. Gray when we had it, and nearly silver when I saw it again when I was fifteen. There was a barbed-wire cut across his chest, a thing you don't often see in mules. They're altogether too wise, usually, to—"

"Blister!" cried the girl. "It's old Blister that you mean!"

He nodded.

"If you found my father, the first of all the five, why did you go away without harming him? Because you knew in spite of anything, that he is a good man!"

"I went away because of you," said the Kid.

"Because of me?"

"You used to ride old Blister."

"Why, I learned to ride on him. He didn't know how to make a mistake. He—"

She stopped, wretchedly tormented. Her lips twitched and her eyes were haunted.

"One day you were riding him up the trail through the hills behind your place. Up through those hills, yonder. You passed a youngster, dressed mostly in rags. He was wearing one shoe and one moccasin. He was sitting by a spring taking a rest, and you told him that if he went down to the ranch house, he'd get something worth while."

"I remember his blue eyes," said the girl, "and—"

She stopped short again, her lips parting.

"It was you!" said she.

"Yeah," drawled the Kid. "It was I, all right. That evening I went down and looked things over. You were in the room where the piano is. Your mother was playing; you were singing; your father was asleep in his chair, but you kept on singing to the open window. You were only a youngster, but you were singing love songs to the dark of that window. And I was out there in the dark, watching."

He made a pause, as if to remember the scene more clearly.

"Since then," said the Kid, "I've come back three times, always at night, and I've always seen you, and I've always gone away. Since that day, when I was fifteen, you've been in my mind as clearly as a thing learned by heart when you're very young."

"I don't exactly know what you're trying to say," said the girl.

"You know very well," said the Kid, "what I want to say. And you know that I won't say it."

He stood up before her. For out of the distance the melancholy sound grew from the horizon, and suddenly she saw that with more than half his mind he was listening to it. It was the lowing of the thirst-tormented cattle by Hurry Creek.

"Whatever happens," said the Kid, "you see that I've put my cards face up on the table. I suppose you'd better show them to your father."

29
Cattle Lover

IN THE SUNSET of that day, the black mare and the silver stallion stood on the crest of a hill overlooking the big hollow through which Hurry Creek ran from ravine to ravine. The light was growing dim, but still there was enough of it for the Kid and Bud Trainor to see quite clearly.

There was a continual shifting and flowing, as it seemed, of the very ground that led down toward the water. It was the troubled maneuvering of masses upon masses of thirsty cattle. Still, from the outer reaches of the ranch, the cattle were drifting in toward the familiar watering place. They could be seen coming, sometimes singly, sometimes in patient files that went one behind the other, winding across the well-worn trails. From the hills on top of which they had a view of the creek, these approaching animals were sure to send out a deep lowing as they were made aware of a new and unprecedented condition there by the water which was life to them.

Sometimes they seemed frightened and remained a long time to gaze. Sometimes they grew excited, and breaking into a gallop, rushed up to join the mob.

There was no sense in them. The cunning of long years on the range was burned out of them. They were simply stupid creatures driven by an inward fire. The bellowing, like the noise of a sea, was so deep and thunderous that at times it seemed far off, and at times it rushed on the ear as though the entire herd were stampeding in the direction of the watchers. Now and then one of the milling currents stumbled on something, like

145

rapid water flowing over a rock; and there was no need for the Kid or Bud Trainor to tell one another what those obstacles were.

Not fifty yards away from them lay a dead cow, with her legs sticking straight out, as though she had been shot through the brain and had tumbled over upon her side. And upon her head sat a buzzard, looking in the sunset light as big as a deformed child. Other buzzards were in the air, though perhaps the near presence of the two riders prevented any of them from joining their companion on the dead cow. But whole drifts of those wonderful flyers sailed low above Hurry Creek, sweeping and sailing without a flap of wings just above the dust cloud which rolled over the heads of the cows and was drawn slowly off on the westering wind.

Through that mist of dust, they could see the surface of Hurry Creek, running red as blood under the sunset, and on the farther bank there was already the shine of a camp fire which grew brighter as the light of the day decreased.

There were Champ Dixon's men making themselves comfortable, and even jolly, no doubt, in the midst of this scene of unspeakable misery and horror.

"That's the way with gents," philosophized Bud Trainor. "You can get a man into a frame of mind for pretty nigh anything. Murder, say. You can get the best sort of people to go to war, and there they'll do all the murderin' they can get a chance to lay their hands on. How many of 'em would stay honest if just the right, safe chance to steal come and nudged 'em in the ribs? Look at me. I sold you right in my own house."

"Bud, never speak of that again," said the Kid.

"You want that I should forget it, but even if I don't talk, it's in my head, all day, every day, all night, every night."

"Don't be a fool," said the Kid.

"I ain't gonna be. But I'm gonna find a way to pay back. I'm gonna find a way to make it right with you, Kid. That's all I've gotta say, and I'll never mention it again!"

He snapped his jaws on the last word.

"What's murder of men?" demanded the Kid. "Men have brains. They have wits enough to hit back. They have guns to help 'em. But a horde of dumb beasts—that's what I don't understand, Bud. Dumb beasts that have done no wrong, because they don't know enough to do wrong. Look at them there! There'll be plenty of crow food on that ground before the morning, Bud!"

"Maybe the boys'll rush 'em before the morning," suggested Bud.

He gestured to either side.

Keeping to the ridges of the hills that made the rim of the bowl through which the creek flowed, all the punchers of the ranch were riding. Slowly they went up and down, never offering to do anything, except keep a sentry beat. But those dark figures, moving black against the sunset sky, were grim enough, and suggestive of the dark passion that was in the heart of every man of them.

"No," said the Kid. "They know the sort of stuff that's down there in the hollow, and they won't rush. Not them!"

He sneered as he spoke.

His voice was rising. His excitement also flashed and glittered in his eyes.

"You'd think," said Bud Trainor, wondering, "that you owned all of those cows, and loved 'em, too!"

"If I were the devil," said the Kid, "I'd get on the backs of these cows and put hell fire into their hearts. I'd run them in a mob on those fences and smash 'em down, and I'd charge them right onto the men and stamp 'em into a big bloodstain in the mud. I'd do it, and I'd enjoy doing it. They're dying, Bud. They're dying tonight, but when the heat of the sun comes tomorrow, they'll drop like flies—all the ones that have been off on the edges of the ranch, already without water for days."

"They'll drop like flies," agreed Bud Trainor. "There ain't any doubt that they'll drop like flies."

"You'd think," said the Kid, "that there wasn't a God, when things like this go on!"

"Look here, Kid," said Trainor, "you've raised your own share of hell in the world."

"I've raised my share, and harvested it, too," admitted the Kid, "and sacked it, and put it away for the winter. I've raised my share, and maybe I'll raise some more, but not till I've tried my hand with this job!"

"Hold on," said Bud Trainor. "How can you try your hand— what job d'you mean?"

The Kid looked sourly on him. His handsome young face was so dark with anger that he seemed ten years older.

"This job in front of us," said the Kid. "I'm going to get those cows to water in the morning, or else I'll throw some lead into Dixon's boys as a fair exchange."

"Don't be a fool," cautioned Trainor, alarmed. "They have the law with them. Even the sheriff admits that."

"The heck with the law," said the Kid. "I'm thinking of dying cows. One wag of their tails is worth all the lives of those dirty crooks yonder!"

"Hold on, Kid. What's your idea?"

"I've got no idea."

"You've got none?"

"But I'll get one before long."

"Where? Where'll you get an idea for the fixing of this job?"

"Oh, I dunno. From the devil maybe, or heaven above. But the idea is sure to come!"

30

Down the Canyon

THE SCENE was darkening. The river tarnished and turned black. The fog of dust which rolled up from the milling cows now was lessening, though now and again the wind drifted a throat-stinging billow of it toward the watchers.

The cattle by this time were becoming more quiet. Numbers of them lay down. Only some hundreds of those most desperate with thirst came sweeping up and down the lines of the fences. The thunder of the bellowing was far less, but still from the hills behind, the newcomers gave voice like mournful drums in a great and scattering chorus.

There was this difference with the coming of the night, for while the clearly seen tragedy of the day had been localized and limited, now the darkness blanketed away the farther mountains and brought down only the nearer hills like black and beastly watchers of suffering. The ocean roar of pain went up against the sky and seemed to fill it. It seeped up from the very ground which actually, or in suggestion, trembled beneath them. Hurry Creek had seemed a little theater during the day where a tragedy was being enacted. Now it included the entire world.

So it seemed to Bud Trainor, as he sat on his horse beside the Kid and looked down on the darkening hollow.

"Suppose Dixon's men wanted to get out of there," said Bud. "They'd have a hard time, I reckon!"

"Why should they want to leave?" said the Kid. "They're holding out for two hundred thousand dollars' blackmail. That's what they want, and as long as they care to camp there, I don't see them running very short of beef, do you?"

The other nodded, and then sighed a little.

"Well," said he, "I meant that if this were an Indian war, the red devils would rather be strung around up here on the heights than to be down there in the hollow."

"That's interesting, but not important," said the Kid. "They could be besieged there for six months, and never have to worry. And if they got tired of that, they could break away. But there's meat enough for them."

"They haven't much wood," objected the other. "They've cleaned up the brush and stacked it in the middle of their camp. You can still see the head of it beside their cookin' tent. But that ain't enough wood for six months' fuel. Not for cooking for that many men! Besides, they wouldn't dare to touch one of the dead cows."

"Why not?"

"Well, wouldn't that make them thieves, and wouldn't we have the law with us, then? Wouldn't Milman be able to raise the whole range to help him, if they did as much as that?"

"You're right," said the Kid, "but they have plenty of provisions with them in there. And—and—and—"

Here his voice faltered and trailed away.

Bud Trainor, for some reason, knew that a matter of importance was filling the brain of his partner, and he held his breath in anticipation.

"Bud," said the Kid at last, "I'm going down into that camp."

"All right," said Bud. "Which recipe for walkin' the air do you use?"

The Kid was silent.

"You might just stroll down through them mobs of cows," said Bud Trainor. "They wouldn't do much more to you than a steam roller would."

Then he added: "I dunno how else you could get there!"

"The ravine! The ravine!" cried the Kid, his voice suddenly ringing out with impatient joy. "What a fool I was not to think of that before!"

"The ravine?" echoed Bud. "You mean Hurry Creek's ravine?"

"That's what I mean, of course. Let's go there and look the thing over!"

Bud gripped the rein of the mare.

"You're clean crazy, Kid," said he.

"Let me alone, Bud. You don't have to go. I'll do this alone!"

"I won't let you go. Not before you listen a minute."

"To what?"

"To that. Bend your ear a little to the north, and just listen, will you?"

It came distinctly through the melancholy booming voices of the cows, a deep and harsh roar which the Kid instantly made out.

"That's the water of the creek. Is that what you mean?"

"Listen to it. Sounds like a lion, doesn't it?"

"Let it be a lion. I'll walk down its throat if I have to. I could drink blood tonight, Bud."

"You're simply going crazy," said the other. "You've never seen the waters in the ravine. Come along with me to the edge of it. If we can't see 'em, we'll hear 'em, at least, at close hand. And that'll be enough for you, if you're in your right wits."

"Very well. Come along then with me."

They cantered their horses forward.

"Who's there?" rang a voice from the darkness before them, and then they made out the silhouette of a horseman, and the starlit glimmer of a leveled rifle.

"Friends!" said the Kid, pulling up the mare.

"What friends?"

"Bud Trainor, and I'm the Kid."

"Hey! Are you the Kid?"

The rifle took a crosswise, harmless slant, and the puncher came up.

"Hullo there, Kid," said he. "I'd been hopin' that I'd see you down here. My name's Bill Travis."

They shook hands.

"Things is pretty bad with the cows," said Travis. "They's a lot laid down that ain't gonna get up in the morning."

"There are a lot who'll get up in the morning and drop before noon, too," said the Kid.

"That's a true thing. Any fool could tell that. Got a chaw with you?"

"I don't carry it. Here's the makings, though."

He passed them over. Dexterously the puncher made his smoke in the dark of the night.

"What are you fellows going to do about this, Travis?"

"Why, what can we do?"

"I don't know. Any ideas among the boys?"

"Nothing except we might stampede the cows to break down the fences."

"It wouldn't work. They'd shoot the head off of any stampede."

"That's what we decided. It won't work. Maybe the old man will have an idea."

"Are they keeping a sentry go along those fences tonight?"

"Sure they are. Three men along each fence. And the others ready to come on the jump, I suppose."

"Baby murder—that's what it is!" said the Kid, his rage breaking out. "Listen!"

He held up his hand in the darkness. The lowing of the cattle swept up around them in waves, as though all the tormented souls from hell were pouring up toward the stars, lamenting.

"Aye, it's pretty bad," said Travis. "Shay and Dixon—they'll sweat for it some day."

"Tonight, I hope," said the Kid, muttering through his teeth.

"What's that?"

"Nothing. You boys are riding these rounds all night?"

"We're riding 'em all the night. If Dixon's crowd starts out to do a little foraging, we'll teach them how the Milman crew can shoot. The boys are pretty hot. Old Tar Yagers, over on the other side of the ranch, is hankering after a scalp or two, and maybe the old man will get a chance, before this fracas is finished."

"Maybe he will," agreed the Kid. "So long. You fellows keep your eyes open, will you?"

"For what?"

"For a signal in the Dixon Camp."

"What sort of a signal?"

"Fire," said the Kid, and rode on without further speech.

Bud hurried the silver stallion up beside him.

"What's that about fire, Kid?" he asked.

But he received no answer, for the Kid seemed lost in thought.

So they came, at last, to the edge of the ravine.

Three steps away the predominant sound was the voice of the cattle from the hollow, but when they came to the verge and dismounted, they could hear nothing except the heavy and continual roaring of the water, like a constant cannonade.

"Listen to it!" said Bud Trainor. "How'd you like to be down there in that, Kid?"

The Kid did not answer.

Presently he drew back from the verge of the cliff.

"You've seen that in the daytime, haven't you?"

"Yes."

"How far is it to the bottom?"

"Forty—fifty feet, I reckon."

"You've got a sixty-foot rope," said the Kid. "Get it for me, will you?"

"What are you gonna do?"

"Bud, for heaven's sake, stop asking questions. I have enough on my mind, just now, without trying to answer you."

"All right," said Bud, "but it makes me pretty sick, even to think about it."

He went, however, to his horse, and took from the saddle bow the long, heavy rope, for he had learned his punching in Montana when a boy, and stuck to the fashion of the northern rope. This he brought back and the Kid, taking the noose end of it, tied it fast about a jag of rock on the very verge of the canyon wall.

Then he got to the end of the line and tested, tugging with all his weight.

"It's sound, if that's what you want to know," said Trainor.

"It's sound," agreed the Kid, and threw the other end down the height.

It disappeared in the darkness of the ravine, but for a moment the upper end jerked and wriggled like a struggling snake.

"Bud," said the Kid, "I'm going down there."

"If you go," said Bud, "I'll go after you."

"You'll stay here," commanded the Kid. "It's my own game and my own business that I'm after. I only want one thing out of you. Give me your hand, and if I don't come back, remember me!"

"If anything happens to you," said Bud solemnly, "I'll keep on the trail of Dixon and Shay till they get me, or I get them. So long, Kid."

"So long," said the Kid, and slipped over the edge of the wall.

31
The Fifth Man Again

YOUTH IS proverbially cruel, whether in its trust or in its distrust. It cannot halt. It will have no half measures. It is an absolute tyrant which pushes all things to extremes.

Now, when Georgia Milman had heard the story of the Kid which inculpated her father, she hesitated for a moment only. The description of her father's face, and the distinguishing little mark upon it, had determined her that the Kid was right.

Yet something might be said.

Men appear in most guilty situations without actually possessing guilt, and that might be true of her father also. So thought Georgia. She wanted an explanation. She wanted it at once. But she went about the acquiring of it in the typically youthful, cruel, headlong fashion.

She could have drawn John Milman aside, of course, but if she did this, she would have to wait, for she found him in the house closely conferring with her mother.

It was his habit when a crisis of any kind came to ask for advice, and the advice which he had come to prize above all else was that which he received from Elinore Milman herself. She was calm, keen-witted, and understood as well as he did all the problems of the ranch and of the affairs which had to do with it.

Accordingly, he was now talking over with her the possibilities of the situation, and there Georgia found him.

He was walking up and down the room—the front room of the house where on that other night so many years ago, she had sung him to sleep, and then sung on to the open window and the soft, impalpable darkness beyond it, not knowing that someone waited there, listening.

And the fact that this was the same room hardened the spirit of Georgia a little.

In that story of the Kid's, she had waited for the things which bore upon her, but he had repressed all emotion, with the restraint of some old Greek poet, preparing an inscription to be cut into stone. There was only a line or two, but it pointed to a great thing, indeed. He had hardly said so much, but most distinctly he had inferred that what had turned his cunning and his anger three times aside from the head of her father was the love of the Kid for her. And she remembered, as she stood there by the door, looking blankly through the window toward the shimmer of the sun on the hills beyond, how she had spoken to that ragged lad, those years before. The bright blue of his eyes had remained in her memory. Now the face itself was distinctly chiseled in her mind. It seemed monstrous that she ever could have forgotten it.

"There are," said Mrs. Milman, who was summing up precisely, "just two alternatives. Either we pay for the cows by the head and send them in to be watered, or else we hire a mob of gunmen and smash Dixon and his crowd with a strong hand."

Georgia opened her eyes. She never had heard her mild mother speak like this before. Milman himself was amazed.

"Which do you advise?" said he.

"I don't know," said Mrs. Milman, half closing her eyes, and by the pucker of her brows seeming to attempt to read the future. "I really don't know."

"It's always foolish to break the law," said Milman.

"It's always foolish to break the law," she echoed. "But it's more foolish to sit and wait—for sure ruin!"

She held up her hand.

"Listen, John!" she said.

And, through the window from the eastward, they could hear a long, dull droning sound—a tremor of deep sorrow on the wind rather than an actual noise.

Milman jumped up, with the sweat running as fast as tears down his face.

He gripped his hands hard together and dragged in a breath.

"I'm half mad with the waiting," he said. "I feel like riding out there and simply going blindly in at them—but there's no use throwing oneself away. The sheriff—my own neighbors—

the law—everything is blind and deaf to me. It looks almost like a hand from heaven striking me, Elinore!"

"Well," said the slender, mild woman, "it's either the hard fist and a crowd of hired guns—or else a miracle."

"A miracle?" echoed Milman heavily.

"The Kid, I mean," said she.

His face brightened for a moment.

"Aye, the Kid," said he. "He's like an answer to a prayer. But what can even the Kid do? He's brought in evidence in the shape of one of their hired gunmen that ought to have been enough to establish our rights in the law instantly—except that the sheriff won't see it that way."

"The sheriff was right," said his wife. "We mustn't throw stones at honest Lew Walters."

Milman made a wide gesture of despair. Then, resuming the subject of the Kid, he exclaimed, "One never can tell. He is the sort of a lad who does the unexpected."

He turned to his daughter.

"Georgia," said he, "we're talking business, your mother and I."

"Yes, and miracles, I hear," said Georgia, with the coldest of smiles.

"What do you mean, my dear?"

"Well, if you're so interested in the Kid, I think you might like to know that I've been talking to him."

"You have? Where?"

"In the woods. In the clearing in the woods, nearest the house. We've been talking for a long, long time."

"I hope it was not a waste of time," said Mrs. Milman, eying her daughter narrowly.

"I never heard so many interesting things," said she.

"Anything that we ought to know about, Georgia?"

"Well, one thing that would curdle your blood," said the girl.

"And what was that?"

"Why," said Georgia, studiously avoiding the eye of her father and giving all of her attention to her mother, "when he was a little youngster of six, his father and mother started to go to a new home—they were just poor squatters, I take it—and when they got to the edge of the desert with their few horses, and their mules, and their burro, and their steers, and their pair of milk cows, along came a band of five scoundrels and robbed them of everything, except the milk cows. Think of that!"

"A horrible thing," said Mrs. Milman a little vacantly. "But we're very busy now, Georgia."

Milman, with an odd pucker of his forehead, looked straight before him.

"You don't understand how horrible it was, Mother," said the girl. "The poor little boy was sick, but his father insisted on trying to cross the desert and get to the new country—the Promised Land to that poor man, I suppose. So they pushed on. The boy grew more ill. The mother was half mad with anxiety. It was a terrible march. They had yoked the milk cows to the light wagon, you see. They lightened the load, throwing away everything but a little food. Still it was hard going through the sand, and the sun was terrible. It beat down, and one of the cows—old Spot—was the first to drop. Then Red went stagger- ing on for a couple of days with the sick boy perched on her back. A frightful march, of course."

"Oh, what a ghastly thing!" said Elinore Milman, all the mother in her roused.

"Well, old Red dropped dead too. But then they were in reaching distance of the edge of the desert. They could see the green mist of the Promised Land. They got through to it, all right. But the mother died in a short time from the effects of that march. The father was broken-hearted, and the Kid grew up with just one purpose in life—to find the five men who had done the thing!"

"I hope that he has!" exclaimed Mrs. Milman. "I imagine that he's the sort of a fellow who would know how to handle them."

"Yes, he got on the trail of them," said the girl. "He spotted the stolen mule nine years later."

Here she let her glance drift across to the face of her father and she saw his eyes widen, and then turn almost to stone.

It was a frightful moment.

If ever fear, grief, and sick consciousness of sin were in a face, it was in that of the rancher just then.

She stared at him. She could have fallen to the floor with weakness and with sorrow. And she was stunned by this second blow even more than when the Kid had spoken to her.

Her mother, finally, attracted by the silence, looked curiously from one of them to the other.

"A grisly story, John, isn't it?" said she.

"Frightful!" said he.

And the word came hoarsely from his throat.

Elinore Milman stood up suddenly.

She faced her daughter and exclaimed: "Did he tell you the names of those men?"

Georgia slumped back against the wall. She was dizzy. The room spun before her eyes.

"He told me—four of them," said she. "Four of them are dead."

She roused herself suddenly. She had not meant to let her mother understand, but Elinore Milman was now as white as marble. Her father was like a man hanging upon a crucifix.

There was no use holding back now. She had said too much. Amazement at her own folly in breaking out with the story before them both closed her lips now. But her mother read her mind.

"I think," said she, "that it's just as well to have all sorts of things out in the light of day. Family skeletons ought not necessarily to be left in dark closets. Don't you think so, John?"

John Milman got to his feet with a lurch and a stagger.

"I'm going out," said he. "Need—little air."

He went past his daughter but he was so blinded that he could not find the handle of the door.

She had to open it for him, and then she watched him going down the hall slowly, with many pauses, supporting himself with a weak hand against first one wall and then the other.

He had been struck down as surely as by a thunderbolt.

And then she remembered what the Kid had done in all the other four cases. There never had been any real use of guns. He had always struck with other means.

And here, incredibly devilish though it was, he actually had delivered his blow against Milman through the mouth of Milman's own daughter.

She had been a mere tool, a foolish, incredible tool, but one with an edge sharp enough to cut her father to the heart.

32
Milman Rides

WHEN GEORGIA turned back to her mother, she was met with a
cold, keen glance that startled her.

"That boy has been telling you a good deal, Georgia," said
Elinore Milman.

"He told me because I asked," said the girl.

"About your father?"

"No, but about what he had done and what he had been."

"You're interested in him, Georgia?"

The girl shrugged her shoulders.

"I think we'd better talk about father," she said.

"Do you?" asked the mother, and lifted her brows a little.

It was a danger sign with which Georgia had been familiar
for years.

"What does he matter," said Georgia, "except that he's a
danger to father?"

"That's what I want to find out," said Mrs. Milman. "I want
to find out what the Kid matters to you."

"To me? Why, I've barely seen him."

"That doesn't matter very much—to him, I imagine. He's
been making love to you, of course?"

"Of course not!" said Georgia.

Then she turned a bright crimson.

"Well?" said her mother, waiting.

"I suppose he did," said the girl. "But not the way you'd
think."

"I don't suppose that he asked you to marry him the first

158

moment, if that's what you mean," said Mrs. Milman, in the same quick, hard voice. "But he's been looking for you a long time, I suppose?"

Georgia, if possible, blushed still deeper. She began to feel that probably even in this matter she had been made a fool of by the Kid. A cold, deep pang of hatred for him slid through her.

"He'd seen me years ago," said Georgia.

"Where?"

"Here. Through that window. One night when you were playing and I was singing, and father was asleep."

"And the Kid was looking about for whatever he could pick up?"

"He was looking for a mule with a barbed-wire scar across its chest. He'd found Blister, Mother, and he'd followed Blister to our house."

Mrs. Milman gripped hard on the arms of her chair.

"That was a stolen mule then."

"Yes. According to the Kid."

"I wish that we had some other name for him. Did he give you one?"

"No."

"Georgia, what is this fellow to you?"

"I don't know," said Georgia, "except that I hate him more than any one I've ever seen."

"You like him better, too, don't you?" asked the mother.

"Yes, I do."

"What else did he tell you?"

"He told me how he had hunted down each one of the other four."

"That must have been a pretty story."

"He never touched one of them. He simply broke their hearts, one after another."

"Using other people for it—as he's used you today?"

The girl lost her color at a stroke, but she answered steadily: "I see that now."

"How do you like him, Georgia?"

"I don't know how to tell you."

"It's the great, romantic thrill, isn't it?"

"What do you mean by that?"

"Oh, the big, handsome stranger with the strange life, and the rather dark past. Isn't that the thing? The Byronic touch, perhaps?"

"There isn't much bunk about him," said Georgia carefully.

She began to think, then she added: "No, there isn't much pretense, so far as I could see."

"And how far do you think that you could see?"

"I don't know. Perhaps not very far. I'm not pretending that I could look through him."

"The mystery is the attractive part, I suppose?"

"Perhaps that's a part of it."

"A good deal of pity, too, for the poor boy and his dead mother and father?"

"I don't think you really have a right to talk about that!" declared Georgia.

Mrs. Milman suddenly closed her eyes.

"No," she said, "I want to be fair. I'm simply trying to get at your mind, Georgia."

"I'll try to tell you everything," said Georgia.

She stood up like a soldier at attention. They had always been very close friends.

"You know a good deal about the Kid, Georgia?"

"I know what he's told me."

"You believe it?"

She pondered again.

"Yes," she said. "Just now, at least, I believe every syllable of it."

"What else do you know about him?"

"The rumors and the gossip, of course, not in much detail."

"Such as what?"

"That he's a gambler and a gunman."

"Two easy words to repeat. But do you realize what they mean?"

"I think so. Not altogether, perhaps. I'm not a baby, though, Mother."

"No," said Mrs. Milman. "You're not a baby, and you've reached the age when you think you know, and think you think. Just try to remember that a professional gambler is a fellow who matches his sleight of hand against the honest chance which other players are trusting. And a gunman is a man who takes advantage of his professional skill, his natural talent, to pick quarrels with less-gifted men, and men who have something other than murder to think about. What chance has the ordinary man against a skilled gambler, or a trained gun fighter?"

The girl nodded.

"I've thought of those things. But I—"

"Well, but—"

"But I don't believe that the Kid ever took an advantage."

Elinore Milman made an impatient movement, but she controlled her voice as well as she could.

"You seriously don't, my dear?"

"I don't," said the girl. "It may be partly because he trusts himself so perfectly. But I think that if he gambles, it's against professional gamblers, like himself. And if he fights, it's with professional fighters, like himself."

A line of pain appeared between the eyes of the mother.

"I've had the same idea myself," said she, "though I suppose I want to make his case as black as possible."

"Oh, Mother," said the girl, "I hope I can be as honest as you are!"

"Then honestly face what a life with him would mean—no home, no children. You wouldn't dare to trust children to the care of such a wild man. You know that?"

The girl was silent. Then she nodded.

"I suppose he told you how much you mean to him?"

"Not one word!"

"Ah, but a look, a gesture can fill up a big page, of course!"

"Not a look, not a gesture. Only that some things leaked through—or I thought they did."

"He's cleverer, even, than I suspected!"

"Perhaps. I don't think so. I think that he's pulled two ways. He hates father. He likes me. And he's determined to break up Dixon's crowd."

"Do you really think so?"

"Yes. Animals mean something to him more than they do to us. I saw his face when he heard the lowing of the cattle at Hurry Creek."

"What are you going to do, Georgia?"

"Wait," said Georgia, "and pray that I never see him again."

Mrs. Milman, staring at the girl like one who hopes against hope, said simply: "I think that you're right, Georgia."

Then she added. "And what about your father?"

"I've thought of that."

"What are you going to do?"

"I'm going to go to him and tell him—"

"Think it over. You'll have to have the right words."

"I'm simply going to tell him that it doesn't matter, whatever he's done in the past. Not to me. Not to you and me, Mother! Am I right?"

Elinore Milman caught a quick breath.

"We can't let it matter. There has to be such a thing as a blind faith and a blind loyalty, doesn't there?"

"Yes," said the girl. "That's just what I feel."

The mother stood up and put her arms around Georgia.

"We're all standing on the brink of ruin," she said. "Yesterday we were rich and happy and there wasn't a cloud in the sky. Today, there's every chance that we'll go downhill and never rise again. Your father's life is in horrible danger from that boy. There's a shame in his past that is never going to take its shadow off our lives, no matter how the affair comes out. All of our wealth seems in danger of being snatched away. And I have you to tremble about and pray for, Georgia. There's only the way to face these things, and that's together, shoulder to shoulder."

"Yes," said Georgia.

She began to tremble violently and suddenly her mother whispered: "I think that you're having the hardest time of all. But now go and tell your father what you've told me, will you?"

"I'll go at once," said Georgia.

She turned to the door and waited there for a moment, breathing deeply to drive away a faintness which was growing upon her. Then, composing herself with a great effort, she went out of the house toward the barn.

She met little, one-legged Harry Sams, with a manure fork in his hand coming from behind the barn. The stem of his corncob pipe had had a new mouthpiece whittled and rewhittled in it. It was now hardly two inches long, and the fumes from the bowl of the pipe kept him constantly blinking. But he was faithful to old pipes, as to old friends.

"Harry," she said, "have you seen Father?"

"Aye," said Harry, "he's gone and got him that white-faced fool of a chestnut gelding, and he's gone off toward Hurry Creek as though there was guns behind him, instead of in front."

The words struck her like bullets. All the sunset blurred and darkened before her face, for she knew that her father had gone off in hope of finding his death.

33

Danger Ahead

THE KID, when he got to the bottom of the long lariat, still found that his feet dangled well above either water or ground. He looked down, but all that he could see was the white dashing of the water—not white, really, but a dusky gray in that half light. He could not tell whether the water ran directly beneath him or if there were a small ledge of rock at the side of the canyon bed.

Hanging by one strong hand, with the other, he took out a match and scratched it. It was only a single spluttering of dim light before a dash of spray put it out, but that glimpse was enough to reveal to the Kid a raging inferno of waters. And, beneath him, a narrow, slippery ledge of rock, hardly a single foot wide.

To the ledge he dropped.

By daylight it would have been a simple matter, perhaps, to get along the place. And he cursed himself because he had not thought of exploring here while the sun was still shining.

He tried matches again and again. But the wind of the water or the flying spray itself instantly snatched away the flame. He had to explore by touch alone. Light there was almost none, Though when he looked up, he could see stars sprinkled across the narrow road which the canyon walls fenced through the high heavens; and there was among them one broad-faced planet—its name he did not know.

The thunder of the creek now pounded steadily, like the continual roar of guns; the solid rocks trembled slightly beneath his hands; and the absence of light gave him only vague and illusive hints of what was around him.

Therefore he closed his eyes altogether for the purpose of shutting out the few, faint rays which merely helped to confuse him, and he began to fumble along the wall of the ravine.

It swung to the left for a little distance. He tried to remember just how the creek had been seen to curve from above, but even this point he carelessly had overlooked. However, that did not matter now. He was committed to that bare, slippery wall of rock, and if he fell from it, he was done forever.

That was not the only danger.

He had hardly made three steps' progress when something crashed behind him, and then a great black form shot by him, low down on the face of the water.

It missed his feet in inches, grinding on the ledge of rock on which he stood. Hurtling onward, it struck on the corner of the next big rock with a staggering shock, then was whirled around the edge.

Vaguely he had seen this, after opening his eyes when the blow came behind him. He knew that it was a tree trunk, torn down from the banks higher up the stream, and now sent like a javelin, flying down toward the lower waters. A second of these might very well strike him and dash him to a pulp, or else flick him off from the wall like a caterpillar from a tree, to be ground up by the teeth of the rocks.

Yet he went on. In fact, there was no return, but the grim steadiness of his purpose never left him.

With closed eyes, and still fumbling, he worked out to a place where the rock ledge shelved away to nothing beneath the grip of his feet. He reached down, pulled off his boots, and prepared to see what naked hands and feet could do with the treacherous surface of that canyon face in the dark, with the spray whipping continually around him.

He found a handhold. His feet, reaching at the rock below, helped him a good deal. He was working his way out and out to the left, where the creek turned its corner, and now he turned the point of it.

It was grisly, hard work, for his weight was hanging almost entirely from his hands. Only now and then did he get any purchase for his feet. And the handholds were hard to find also. He had to hold by one hand and with the other fumble before him, vaguely, up and down, until he found some small projection, or some crevice into which even the tips of his fingers could be fitted.

Sometimes he was swaying up. Once he descended until his feet thrust into the water.

The current jerked at him like a hand. He almost lost his hold. For one breathless moment he thought that he was gone.

But his hands were strong, and his hold remained true.

In this manner he found that he had turned the corner. But now his position was not much better. There was still no foothold beneath him, and his arms were now aching to the pits of the shoulders. They were so extremely tired that they shook with a violence which of itself threatened to shake him loose from the wet rock.

And there was no light!

He opened his eyes.

Yes, far away to the left there was a red star shining toward him. It glared at him like an eye, threateningly. But suddenly, his eyes opening more clearly, he saw that it was the flame of the Dixon camp fire.

That, which should have depressed him still more, gave him a sudden hope, and with the hope came strength.

He could not have endured the strain of going back to the last ridge which he had left. The very idea of turning back, however, had not come to him. And he worked on, gritting his teeth until his jaws ached as well as his arms.

Then, fumbling forward with his left foot, he touched a firm support.

He rested his whole weight upon the rock beneath. It was strong and firm.

At this the relief was so great that the blood bounded violently into his head, and he was dizzy. But he clung, fighting his way through the first moments of the reaction after the strain was over.

Still his body was shaking a little, and his arms were numb, but he began to breathe more easily, and his mind was more at ease also.

Those who have passed through the desperate gates of an enterprise feel that the early danger must assure them of better luck further on. At least, so the Kid felt, as he stood there in the dark of the ravine, with the chilly drops of snow water flicking at him.

The canyon walls opened here perceptibly, moreover, and there was sufficient starlight to enable him to see dimly what was before him.

It was no easy road. Here the ledge ran a little distance. There it disappeared entirely. But the walls were not so perpendicular and the weight of his body would in no place fall so sheerly upon his tired hands and upon his shoulders.

He swung his arms. He kneaded them with his shaking hands until the flow of blood subdued their aching. And when at last he felt sufficient master of himself, he resumed his progress toward the mouth of the canyon.

He had had practice now; besides, he had some sight to help him, so that the work went on more easily, and he made good use of all his advantages until he came to where the very lips of the ravine spread out wider and wider, and the opening flood of the river flattened and lost its noise over a more ample bed. Its speed was quenched, in the same manner and moment, for a final reef of rocks in the neck of the canyon had chopped up the waters and taken their headway from them.

Now, all in a moment, the water slackened and spread out shallowly across a bed four times as spacious as that into which it had been crowded by the narrow walls of the ravine. Here, flat-faced, gently, it ran into the open valley, heading toward the other dark throat into which it was soon to fall and again begin to rage and roar like a lion.

And the Kid, soaked to the skin, tired, and aching from his labors, looked out on that flow of water as a strong and busy man looks out upon one placid moment between strenuous days of action and of danger—one walk through the green country, one solemn moment of peace.

Yet there was no peace for him.

He had performed all of these labors merely to bring himself to the door which opened upon the real peril. And of all the arduous tasks which he had taken in hand in his days, none was comparable with the thing which lay before him.

No strength or craft of hand, he knew, could ever make him equal to the assembled strength which Dixon had gathered here.

If he were superior to each of them by the flickering, broken part of a second in speed of draw; if he were a finger's breadth closer to the bull's-eye when he fired, these advantages which meant life and victory in a single combat were nothing compared with the overwhelming odds which he would have to encounter.

No, there was now nothing left for him except subtlety and silent craft, like an adventuring Indian in a camp of the enemy.

The Kid, taking stock of these truths, gravely advanced still farther, until he was on the exact verge of the canyon mouth, where a little shore of gravel went down to the waters.

From this point, he could see all that the hollow contained. He could see the mist rising faintly against the stars above the uneasy cattle. He could hear the desperate moaning voices of the thirst-starved creatures. That sound made the roar of the river at once a small thing.

He looked down on the red beacon of the camp fire where his enemies were. He looked away to either side, where the soft curves of the hills undulated against the sky line; surely those hills never had seen a stranger thing than he would attempt this night!

Then, narrowing his eyes, he crouched low, his head close to the water, and scanned the shore on each side.

He was inside the lines, He could see, here and there, the flicker of the barbed wire which made the outer defense. He could see also the occasional form of a guard marching as a sentinel up and down the fences.

Now, as he watched, he saw the vague outline of a man come from the camp fire and walk down to the water's edge. There the fellow stood. It was Dixon, perhaps rejoicing in the mischief which he was working, and grinning as he listened to the noise of the tormented cattle.

His own mind flashed back to another picture—the sunwhitened desert, and the two poor cows struggling and swaying under their unaccustomed yokes.

Then he stepped with his naked feet into the cold waters of the stream.

HIS REVOLVER he kept above the surface of the stream, which was now not more than three or four feet deep. But though it was shallow, and slid along a fairly flat surface, there was amazing force in it still, the last effect of the long impetus which it had received in shooting down the flume of the ravine.

He had to lean upstream at a sharp angle, with the current heaping shoulder and even neck high as it bubbled and rushed and gurgled loudly.

His nerves were as good as those of any man, but before he was halfway across the stream, walking in the dim, red path of the light from the camp fire, he made certain that the men on the shore must have seen him. If they had not seen, they must have heard. Surely they were watching there, laughing in the dark of the covert, and grinning at the poor fool who was walking into their hands.

Then he remembered that there were other noises abroad in the valley besides the intimate voice of the river just under his ear. There was the dull and distant roaring of the penned-up waters in the canyon above, and a deeper, fainter call from the lower ravine; above all, the solemn music of the lowing cattle flooded across the hollow.

No, he could not be heard, but surely he was seen!

The long, red arm of the firelight stretched toward him and caught him by the throat.

He thought of lying flat on the surface of the stream. It would shoot him like a log safe past the fire, past all the

168

watchers, and at the mouth of the lower canyon, he would struggle on shore and try to escape.

That thought of flight tempted him mightily. He fairly trembled on the verge of giving way to it.

But he went on.

The strength of the resolve which drove him had a pull like that of gravity and carried him step by step against his reason. And then the ground was shoaling beneath him. The suction grew less in the shallows, and finally he crawled out on his hands and knees.

There on the shore he lay flat.

He was shuddering with cold. He was helpless with it. Any yokel, any cowardly boy might have mastered him then, he felt. The snow water had sent its numbing chill through him to the bone. His breathing failed. The tremors shook him more than earthquakes shake cities.

But he had to lie quietly while he took stock of the situation before him.

He was not nearly as close to the camp fire as he had thought while striding across the creek. He lay, in fact, some distance to the north of it, and between him and the flames stood a row of three wagons. Their wheels looked enormous and misshapen. They seemed to be broken and flattened on the lower surface that met the ground. Their shadows went wavering across the ground. Sometimes it was as though the wheels were turning.

Around the fire three or four men were sitting.

Others, wrapped in their blankets, apparently were asleep, or trying to sleep. And it seemed to the Kid that this was the ultimate prooof of their brutality. They could sleep while that sound of agony from the thirsty cattle moaned and howled across the valley! That water which had tugged at him which had swept by him in countless barrelfuls, in unnumerable tones, which had frozen and shaken him, how sweet it would have been in the dusty, dry gullets of those thousands and thousands of dying beasts. All the sweetness of life would have been in it.

A blast of heat came to him out of memory as he thought again of the unforgotten picture of his boyhood—the creaking wagon, and the two old cows swaying and staggering before it, halting in their steps, but leaning again on the yoke and slowly drifting the miles behind them. He himself had had the thirst of fever in his body on that day. He had it again now. A flash of burning heat, and of hatred for these men or devils who were with Dixon.

When he looked more closely toward the fire, he saw that on the opposite side, with the full red flush of the flame in his face, sat Dixon himself, looking rather old and stoop-shouldered, as almost any man will, who is sitting cross-legged on the ground.

Suppose that Dixon guessed, even faintly dreamed, that his enemy had broken through the invincible outer lines and was lying there in easy gunshot? Oh, so easy to draw a bead even from this distance, and by pressing the trigger, beckon the brain and heart of the enterprise out of existence!

He could not do it.

His philosophy, blunt and uncertain on many points of life, was in one respect absolute and true. He could not strike from behind or from the dark. There was no Indian in his nature to excuse such ways of fighting.

But he felt, at the sight of Dixon, a calm heat of anger rise that made him forget the river water and its cold hands.

He got up to his knees and went slowly on, still pausing to turn his head from time to time, until he reached a thick, solid wedge of shadow that extended behind one of the wagons.

When he came to this, he rose, and as he rose, he saw suddenly that a man was standing before him!

The breath was pressed from him by that sight. His mind spun about. It was as though a spirit had risen through and out of the solid ground.

How long had the man been there, lost in the shadow, calmly watching the progress of the spy, the secret enemy? Who was he that he dared to take that advance so calmly?

These questions rushed through the mind of the Kid in a broken portion of a second.

"Where'd you get the redeye that knocked you out, buddy?" said the man. "You know where you been? You been crawlin' around, this side of the water, like a sick snake! Did Bolony Joe open up that keg of his for you, or d'you tap it for yourself? Old Champ will sure raise a riot if he finds out. You better not let him see you!"

"You're a fool," snarled the Kid in apparent anger. "I got a slip and fall down there on the edge of the water, and I got soaked, and turned my ankle. The ligaments are about pulled out of place. Get out of the way, will you, and leave me be with your fool ideas!"

"Who are you?" demanded the other, taking a step closer. "Who are you to be orderin' me around? I'll tell you a thing or two, old son, if you was ten Champ Dixons rolled into one!"

He came closer. The Kid was silent, but putting down his right foot on the ground, he made a slow, hobbling step, and groaned aloud.

The other was not moved. He had come much closer.

"Yeah. You come out of the river, all right," said he, "but I dunno that I recognize you. What's your moniker, son? I don't seem to place your head and shoulders, sort of, among the boys. What's your name?"

"I'm the Kid," said he.

This name made the man jump back a good yard in surprise and in fear.

Then he began to laugh. He laughed with deep enjoyment.

"Yeah, you're the Kid, are you?"

"I'm the Kid," said he truthfully.

"I didn't know you, Larry," said the other. "I wouldn't never of guessed you, except you begun kidding, like that. It's a funny thing the way night changes things. Your voice is changed too."

"How could it help?" said the Kid, "and me doused in that ice water and pneumonia likely, coming on!"

"Here," said the other. "I'll give you a hand back to your blankets. Where'd you bed down? Over by the fire, or in one of the wagons?"

"Leave me be," said the Kid. "I don't want any help. Keep out of my way, that's all. There's too darn many boys and fools along on this trip to suit me. They got the place all cluttered up!"

"Aw—go to the dickens," said the other suddenly. "You've got your stomach soured and your head turned because some of the boys has been fool enough to laugh at some of your bum jokes. I'm glad you've turned your ankle. I wish you'd broke it, and your head along with it!"

"I'm going to wring your neck," said the Kid, "when I get fixed of this."

"Yeah?" demanded the other. "You're gonna wring my neck, are you? Why, you sucker, I could eat you in a salad and not know that you was there. You make me sick!"

He turned on his heel with his final declaration and strode away.

He had used the strongest expression that the law allows.

Swearing in its most violent forms is as common as dust on the Western range, but there is nothing in the entire, powerful range of the vocabulary which has the meaning of the heartfelt statement: "You make me sick!" It takes the heart out of the man addressed. It leaves him crumpled. It does not even lead to a fight, usually. And the victim feels that he has been criticized, not insulted.

"You make me sick!" said the puncher of the Dixon crowd, and then walked away.

But the Kid, behind him, felt none of the usual qualms following this speech. Instead, he could not help smiling. And that little touch of triumph warmed his blood as thoroughly as an hour beside a steaming fire.

He went on in the same hobbling gait until the other had disappeared among the shadows.

Then he stepped out freely and silently, and in another moment, found himself between the last wagon and a heap of stuff which had been in part unloaded from it.

Between the two objects he was comparatively safe.

And now that he was here, what was he to do?

He had not, in fact, the slightest idea. He had come down here with a vague purpose of making trouble for the Dixonites; and he had even a sort of dream-like consciousness of what that trouble might be.

In the first place, he might, however, work among the heaped pieces of freight and come close enough to the fire to overhear some of the talk. If he could learn the intimate plans of the enemy, that might give him a clue on which to build his plans. So he went forward among the coils of barbed wire, glimmering like silver where the highlights touched them. And there were boxes of provisions, a pile of extra saddles and other equipment. Through these he wriggled, until he had the groups around the fire under his eyes.

EIGHT MEN were in view. Of these, five were obscure heaps in their blankets, sleeping the sleep of the tired. Only one face could be seen. The man lay on his back, his mouth open. Now and then he snored and snorted in his sleep.

It was Peg Garret, well-known to the Kid, who recognized that face and remembered the villainy of the owner of it. It was as though he were suddenly put in touch with the evil of the entire crowd. Hand-picked for cruelty and hard hearts, beyond a doubt.

Two others sat with a blanket between them, rolling dice, muttering, throwing out and raking in money as they won and lost. For such a quiet game the stakes were high, which told the Kid that these rascals had had a fat advance payment for this work of theirs. To their right was Champ Dixon, with his profile toward the Kid. As for the two gamblers, they were Dolly Smith of gun-fighting fame, a little, blond, smooth-faced boy of nineteen with a reputation like dynamite; the other was the somber face of Canuck Joe, who had a passion for fighting when the lights were out. Bare hands were his favored weapons then, or a knife to feel for the throat of another in the dark.

Just then, into the light of the fire stepped a beetle-browed youth who took out a red-and-yellow handkerchief and with it wiped his eyes. For the thin dust cast up by the milling cattle was constantly blowing in the air. Usually, it was hardly perceptible, but now and again a denser cloud would roll in, red-stained above the fire. One of those clouds was passing now, and the newcomer snorted and grunted.

"Damn dirty work," said he.

"What's doin', Jip?" asked Dixon.

"Aw, nothin' much," said Jip, whose voice the Kid recognized as that of his recent companion in the shadow. "The cows is still workin' up and down the fences, but they ain't gonna bust through. The boys is keepin' them back, and the cows is gettin' used to holdin' off. They ain't got no nerve, these here beeves. They got no more nerve than old man Milman and his crew. They're tender, that's what they are."

"Yeah," said Dixon. "They're tender. I seen five thousand head down on Chris Porter's ranch in Arizona that would of beat in a stone wall with their heads if they wanted that bad to get at water. They ain't got no brains, these cows. They're stall-fed, what you might say."

"Yeah, they're stall-fed," said the other. "Darn the dust. I'm gonna taste it for a month."

"No, you won't, son. One shot of redeye will take the taste out of your mouth."

"Tell Bolony Joe to open up and pass around a little of the hot stuff, will you, Champ?"

"Will I? I will not," said Dixon. "I ain't gonna have no bunch of drunks on my hands."

Jim made a cigarette.

"Larry has gone and got himself a sprained ankle," said Jip.

"Hold on!" exclaimed Dixon. "How'd the fool do that?"

"Aw, he just goes down and gives himself a tumble by the creek, that's all."

"Did he sprain it bad?" growled Dixon.

"He can't walk, hardly. That's how badly."

"If he can walk at all, he can ride a lot."

"Aw, maybe."

"Where is he?"

"I dunno. I don't care. He makes me sick," observed Jip.

"What's the matter with you and Larry? Larry's all right," broke in little Dolly Smith.

"Is he? You have him then. I don't want him," said Jip. "He's too blame sour. Somebody's gone and told Larry that he's funny."

"He is funny," said Dolly. "I always get a good big laugh out of Larry. The way he has of talking makes me laugh."

"It don't make me none," replied Jip. "He makes me sick. That's all."

"What for does he make you sick?"

"He's so blame sour. I wanted to help him to his blankets. He cursed me. That's what he done. He's sour."

"Give him some castor oil, Champ," advised Dolly. "He's very sick. Larry makes him sick."

"Yeah?" said Jip, raising his voice. "You don't make me none too darn well, yourself, as far as that goes."

"Is that so?" said Dolly, jerking up his head like a bird on a branch that sees trouble ahead. "Maybe I'm gonna make you feel a lot unweller, before I get through."

"You little sawed-off, pink-faced, pig-eyed runt," said Jip, thoroughly aroused. "You come out here and I'll tell you something that your ma and pa would like to hear!"

"You set where you are," broke in Champ Dixon. "Jip, you back up."

"I ain't gonna take none of his backwash," declared Jip.

"Who's started all the fuss?" asked Champ. "You have. You come in here and break up the party. How old are you, kid?"

"I said that Larry was a bust," said Jip. "I told him to his own face. 'You make me sick,' I says to him. I told him off, is what I done."

"If you said that, Larry would punch you in the eye," observed little Dolly Smith. "You wouldn't never dare to say that to Larry. He's got a wallop like a mule. I seen him once in a Phoenix barroom when a couple of elbows comes in to straighten out a fuss. They started something when they got to Larry. And he done all the finishing. You keep your hands off of Larry, kid, or you're gonna lose about ten years' growth one of these days."

"Thanks," said Jip. "I tell you, Larry makes me sick. His idea of kidding, it makes me sick too. 'Who are you?' says I, as he comes crawlin' along. 'I'm the Kid!' says he."

Both Dolly and Canuck Joe put back their heads and laughed at this last remark.

"He said he was the Kid," Dolly Smith said, chuckling. "That's pretty good, Canuck, ain't it?"

"That's kind of funny," said Canuck Joe, and laughed more loudly than before.

"Shut up your faces," said one of the sleepers, wakening.

"Yeah, pipe down," advised Champ Dixon. "The boys has gotta get some sleep, don't they?"

"I'll tell you the trouble with you Dolly—" began Jip.

Champ Dixon raised one finger.

"Jip, you hear me? You back up."

Jip glowered at his leader.

But that raised forefinger and that quiet voice had a meaning that was very definite. He turned on his heel and retreated into the night, declaring over his shoulder, that he was "sick of the whole business anyway."

Dolly Smith glared after him.

"Jip is only a fool kid," said Dixon. "He's all right."

"Is he?" said Dolly coldly. "Where's his call to come around here with his back fur all standin', I'd like to know? You hear that, Champ," he went on, "when Jip asked Larry who he was: 'I'm the Kid,' says he. That's pretty good, ain't it?"

"Yeah, that's rich," Champ Dixon said, laughing. "The Kid is gonna come a bust one of these days," he added darkly.

"Sure he's gonna come a bust," remarked Dolly Smith. "But I don't wanta try the bustin'. Not till I've got my full growth. He's too hot for the kind of gloves that I wear."

Canuck Joe thoughtfully spread out his own great hands and examined them in the firelight as though they had a special and new meaning to him at that moment.

"I dunno," said he, doubtfully.

"You never seen him go," said Dolly Smith. "I seen him go, though. Have you ever seen that sweetheart work, Champ?"

"Yeah, I seen him work," said Champ.

"He loves it, don't he?"

"Yeah, he loves it, all right," said Champ.

"He's a ring-tail little snake-eatin' weasel, is what he is," said Dolly Smith fondly. "I seen him work one evening in Carson City. The dust he raised, you couldn't see your way for a week, in that town. I wonder how Chip Graham is? I wonder what they'll do with Chip?" he continued, altering his voice.

"Shay's gonna take care of that," said Champ Dixon curtly. "There won't nothing happen to Chip. Shay ain't that much a fool to let a good boy like Chip down. He'll stand by him."

"He better, I'll tell a man. If anything happens to Chip, there's gonna be a bust, I tell you. I'll be right there at the busting, too. Too bad you couldn't get the Kid in on this here deal."

"Well I tried to."

"What did he say?"

"I'll tell you something, Dolly. The Kid's gone and got a swelled head. That's what he's gone and got."

"Yeah?"

"You never seen no sign?"

"No, I never seen none."

"Education," said Champ Dixon with a sigh. "That was the spoilin' of him. He figgers that he's different from the rest of us. Besides, the newspapers is always givin' him space."

"He ain't no circus performer, though," said Dolly loyally.

"He won't throw in with nobody. He's got a swelled head," insisted Champ Dixon.

"Maybe he's got a swelled head," assented Dolly. "I wonder what he's doin' now?"

And, turning his head, he looked straight back at the point where the Kid lay, listening!

"He's tryin' to think out some way," said Champ Dixon. "But he ain't got a chance. There ain't no way."

"No, I guess there ain't no way," replied Dolly. "Hard nuts is his meat, though."

"Yeah, hard nuts is his meat. But you tell me how he's gonna get inside of that wire, will you?"

"Yeah, how's he gonna do that?" admitted Dolly. "I seen him work, though. The dust he raises, you wouldn't hardly believe. I'm gonna turn in. When do I go on watch?"

"Two hours more."

"What's gonna be the end of this job?"

"The Kid's gonna have a bust," said Champ Dixon, clicking his teeth. "That's gonna be the end. And Milman is gonna eat out of our hands."

"Well," said Dolly, "I'd as soon that it was finished. It's dirty business. Them cows—"

And he rose and went toward a wagon and climbed into it over the doubletrees.

36
Chuck

THERE WAS NOTHING particularly gained by listening to this conversation, the Kid decided. He had learned that there was a certain amount of fundamental decency in Dolly Smith. He had learned that Champ Dixon kept his crew of barbarians controlled in the hollow of his hand. He had learned, finally, that he himself was looked upon as the single danger to the camp, and that danger they considered small.

"The Kid's gonna have a bust," Champ had declared with a prophetic solemnity and the words rang and re-echoed through the mind of the boy as he drew back again from the fire, working his way slowly among the boxes.

The cook came out from his kitchen tent carrying a bucket of steaming coffee, and the Kid paused in his retreat to watch the other put down the bucket where the heat of the fire would warm it. Then Bolony Joe—gaunt as a crow, and evil of face—took some wood from a great heap which towered a dozen feet into the air and freshened the fire.

"You gents ain't got the sense to keep up your own fire," said Bolony. "Well, you can have cold coffee, then. I'm gonna turn in. This is the worst job that I ever cooked for. They's dust in everything. I hope you bust your teeth on the grit in that corn bread. I'd rather cook in the inside of a sand storm. I'm gonna turn in."

"Take it easy, Bolony, will you?" said Champ Dixon soothingly. "That was a fine mulligan that you cooked for supper."

"There wasn't enough tomatoes in it," said Bolony. "You

178

can't make no good mulligan without no tomatoes. I told you that we oughta have a lot more tomatoes. Didn't I tell you?"

"Yeah. You told me. I ordered 'em. It was the fool of a kid at the grocery store."

"Well, you can't do no cookin' with nothin' to cook with," said Bolony. "That's all I gotta say."

"You can," said Champ Dixon. "Because you got brains, Bolony. I seen a lot of them fancy French chefs that had everything in the world and they couldn't cook one side of you, Bolony. Because you got brains. You gotta have brains to be a cook."

Bolony cleared his throat and frowned to keep from betraying pleasure with a smile.

"That baked ham was pretty tough at noon," he said.

"That was the best ham I ever put a tooth into," said Champ Dixon. "I never seen no better cooked ham. All the boys said so. Look what they done to that ham, I mean!"

"Well," said Bolony, "they dunno nothin' about eatin'. There ain't any call for a cook on this outfit. An Injun would do for them. They dunno enough to know what they're puttin' in their faces. I got some dried apples, Champ. How about some apple pie for breakfast?"

"Bolony, I leave it to you. I never heard of a thing like apple pie out in camp. You sure got the ideas, Bolony."

"Yeah," said Bolony. "Soft-soap the cook. That's the way it goes. A lotta soft soap to make the dog feel good. I'm gonna turn in. S'long, Champ."

"So long, Bolony."

The cook turned away, and Champ Dixon, for a moment, smiled faintly to himself. The Kid, in the farther darkness, was smiling also.

But then he turned seriously to whatever work he could find to do. The very appearance of Bolony Joe had put an idea in his mind. Cows die slowly on a Western range, with their water supply cut off. But hungry men go on strike far sooner. The appearance of Bolony Joe and the sight of the kitchen tent did the rest for the Kid. He started worming his way toward it at once.

When he passed the big woodpile, where the accumulated brush had been heaped, he was able to stand up and go more freely, for the shadow which it cast concealed him well enough.

So he came to the kitchen tent.

Outside of it was the well-built fireplace over which Bolony Joe gloomily performed his duties. The Kid gave a rather friendly glance at the dimly glimmering embers of that fire. Then he passed into the tent.

He was amazed by what he found within it.

Certainly Billy Shay and Dixon, in equipping this expedition, had not spared expense. They knew that high wages are the first requisite to keep men happy; and right after money comes food. There were rows of tins and heaps of boxed goods. There was a thin odor of hams and bacons, the rankness of onions; the peculiar, earthy smell of potatoes. A pang of hunger struck the Kid. It was so keen that he shook his head and smiled at himself.

From the last of the cook's fire, he gained enough light to see a good deal of the interior.

Yes, every provision had been made. There was even an oil stove, in case there should be some interruption of supply of wood for the fire. To feed the oil stove, there were two ponderous tins of kerosene. And the clutches of the Kid were instantly upon them.

He had unscrewed the top of the first and begun to pour its contents over the boxes, when a sharp rattling of rifle shots to the east of Hurry Creek halted him.

He went to the door of the tent to watch and listen.

It might be that Milman had gone around by the distant road to the far eastern side of the creek, and from that quarter, was about to deliver a suprise attack with a rush.

If that were the case. Heaven help him and his men. They never could deal with these practiced ruffians!

The whole camp was instantly in an uproar, as the shots resounded. But the uproar did not last long. There were only a few shouts to make sure that every man had turned out for the alarm. And then came the bustle of quick, sure preparation. These men knew their posts and went instantly toward them.

Bad fortune was reasonably sure to come to all who tried to rush that fortified camp with those repeating rifles in sure hands! The Kid, gritting his teeth and grinning in impatient anger, waited there at the door of the kitchen tent, and gripped the handles of his Colt.

If the attack really were pressed home, he would have to strike in order to help Milman's forces. He would have to strike, and then die like a rat in a trap.

A fine ending, indeed!

However, the rattling of the rifle shots suddenly ended, and then a voice was calling from the eastern fence of barbed wire.

Some one called for a lantern. There were shouts back and forth, but the Kid thought that these calls were signs of rejoicing, rather than of mere battle excitement.

The lantern was brought, on the run, setting the camp aswing with gigantic, grotesque shadows. Then back came the light, and a group of men with it. In the center of that group, the Kid saw a limping form—a tall, spare man.

It was Billy Shay!

Even from a distance the first hint of the long, white face was enough to make him guess the identity of the newcomer. He was being surrounded by rejoicing cohorts.

"I couldn't get through with nothing, boys," said he. "All I could bring you was myself, and I had a hard job of that. They shot my hoss from underneath me!"

"We got you, Billy, and that's good enough for us," said Boone Tucker. "We'd rather have your long head around here than ten extra men, if it comes to a show-down of any kind."

"I wanted to be in here with you boys," said Billy Shay genially. "I didn't want somebody else to be running into the danger for me. I wanted to be in the same pot and stew with the rest of you."

"Yeah," said Tucker, "You're all right, Billy. None of the boys will ever forget this!"

"You got the right nerve, Billy."

There was a chorus of appreciation.

In fact, the Kid was astonished by the risks which the gambler must have taken in order to get there. It was not like Billy Shay to run unnecessary risks, though he was known as a savage fighter in a pinch.

"How did you get through, Shay?"

"Why, I had a hard job. They're watching the gap on both sides of the creek as though it were a bank. Then there were the cows between the Milman riders and the fence. Those cows were kind of shifting around, though. Pretty soon there was a gap opened up through them and I made a dive for it straight for the fence. A couple of the Milman punchers seen me and opened up. They can shoot, too, that crew. Even by night. Starlight is good enough for those gents."

"They nick you, Billy?"

"No, not me, I guess. But they nicked the hoss. I almost got to the fence when I felt him sag one step, and the next step he went down. The sagging, it gave me a hint of what was likely to come, and I was riding loose and light, ready for a tumble. I guess I went a hundred feet, when he flopped. But I come up, all right. I was just a little dizzy from the whang as I first hit the ground."

"You've got your coat about tore off."

"Well, I'm here, and that's the main thing."

"Yeah, that's the main thing. How's everything in Dry Creek?"

"They're still talkin' about the Kid and what a fool he made of me," said Shay, with astonishing frankness. "They dunno that the game ain't ended."

"Nope. It ain't ended yet. That's true, Billy!"

"When I heard that the Kid was out here with Milman, I decided that I'd better come out myself and get into the business. See the Kid?"

"Yeah. He come down with Bud Trainor. We tried to catch the two of them, when they wouldn't join. But they got away, and they took off Chip Graham and the Silver King."

"The heck they did!"

"The heck they didn't. The Kid flipped Chip with a long distance shot. I seen the shooting. You wouldn't've believed!"

"The Kid," said Shay, "is gonna come to the end of his rope and bust his neck, pretty quick. Is this here the cook tent?"

"Yeah. You want some chow?"

"Is Bolony around?"

"He's turned in, and the shootin' didn't turn him out."

"Yeah, he's ornery. But I'll get along without chuck. I'll just take a look inside of the tent, though, and see how things look."

37
One Match

THE KID, when he heard this, looked desperately around the little tent, but he could think of nothing that would enable him to hide himself. He could only lie down on his face beside the row of boxes to the left of the entrance to the tent.

There he waited, gun in hand. If Shay looked down at him, it would be Shay's last look in this world, to be sure, but it would also be almost the last moment in the life of the Kid.

Then, though there was no sound, he felt, like a mental shadow, that some one had leaned into the tent.

"Why, there looks to be a lot of stuff in here," said Billy Shay. "Hand me a light, somebody."

"Where's that lantern?" said another. "Hey, Sam, bring the lantern back here, will you?"

"Does he feed you well?" asked Shay.

"Sure. There ain't a better camp cook than Bolony Joe. Outside of his disposition, I mean, but cooks can't help bein' that way."

The light of the lantern flickered closer to the entrance of the tent.

"Well," said Shay, "if you boys are being treated right in the grub line, I won't bother to look over Joe's stores. He most generally has the right kind of a layout."

The figure withdrew from the tent entrance, and the crowd moved off toward the camp fire again.

And the Kid waited for the thundering of his heart to quiet again.

183

At last, he resumed his work, methodically, where he had left off. The stores inside that tent were thoroughly drenched with kerosene, and still only one can was used.

The next can, he opened, and carrying it around the side of the tent, he laid it on its side. At once the slim, silver tide flowed out, with a soft gurgling, in the direction of the big woodpile. On the other side of this, again, the fire had been built high, and the flames were wagging their heads wildly above the pile, above the wagon tops, so that an uncertain light began to flicker all over the near vicinity.

The Kid, when he saw that the oil was actually flowing on under the pile of wood, went back to the cooking tent and cast a final glance around him.

Between him and the eastern fence the horses were grazing, hobbled. They were in a close group, and the Kid, looking them over, could guess their quality by the length of their legs, if in no other way. They had not the roached backs and the stubby underpinnings of the usual mustang. No, such men as these whom Shay and Dixon had gathered were more likely to be mounted upon hot-blooded horses of price.

And a new thought came to him, wilder and more impracticable than the one which already had entered his mind. But suddenly he thought of all these men reduced to their own feet for locomotion. They would be like fish out of water—a hungry crew without means of attack or of retreat!

Like all men who rode through that country and sometimes wished to take short cuts across the open, he carried wire cutters with him. He went with them now straight to the nearest section of the fence. The guards who walked up and down, on that side, were not in motion just now. They were bunched, instead, at the place closest to the camp fire, so that they could overlook the celebration which, in a mild way, followed the arrival of Billy Shay.

So the Kid cut the wires. It was a thing that had to be done with care. For the wires were stretched tight, and were sure to spring back with a twang as loud as a bowstring if they were severed carelessly. Therefore the Kid first balled a handkerchief inside his hand and with this as a defense, gripped the top wire and gave it a strong pull. Then he used the pliers, cautiously, and made the snipping sound as faint as possible. The loosened wire, jumping hard against the pull of his arm, he held securely, and then coiled it back at the foot of the left-hand post. The second and third he severed in the same manner.

And here was the gap in the inside line of the Dixon fortifications!

Before it the cows wandered, their eyes lighted by the tossing and falling flames from the fire. They went slowly, hopelessly. Not far away he saw a group of several lying down, their heads dropped low. They might be dead, for all he knew. Surging against this obstacle, stumbling and sometimes falling upon the prostrate forms, the main currents of the thirst-tormented beasts were moving.

He noted this and then, with a glance to the left, saw that two of the guards had resumed their beat and were coming rapidly toward him. The Kid melted back among the grazing horses.

He ground his teeth at the thought that there would not be time for the last maneuver which he had conceived. If only those guards had kept near the fire for a few more minutes—

But they came on, talking to one another. They reached the gap which he had cut in the fence—and they walked straight past it!

They, as well as the cows, seemed to take it for granted that nothing could be wrong with this fence, so lately strung!

And the Kid fell instantly to work.

His knife was in his hand, and moving among the horses, he made that sound, half-humming and half-hissing, which seems to attract the attention and soothe the nerves of horses more than any other noise in the world. With one hand extended to touch them gently on hip, on neck, and on shoulder; the other hand bearing the knife went down, and one touch was enough, for the blade was as sharp as a razor edge. One by one, he carefully parted those bonds, until, at last, there was a free band of horses.

And now he was ready for the last work; the last touch. If he succeeded, it would be a feat which even the wild West would not soon forget, and it would wreck the proud hopes of high robbery which were now filling the brains of Dixon and Shay.

He went hastily back to the cooking tent. He did not stay there long, for he was in great haste. He must act before the horses had begun to scatter and attract attention. He merely scratched a match and tossed it, flaming into the interior of the cook tent.

An explosion followed, a muffled sound like the clapping together of two enormous pillows.

The tent lifted half a dozen feet, ripping away from its fastening ropes, as a puff of bluish flame accompanied the explosion.

This flame died down to a fierce weltering, which ran along the ground and instantly, reaching the spot where the oil had run under the big woodpile, converted that heap into a tower of shooting fire.

All of this happened in the first second. The Kid observed it on the run, for he had headed straight back toward the nearest flank of the horses.

They, astounded by the first explosion and the shooting fireworks, hesitated an instant in a blind terror before they fled. And still they were not under way when the Kid, like a panther, leaped upon the nearest back.

The firmness of the barrel under the grip of his knees, and the length of the animal's neck told him instantly that he had made a wise selection. He whirled his hands above his head and gave an Indian yell. To the eyes of the horses, it was as though a second explosion had occurred in their very midst and had dropped a man on the back of the tall gray gelding. And this, in turn, plunged forward, and reared against the body of the animal which blocked its flight.

And, to spur them forward, from the men at the camp fire, amazed by this sudden disturbance, there went up first a wild shrieking of fear and bewilderment, and then a howling of rage.

That uproar frightened the half-maddened horses still more. And those nearest to the fence at this moment found the gap which the Kid had cut. And through it they went like wildfire!

They found their own free way through the herd of cattle like hawks through a flock of crows.

The thing was done. Dixon and Shay and all their men, without a single horse to back, without food of any kind, without even oil or wood for a fire, now had the tables turned upon them and were held in the hollow of Milman's hand.

So the Kid saw it, and so it seemed to be. And still, as he waved his arms to steer the horses in front of him through the gap, he shrieked and yelled like an Indian on the warpath.

Rifles began to click and he heard the waspish sound of bullets kissing the air, but it seemed to him that the game was as

good as over when, as if out of the bowels of the earth, the form
of a cow heaved up before him.

The gray gelding, right gallantly, gathered and strove to clear
the obstacle.

Had the warning been one hundredth part of a second
sooner, he would have succeeded, but as it was, his forelegs
touched the back of the steer. The gelding spun in a frightfully
sudden somersault, and the face of the solid earth leaped up
and struck the Kid so that he was senseless.

38
The Verdict

WHEN HIS SENSES came back to him, he felt warmth in his face,
and then a dazzle in his eyes. There was a dull roaring, and
through the roaring a voice was saying "He's comin' round."

"Aye," said another, "a little thing like havin' a hoss fall on
him and two or three thousand cows walk over him, that
wouldn't bother the Kid, much. Just sort of rock him to sleep."

The Kid wakened utterly, and sat up at the same time.

He found that his hands were lashed together and his feet
similarly secured, and he was sitting in the light of a towering
mass of flames that seemed to split the dark of the heavens
asunder. Every star was put out by this radiance.

It was the total supply of fuel for the Dixon camp. The
incendiarism of the Kid had been even far more successful than
he had expected to make it, for two of the wagons were rolling
in sheets of fire and a third, badly damaged, had been partially
salvaged by rolling it down the slope and into the shoal waters
of Hurry Creek.

As for the wood, it could not be saved, for the oil, running
out quickly on all sides of the pile, made a no-man's land that
weltered with fire and on which men dared not step.

The Kid, wakening, saw these things, and one besides—this
was the face of Billy Shay, white as the belly of a fish, with the

little eyes glittering and fixed. They were not fixed upon the destruction around, but straight on the Kid himself.

It was a nightmare effect from which the Kid looked hastily away. He saw that the rest of the crowd stood around in attitudes of helpless surrender. There was only one figure in motion, and that was the lean form of Bolony Joe, striding up and down near the spot where the cook tent had stood, once so filled with camp necessitites and camp luxuries; now a charred and steaming mass of wreckage.

Certainly the blow had fallen with full weight, and the end had come suddenly to the hopes of Shay and Dixon and their crew.

Shay came suddenly to the Kid and stood before him.

"You've won, Kid, and I've lost," said he, "and I've won, and you've lost!"

The Kid said nothing. There was simply nothing to say.

Dixon came up also, smiling. But there was something tigerish behind that smile of his.

"How did you manage to do it, Kid?" he asked.

"Oh, I just came down the canyon," said the Kid. "That's how I got inside the lines. If that's what you wonder about."

"You came down the canyon?" exclaimed Canuck Joe. "Nobody could come down that there canyon. The water'd kill a whole tribe of tigers in no time, inside the mouth of the canyon, and there ain't any way along the walls of it."

"There is a way, though," said the Kid. "I found it. Mostly climbing with my hands."

Canuck sharply turned his back.

"He climbed along that wall with his hands!" said he.

And then he made a hopeless gesture of surrender with shoulders and arms.

"Then what did you do?" asked Dixon.

"I had a little chat with Jip. He found me crawling along from the edge of the water and when I stood up, he mistook me for Larry."

Jip himself, his face suffused, his eyes brilliant, thrust out an accusing arm.

"It was you! It was the Kid!" he shouted. "Well, cuss me white and black!"

"Then you fixed things?" said Shay.

"Then I fixed the things in the cook tent. I was lying down in there taking a little rest when you suddenly peeked in, Billy."

The face of Shay contorted in the uttermost hatred. But he smoothed out his expression almost at once.

"You're a bright boy, Kid," said he. "You shine pretty nigh enough to light your own way through the dark."

"Thanks," said the Kid.

After this, a little silence fell.

The men had gathered around the captive, and they stared at him as at an inhabitant of another world. They measured him with their eyes, and they shook their heads at one another.

The Kid, for his part, looked away from them and across the waters of Hurry Creek. They were brightly lighted by the leaping flames from the woodpile, and the same illumination glittered on the eyes of the cattle massed beyond the fences. Still at those fences, guards went up and down. Beyond the masses of the cows, the Kid saw, or thought he could see, dim shapes wandering along the hills. It might not be his imagination, but actually the forms of the men of the Milman ranch.

Shay raised a hand, suddenly.

"Now, boys," said he, "we're gonna have some voting on this here. We're gonna find out what we'll do."

"Why," said another, "I suppose that we'll stay right on here and have cold water for breakfast and cold water for lunch and cold water for supper. We can smoke cold water, too. Yeah, that looks like the right thing for us to do."

This was Three-finger Murphy, a sour and evil-looking man.

Shay turned on him in a quiet fury.

"You talk like a fool!" said he. "Are there any men here in this bunch?"

"Pick your words a little finer when you wanta talk to me," said Murphy. "I ain't here to soak up any of your back talk, old son!"

"Soak up some of mine, then, will you?" asked Dixon. "Or d'you think that your ugly mug is popular around here with me?"

"Gonna gang me, are you?" asked Murphy, almost good-naturedly. "Well, boys, I'll take you, one at a time."

"You are a fool, Three-finger," said another voice. "Shut up and let's talk sense. Of course, we ain't gonna stay on here."

"If we move, we move at a walk," said Jip. "What I wanta know is, do I get salvage for that gray gelding that the Kid rode to death, out there?"

"I paid eight hundred bucks for that bay mare of mine," broke in Peg Garret. "If that means something to you, tell me when I get paid off for that?"

"If some of you," said Billy Shay, "had had your eyes open and the wool out of your ears, you'd've seen the Kid walkin' up into the camp, dripping water as he come. Jip did see him, and played the blockhead. I never told any of you that I'd guarantee the hosses that you was riding."

The Kid bowed his head and smiled a little.

The trouble which had started in that camp was likely, it appeared to burn even longer than the pile of wood.

"I'm talkin' about the Kid, first," said Shay. "What're we to do with him?"

"Turn him loose," said the voice of young Dolly Smith suddenly. "Turn the Kid loose."

All heads turned suddenly toward the speaker, and Dolly was seen to be highly excited, and flushed of face.

"I'll tell you what," said Dolly, "there ain't anybody that's done what he's done tonight. He's all off by himself. The rest ain't nowheres. I say, turn the Kid loose. He's raised hell with us, but he'd've got clean away, if he hadn't had a touch of bad luck. I seen the cow that started up and tripped the gray gelding for him. Aside from that, we'd all be out of luck."

"Is there anybody," said Shay, "who feels about it the way that Dolly Smith does?"

The voice of Three-finger Murphy unexpectedly said: "I feel that way about it. The Kid ain't no friend of mine, as you all of you know, if you know anything. But a gent with the nerve and the brains that he's got, had oughta have a chance to try his luck again. I say, turn the Kid loose."

The Kid, frankly astonished, turned a more or less bewildered eye upon the last speaker.

"Three-finger," said he, "you're all right, Right here I take back what I said about you and Buck Stacey."

"It was Buck that put the light out," explained Three-finger.

"I believe you," said the Kid.

And Three-finger smiled with profound pleasure.

"All right," went on Shay, very calm, now. "There's two that vote for turning the Kid loose. What do the rest of you say?"

This question met with a deadly silence.

Suddenly Peg Garret exclaimed: "You boys think that you know something about the Kid. Well, I know something, too, and what I know is that he's one that never forgets. He's agin' us now, and he'll always be agin' us. They's gonna be a time, if he gets loose, when he'll pick up some of us by ones and twos, and them that he picks up ain't gonna get home none too quick, and they ain't gonna feel none too good on the way."

"Peg is agin' turnin' him loose," said Shay. "Who else?"

A big man, gray before his time, with a battered, evil face, exclaimed in his deep voice: "I'm agin' turnin' of him loose."

"Hollis, he says that he's agin' it, too," said Shay, nodding.

"Who else? You see that I'm givin' you your fair chance, Kid?"

"Yeah, I knew beforehand just what sort of a chance I would have," said the Kid.

His voice was not bitter, and his manner was simply that of a man who is mildly interested, mildly curious in the procedure that went on all around him.

Then three or four more said hastily that they thought it was folly to turn the Kid loose. He had proved himself their enemy. Gratuitously, he had taken the part of the rancher against them, though they were really his kind. He had gone out of his way to injure them, and he had taken a desperate chance, this evening, to ruin all their work. He had succeeded, but he ought to pay a penalty.

That appeared to be the consensus of opinion.

"All right," said Shay, with a wicked glint of pleasure in his eye, as he glanced toward the Kid. "And what'll we do with him now that we have him?"

"Aw," said Peg Garret, "you better put him in a glass case and show him around the towns, at a quarter a look. People'll be glad to see a killer like him, and they'll pay dead easy for the chance."

Young Jip, his lips sneering and his eyes hard, broke in: "He busted the neck of my gelding. I'd like to see his own neck busted. He's asked for trouble. He's got trouble, And if I was you, I'd certainly hang him!"

Dolly Smith broke out: "I won't stand for it. He's a better man than you ever were, Jip, you cur! I'd—"

"Why, dang you—" began Jip, reaching for a gun.

The hand of Dixon, however, already was filled with a weapon.

"The first sign I see of a gun play," said he, "I'm gonna turn loose on both of the fools that start anything. You hear me, boys? Now, let's have some sense talked, here. Jip says to hang him. Who else votes the same way?"

"I do," said Garret.

"And me!" said Dixon.

"And me," said Shay.

Then, in a chorus, came in several of the others.

"Otherwise," said Shay, "we'll never have him off our trails. Kid, I'd almost like to ask you if you didn't swear that you'd get me, one day?"

"I swore it," said the Kid, "and I sent you word that I was coming."

"You'd likely be breaking your oath, now?" demanded Shay, with his white-faced sneer of malice.

"I never broke my word in my life," said the Kid, without emotion. "If I live though this, I'm going to get you, Shay, as surely as you got my old partner!"

"You see what he is!" exclaimed Shay. "Now, boys, what's the answer?"

"Shoot him," said Dixon. "He's been a brave man. He deserves something better than hanging."

"I'd drown him," said Shay, with horrible malice. "I'd drown him like a blind puppy, if I had my way, but I'll do what the crowd says. Shooting it is. Some of you stand him up."

"Oh, I can stand, all right," said the Kid, rising to his feet.

"Stand back, all of you," said Shay. "I ain't gonna ask any of you to take this job and dirty your hands by the shootin' of a helpless man. But since it's gotta be done, I'll manage to do it myself."

"You're a fine, public-spirited fellow, Billy," said the Kid.

And, throwing back his head, he smiled straight at the gun which was being lifted in the hand of the gambler.

39
Davey Rides

WHEN MILMAN left his ranch house on the dead gallop, the horse straining and struggling forward under the spur, there was very little care in his heart except to finish the miserable business of life at once. But when he came in the darkness to the rim of the hills which overlooked Hurry Creek, he had a sudden change of heart.

Here was his father's work and his own, represented by those milling thousands of cattle. The stinging dust which rose unseen from the hollow to his nostrils was to him as bitter as poison, and as he stared at this dim picture beneath him, and the red streak of the camp fire across the face of the river, there was another fierce desire in him, coming before that of death.

He would die, and gladly, but first he must do his best to solve this situation; cut this Gordian knot.

One of the punchers who drifted up and down the hills, on guard, challenged him, and instantly recognized the voice of the rancher.

He had news that was news indeed!

Bud Trainor had seen him and reported that the Kid, single-handed, had descended by a rope into the upper ravine of Hurry Creek, in the hope of reaching the camp of the enemy.

The mind of Milman whirled in infinite confusion.

This youth whom he dreaded, this same youngster who in a day had ruined Milman in the eyes of his family, this was the same who now ventured his neck most desperately to defeat the

Shay-Dixon crew and rescue the water-starved cattle in the hollow!

Milman strove to fit the two halves of this idea together, but it was a puzzle beyond his ability.

"He went down Hurry Canyon?" said Milman. "But I tell you, there's no way for a man to get down Hurry Canyon!"

"That's what I said. That's what Bud Trainor thinks, too, but he won't let himself be honest. He says that the Kid has got to live. It ain't possible for him to die."

The puncher chuckled.

"From some of the things that I've heard about him," said he, "I reckon that there's a little truth in that!"

"The walls are as slick as the walls of a house!" exclaimed the rancher. "And they're wet with the spray of the creek. How could anybody be crazy enough to tackle such a job?"

"I dunno," said the other. "It ain't my style of a job, I know. I can ride any rope and brand. I can't be a fly and walk on a wall, though, or a ceiling. But the Kid ain't like the rest of us, chief."

"No," said the rancher solemnly. "He's not like the rest of us. He's different flesh, and has a different brain and soul, I think, as well. What else did Trainor say?"

"Not much. Trainor is half out of his wits. He's pretty fond of the Kid, I reckon."

"Will you tell me, if you can, how any man could be fond of a striped tiger of a man like that boy, the Kid?" asked Milman, the words breaking from him.

"Why, I dunno," answered the puncher. "But I've heard that the Kid's word is better than another man's bond; that he never took an advantage; and that he sticks by a bunky to the end of time. They's a lot of men inside the law that you couldn't say that much about!"

"True!" exclaimed Milman. "There are a lot of men inside the law who can't claim such qualities. What else did Trainor say? Did the Kid have a plan of any sort?"

"He had a plan," said the other, "but he wouldn't tell Bud. I think he told Bud that if he got to work in the Dixon camp, there'd be a signal that we all could see. Trainor has gone around to the other side of the hollow, so's to be near to the scene if it comes to a fight."

"I'm going to the same place," answered Milman, and straightway cantered off toward the south, to find the main road that bridged the lower canyon of Hurry Creek.

He rode steadily, and he rode hard, the good horse stretching out gallantly beneath the weight of its master. And so the road rang under the iron hoofs, the bridge thundered underneath, and the rancher, over the rail, got one glimpse of the dark and roaring hollow of the canyon.

He thought of a man working with hand and foot through the spray and the darkness of such an inferno. And for what? For the cattle owned by another man!

Bewilderment again surged in a wave over the brain of Milman.

At the first gate, he turned in from the road, and headed across the hills until he came out on the verge of them, after making the long detour. From that verge, as he drew the horse down to a milder gait, he could see the camp fire in the hollow, and the dust from the moving cattle blew again to his nostrils.

A moment later, he saw a swift shadow speed across the lowland, and a crackling of the rifle shots welled up to him, sounding wonderfully faint and far away, almost like bells of an unseen village.

He hurried on again, his heart in his throat. It seemed to him that the final fight might be about to commence, and he doubted the end of it. He had good men—men who could shoot straight enough at a deer, but men are not deer, and the best of game hunters may make the worst of soldiers.

Sweeping down to the lower plain, he found, beyond the outskirts of the massed cattle, several of his riders, and Bud Trainor among them.

They reported that a rider had come in from the outside and slipping through a gap among the cattle, had safely reached the lines of the Dixon camp, in spite of their shooting. Who the stranger was, they could not guess, unless he were simply a hired gunman sent up from Dry Creek by Shay, perhaps bearing a message of some importance to the camp to maintain the spirit of the defenders of those two lines of barbed-wire fences that controlled the priceless waters of Hurry Creek.

Bud Trainor, in the midst of this explanation, began to argue with another rider, a very small figure of a man, as it seemed to Milman, and mounted on a mere pony of a mustang.

"You get the dickens out of here and go home!" commanded Bud. "Whatcha doin' away up here, anyway? Get out of here and go back, as fast as you kin!"

"You can't chase me out of here," said the piping voice of a child. "You ain't got a chance to chase me out of here! Not all the way back home. I heard that the Kid was up here and that's why I come, because him and me is partners!"

"Who is it?" asked Milman.

"It's a fool kid cousin of mine," declared Bud Trainor. "This kid Davey is always up to his neck in trouble. And here he is ag'in. He couldn't fill one leg of a pair of trousers, but he thinks that he's a man. I never see such a young fool!"

Milman, in spite of his manifold troubles, began to laugh a little.

"You'd better cut back to the road, young fellow," said he, "and then follow it up to my ranch house. You'll be welcome there, and you can turn into a good bed. My wife and daughter will take care of you. But tell me one thing. What makes you a partner of the Kid?"

He asked with the keenest curiosity. Once before, on this night, he had heard a testimonial to the many qualities of the Kid. Here was a boy, finally, to add his word.

"Why, I dunno," said Davey, after an instant of thought, "but him and me, we just sort of hit it off, together!"

The punchers laughed uproariously.

"All right," said Davey fiercely, "you laugh, but I'd be in at the death to help the Kid when a whole lot of you would be scratchin' your noses and holdin' back!"

They laughed again, but not quite so loudly.

"Now, you get out of here. They's likely to be trouble, and bad trouble!" said Bud Trainor.

But, before he could speak another word, a thing happened which took the attention of every one quite away from Davey Trainor and his odd affairs.

For, from the center of the heaped shadows of the Dixon camp, a column of bluish flame shot up, and then the whole mass of the big woodpile put up an arm of towering fire that clutched at the very sky.

"What in the name of thunder is happenin' there?" asked one puncher.

"It's an explosion," guessed Milman. "Some of their gunpowder has caught fire—"

"It's an explosion, all right!" shouted Bud Trainor. "And it's the Kid that's exploded it. It's his signal. It means that he's at work! Heaven bless him, there ain't another man like him in the world. He's gone and done it ag'in! He's gone and done it, d'you hear? He's in there raisin' the devil with the whole crowd of them!"

Here there arose a prolonged rattling gunfire from within the camp, or from that direction, the sounds coming back from the hill faces like hollow hands clapping violently together. An odd time and an odd scene for applause!

Then, through the mass of the cattle, which divided a little to this side and that before the charge, streamed thirty or forty swiftly galloping horses, with no visible riders on their backs. Many of these took a noble header over some cow which could not get from the path, but, rising again, the band streamed on up the bottom of the hollow, cleaving a way as they went, like a flying wedge.

"It's the Kid! It's the Kid!" screamed little Davey Trainor.

All the punchers in the Milman service on that side of the hollow were riding, now, toward the point at which the frightened horses were issuing from among the cattle masses.

But Davey was there the first of all, and bending low, so that he could examine the silhouettes of the animals one by one, more closely, he strained his eyes to make out the form of a rider on one of them.

There was nothing to be seen. There was no rider, however flattened on the back or, Indian fashion, along the side of one of those racing horses, that could have escaped the glance of the sharp-eyed boy.

In the meantime, the inferno of flame continued to whirl upwards into the air from the camp of Dixon, throwing out long arms which vanished almost as quickly as they appeared.

"It's the Kid's work," said Milman suddenly. "No other man could have done so much, and the fire and the escape of the horses cannot both be accidents!"

"But where's the Kid now?" demanded Bud, excited. "He ought to've been on the back of one of those hosses. And where's Davey? Davey, you little fool, where are you?"

But Davey was gone!

40
For the Sake of Cows

HE HAD GONE OFF, perhaps, to the top of one of the nearer hills in order to get another view of the camp fire and to strain his eyes toward the figures which were near it. For, from that distance, they could see forms indistinctly, moving about in the yellow red of the firelight.

Those who waited in that excited group had something else to think of, a moment later, for a rider came up to them at wild speed, and young Georgia Milman's voice called out frantically to know if her father was there.

"Aye," said Milman, after a moment of hisitation. "I'm here, Georgia. What brought you out?"

He rode out to meet her, and she, wheeling her horse, went with him a sufficient distance to cover the sound of their voices from the ears of the others.

"What is it, Georgia?" he asked her.

She was half weeping with relief at finding him.

"I've come like mad all the way from the house," she said. "I saw Tex Marshall on the other side of Hurry Creek and he said that you'd come around here. Father, I've come out to tell you that Mother and I don't care what's happened in the past. We don't care. You're ours."

He reached for her through the starlight and found her hand in his with a strong grip, worthy of a man.

"Your mother, too, Georgia?" he asked her.

"Yes, Mother, too. Of course!"

"She's always known that there was something wrong," said

Milman. "But—I can only thank God and the two of you. Georgia, some day I'll be able to tell you a story that will be hard to believe. So hard that I couldn't try to tell it today, when you taxed me."

"I believe it already," she told him loyally. "Oh, Dad, it's the three of us against the world. D'you think Mother or I could fail you now, when the bottom is falling out of everything?"

Something like a groan welled up in the throat of Milman. He crushed Georgia's hand and then let it fall.

"I'm going to talk it all out to the two of you," said he. "But not now. There's something else to think about now. You saw the explosion?"

"Where?"

"In the hollow there in Dixon's camp."

"Explosion?"

"Doesn't that camp fire look big to you?"

"Yes it does. What happened?"

"That's what we don't know. We only know that the Kid left Bud Trainor and lowered himself by Trainor's lariat into the gorge of the upper creek. He was trying to get to the camp of Dixon, inside the fence lines where they've been keeping watch. We don't know, but we suspect that the Kid may have caused the explosion that we saw in the camp—and the woodpile caught fire from it. Then there was a stampede of the horses from the same direction. They broke out through the herds. We don't know what to make of it—"

"And the Kid didn't come out with the horses?" asked the girl.

"No."

"Then he's back there in the camp!"

"We've no proof at all that he ever reached the camp. It seems humanly impossible that he could have got down the wall of the ravine and—"

She cried out, choking away the sound miserably at the end.

And that cry stabbed her father with a quick and frantic pain.

"You care a frightful lot about him, Georgia?" said he.

"Aye," said she. "A frightful lot!"

"He's tried this crazy thing for your sake, Georgia?"

"For me? For me?" said the girl, agony in her voice. "No, no! Don't you see that what he means to do is to smash you as he smashed the other four? How could he try to do anything for

my sake, then? It's not for me. It's the misery of the poor dumb
cows that's making him try to do what no man can win through
to!"

"I don't know what to make of him," declared the father.
"There never was another man like him. Who else in the
world would try such a thing—for the sake of dumb beasts?"

"There are no other men like him," she said. "But what will
become of him and all of us, I don't know. I don't dare to guess.
But he's down there in that camp, I'll swear."

"What makes you so sure?"

"Because he couldn't fail. There's no failure in him. He could
die. I know that. But it will take men to kill him. It'll certainly
take men to kill him!"

They went back to the rest of the watchers and all stared
anxiously down toward the fire. It no longer threw up flames so
brilliantly. The strength of the burning had rotted away the
woodpile and allowed it to spill out on the side. A strong glow,
constantly reddening, was thrown up from this mass, but the
light was much less clear and far-reaching.

"Who has a strong pair of glasses?" asked Milman.

"I have a pair," said a puncher, "but they really ain't any
good for night work."

Then a rider came up to them, sweeping from the hollow at a
gallop, in spite of the slope.

And, as he came in, the shrill, piping voice of Davey Trainor
cried out: "He's in there! He's in there! I seen him!"

They swarmed suddenly around the boy. Here was excitement. The passion that was in him seemed to illumine his face
far more than the starlight.

"What did you see, Davey? Where've you been?"

"I wanted to go look. I couldn't stay out here with the rest of
you just millin' around and doin' nothing'. I went and had a
look. You can get through the cows. The worst ones is out on
this side. The ones inside is pretty nigh dead with the thirst. I
got through, anyway. I got through, and I seen him!"

"Who, who? Davey, who d'you mean?"

"Who do I mean? I mean him that started the fire, and that
busted the fence, and that burned up their chuck and that
burned up their wagons and their wood supply, so's they're as
bare as my hand of everything that folks would need. The Kid
—the Kid, of course! There ain't anybody else that could do
such things, is there?"

"He's there!" cried Bud Trainor. "I might've knowed that it was him. I did know it. I felt the ache of it in my bones!"

Tears began to stream down the face of Georgia.

She pressed her hands against her eyes, but the tears pressed through and her hands were wet.

It was the end, she felt. Yet she controlled the throes of her sobbing. Dimly, she heard the voices of the men.

"Who's gonna do something?" demanded the voice of Davey Trainor, sharp and biting as the noise of a cricket on a hearth. "Who's gonna get started and do something for the Kid? He wouldn't leave a partner down there with them crooks! He wouldn't just sit around and look and talk. He'd be down there sure raisin' hell for the sake of his bunky! Who's gonna start something up here, for him? I'll make one!"

This fierce and piping voice silenced them, for a moment.

"There are twenty men down there," said one of the punchers, sullenly. "I'd take a chance for the Kid. But not no chance like that. It ain't a lot of wooly lambs that are down there with Dixon."

Milman took charge of the cross-questioning of the lad.

"Tell me, Davey, just what you saw?"

"I'll tell you," said Davey. "When I got through the cows, I come to a place where I seen that there was three or four gents workin' to patch up a gap that had been broke through the wire fencing. They was cussing a good deal.

"I worked along, keepin' on the edge of the darkness, which wasn't none too hard, because the light of that fire's so bright that all of them that are near it are sort of blinded, I reckon. Fifty feet from the fire, it's like they was lookin' at black windows. They couldn't see out no farther. Anyway, I worked down the line.

"That camp is sure a wreck. The cook tent is just a black mess, that's all. Everything is gone, includin' their hosses. All that they got on their hands, it's a pile of saddles and such."

"But the Kid, the Kid!" exclaimed Milman impatiently.

"Yeah, and I'm coming to that. I got up the line, closer to the fire, and there I seen a lot of the men standin' around, and whisperin', and shakin' their heads at each other. You'd think that they was standin' around and lookin' at the devil or a ten-foot rattler. But it was the Kid. He was stretched out, there. They had his hands and his feet tied. I gathered from what I heard them say that he'd 've got clean away on the back of one of the hosses, if it wasn't that the one he was ridin' bareback had had a tumble and broke its own neck, and dropped the Kid. He was senseless, but while I was there, he woke up, and sat up. Jiminy, before that, I pretty nigh thought that he was dead!"

"What else?" asked Milman. "What else did you see?"

"D'you think I'd wait there?" demanded the youngster. "D'you think that I'd wait there till they murdered him?"

"Murdered him?" cried out Georgia Milman suddenly, and her voice rang sharp and thin in the air, almost like the excited yipping of Davey himself.

"Sure they'll murder him," said Davey, "unless we do something about it. Surely they'll murder him. D'you think that that bunch of yeggs would ever let the Kid loose to go wanderin' around and pickin' 'em off? Why, it would be pretty jolly for the Kid, wouldn't it, to have that many gents to trace down and bump off? It would keep him happy pretty night all the rest of his life, wouldn't it?"

"I suppose that it would," said one of the punchers. "What can we do?"

"Ride down, ride down!" said Davey desperately. "Ride down and make a try. They's five of you here. You're something. You can make a try for him. You can sure make a try to help him. You wouldn't be letting the Kid get bumped off, Buck, would you? You wouldn't let the Kid go like that, Charlie? I know you wouldn't. Mr. Milman, you say something to 'em!"

"There's nothing for me to say," said Milman, after a moment of quiet. "I know that I'm going down to do what I can!"

"There are twenty of them, father!" cried Georgia. "What could you do? It's a lost cause. You're only throwing yourself away!"

But her heart leaped in her throat, and she knew the answer almost before she heard it.

"It may be a lost cause," said Milman, "but it's my cause. And if the Kid is brave enough to die for us, we'll have to die for him. Georgia, so long for a little while!"

He rode off.

"I'm number two in this party!" said Bud Trainor, and instantly his horse was beside that of the rancher.

41
Two Against Twenty

BUT THE OTHER three cow-punchers did not move to join the two. Two against twenty! Aye, or even five against twenty, considering who the twenty were, seemed sickening odds. Besides, these were not gunmen or professional fighters. They had been hired to ride range, not to shoot it out with such as the Dixon crowd. They milled about a little, uneasily, until one of them said: "I got a wife and two kids that live on what I make. I reckon that I ain't afraid to be ashamed."

The other two said nothing, but they seemed willing to allow the other's speech to stand as a lead for them.

Little Davey Trainor suddenly cried out:

"You ain't punchers! You ain't Westerners! You're a bunch of yaller-livered, no-good skunks! I'm gonna tell every man on the range about you! I know your names, and I won't forget 'em. The Kid's down there doin' your work. The Kid's gonna die for what you should've died for——"

He looked about him, and suddenly he saw that the girl had ridden off into the dark of the night.

Instantly he pulled his own mustang about and was beside her.

"Whatcha gonna do? Where you headin'?" asked the boy.

"Go back, Davey," said she. "Never mind where I'm going."

"You're gonna go in there!" exclaimed Davey. "You figger on follerin' your daddy."

"It doesn't matter what I figure on. This is no place for you,

203

Davey! Go back, and try to talk those three punchers into coming along."

"They can't be talked into nothin'! They wouldn't budge. You couldn't pray 'em into budgin'. Dog-gone it, though, you can't go in there! D'you think that those thugs'll be able to see that you ain't a man? D'you think that they'd care, much, even if they knew? They'll shoot at everything that budges, after a while!"

"Davey," said the girl, "I know that you mean well, but don't try to persuade me any more. There's no use. I'm going to ride in there. Nothing can stop me. Go back and try to find some of the other men. We have something besides cowards on our ranch!"

"Ride back for 'em yourself," said Davey. "You ain't a man, and I am. I'm gonna go in there and see what happens!"

"Davey! Davey!" she cried at him. "You silly child—you great, silly baby, what can you do?"

"I've got a gun, and I can use a gun," declared Davey. "That's what I can do. Is that enough?"

And then, as they entered the outer fringe of the cattle, there was too much work for them to allow further talk.

It was no easy thing.

Wandering on the outer edges of the hollow, masses of the cattle stirred here and there, wakeful with thirst, uneasy, prevented from getting on by the more solid masses of living flesh which barred the way toward the desired creek.

Among those crowds they had to go. It seemed impossible, at first, but they knew that a recruit to the Dixon crowd had gone through, and they knew that the boy himself had gone back and forth, and that the horses had burst through the mass.

What was the fortune of Milman and Bud Trainor, they could not guess. The double dark of the night and of the dust clouds shut them from sight as soon as they entered the herds.

Now and then, with a loud bellowing, a section of the herd would loom at them, with vaguely glistening horns, and terrible eyes, but the sight of the mounted men made them turn back.

It was as though they passed into a whirlpool of many currents, conflicting, and the waves of it armed with horns that looked long enough to impale horse and rider with a single thrust.

So they went on, the girl holding her breath with fear; then half choking in the dust.

She arranged a bandanna over her mouth and nose and breathed through this with an effort. Yet the choking effect of the dust was thereby much lessened.

It was a nightmare, and beyond this evil dream lay another far more horrible, toward which she was going. What she could do, she could not guess. To see the tragedy that must occur was abhorrent to her, but yet she was drawn on as by a magnet of an overwhelming power.

On the whole, the problem of getting through was not half as desperate as it looked from a distance. The courage of the lad in first facing that tangle of dust and stamping hoofs and horns staggered her, however. He was before her, now, leading the way, parting the currents of danger, as it were.

And, with another leap and ache of her heart, she knew that here was the promise of such another manhood as the Kid's. Something great for good, or for evil. No man could tell for which.

But goodness began to appear to her struggling mind in a new light. It seemed not so very difficult to dodge all evil by denying all temptation. Good women did that, closing their eyes upon what is dreadful and horrible, what is wild and enchanting in its wildness. Good men did it, also, keeping to a straight and narrow path, and blinding themselves to the possibilities which lay right and left. Yonder three punchers, for instance, were good men, who would have died rather than not do their duty. But for this thing which lay outside and above their duty, which was extra reasonable and had nothing to do with law, that wasn't business for them. It was the business of the professional gambler, the gunfighter, the manslayer. It was the business of the Kid!

How to rearrange her ideas she could not tell, but she knew that the Kid began to appear before her mind luminously, a moon of brightness among starry mankind, making them very dim indeed.

And then, the dust mist before her began to be stained by the faint rose of the firelight. The dusty herds grew more dense. They would never have gotten through had it not been for the tactics of the mustang on which the lad was mounted before her. That mustang had been trained for many a long year in the ways of the range and of range cattle. He went at the steers and the cows with teeth and striking forehoofs. He went through them as a sheep dog goes through a well-packed flock of sheep, making them crowd to either side and leave a narrow channel through which he runs. In that thin wake she followed, taking advantage of it by pressing up close to Davey. And, now and then, she could hear his thin, piercing voice, shouting cheerfully back to her above the mighty thunder of the lowing.

There were waves of that sound, and then moments of almost utter silence, except for the melancholy music from the hills that rimmed the hollow.

In one of those spells of silence, they came through to the final rim of the cattle, and saw before them, here and there, the gleam of the triple rows of barbed wire, and the dull silhouettes of Milman and Bud Trainor just before them, very close to the rim of the encampment.

Now the girl could see the blackened debris of what had once been the excellent camp of Dixon and Shay. Yes, that was the work of the Kid. There was a thoroughness about the destruction which seemed to identify it as his, immediately.

She looked to the left. Two men walked up and down the fence, with black-snake whips, striking at the faces of the cattle which came too close. The two men were so near that it seemed miraculous that they did not see the four interlopers out there on the rim of the cow herds.

But the glow of the fire prevented, no doubt, blinding the watchers, as little Davey had pointed out before.

It was not so much of a blaze, now, but the glow was intensely bright, as it struck up from the masses of embers. When a gust of wind struck it, the light pulsed brighter, and took on a more yellow and penetrating color.

And the first of those brighter pulses showed her, at the right of the fire, the group for which she was looking. It was very close at hand. She could see every feature of every man that faced her.

The Kid stood there with his hands and feet lashed, his back to her. Facing him was a loose semicircle of Dixon's men; and just in front of him was Shay, his long, white face inhumanly ugly as he balanced a revolver in his right hand.

"I'm going to hold up a minute, Kid," said he. "If you got anything to say, we'll try to remember it for you."

The Kid answered, and his voice was clear, free, and almost joyous.

"I can talk for quite a while, Billy, but I don't want you to make your wrist ache, holding that heavy gun so long."

"Don't worry about me," said Billy Shay. "Just talk your heart out, if you want to, Kid."

"Well, there are only two or three things. You know Bud Trainor, some of you?"

"Yeah, I know the sucker," said a voice.

"Well, tell Bud to forget about this. Tell him that was one of my last wishes. He might have an idea that something was expected of him."

"Not if he's got sense," said the other. "But I'll pass your word along to him."

"Another thing," said the Kid, "is that I'd like to have my name scratched on a rock, and the rock put at my head, so that if the Milmans get around to burying me, they'll know who is lying here. My name is Benjamin Chapin, alias a lot of things."

"What makes you tell us?" said Billy Shay, curiously. "After you've covered it up for so long, too!"

"I'll tell you why," said the Kid. "There's one person in the world that I wish to learn it, and this is the only way I can make sure that the news will travel."

"It's a girl, Kid, I suppose?" said Shay.

"Billy," said the Kid, "a warm, sensitive, proud heart like yours is sure to get at the truth of things. Yes, Billy, it's a girl."

"Yeah, you been a heartbreaker all your days," said Billy Shay. "I'm supposin' that she'll bust hers when she learns how you dropped."

"Thank you, Billy," said the Kid. "There's one other thing. I think that Bud Trainor may do as I want and keep his hands off you. But there's another who won't. Boys, watch out for him, when little Davey gets man-size."

"Is that all?" asked Shay.

"Yes, that's all, Billy. Go ahead."

"No prayin', nor nothin' like that?"

"Prayers won't help a man like me," said the Kid cheerfully. "I've done too much that was wrong. You boys will know when you come to my place. You'll understand what I mean when I say the prayers don't help. Excuse me for talking a little bit like Sunday school. All right, Billy."

"Now for you," said Shay, stepping a little closer, and his face twisting into more consummate ugliness. "You've hounded me, and you've dogged me. You blamed your partner's death on me. You're right. I plugged him and the reason that I plugged him was because he was your friend. You done me

shame in Dry Creek. It ain't a thing for me to live down. But I'll
have the taste of this to make me feel better. Kid, you're gonna
see the devil in another quarter of a second!"

And, with this, he jerked up the gun until it was level with the
head of the Kid.

A report sounded, but no smoke issued from the revolver in
Billy Shay's hand. It was a sound closer to the girl, and with a
wild glance, she saw that a rifle was couched against the
shoulder of Bud Trainor, as he sat his saddle in the dust cloud
near the fence.

The head of Billy Shay jerked back. He leaned. It was as
though he wished to recoil from his victim, the Kid, but could
not move his feet. Back he leaned. His body was stiff. He
reached an absurd angle. It seemed as though he must be sustained by the counterpoise of some other weight.

And then he slumped heavily to the ground, with a distinct
impact.

There were guns in the hands of the entire semicircle of
Dixon's men, but, with amazed, uncomprehending faces, they
stared into the dust fog, and could see nothing. The firelight
which made them easy targets had blinded them thoroughly.

Then Dolly Smith leaped to the side of the Kid.

"Drop, Kid, drop!" he screamed, in a voice femininely high.

And, beside the Kid, he slumped to the ground, where the
fallen body of Shay lay like a shallow bulwark between them
and the other guns.

42
Heroes

THE GIRL, watching with fascinated eyes, frozen in her saddle,
saw the gleam of a knife in the hands of Dolly Smith as it made
the two quick slashes which turned the Kid into a free, fighting
man.

Then she heard the cry of her father's voice, as he shouted: "Charge them, boys! Blow them off the face of the earth! Charge 'em! Charge 'em!"

And there, behold, black and huge between her and the firelight, appeared the form of John Milman as his horse rose for the leap and then sailed over the top strand of the barbed wire.

"Charge 'em" shrieked the higher, more piercing voice, and she saw little Davey go over the fence a short distance away, an old revolver exploding blindly, uselessly in his hand.

Bud Trainor shouted also. It was the whoop of a wild Indian. And he, too, had taken that fence with a bound of his horse.

How the silver stallion shone as it sailed across the rose hue of the firelight!

And Dixon's twenty heroes?

There were not more than a dozen of them in that group, in the first place. Others were off guarding the fence lines. But of the dozen who were there, it seemed that not one took any care of standing up to fight the thing out.

The surprise was complete.

They had seen that one of their best men, in the crisis, had gone over to the enemy. And then there was the spectacle of the riders plunging over the fence, shouting, calling out as if to a host, and looking greater than human in that fantastic-like haze as they rushed through the dust fog.

Dixon's crowd did not lack leadership.

It was Champ Dixon himself who turned with a yell of fear and showed the way. But he was fairly passed by most of the others in the flight that followed.

Perhaps half a dozen wild shots plowed up the ground or uselessly whirred through the air. And all in a trice the ground was vacant.

The Kid and Dolly Smith—for Smith had armed the Kid in the first moment the latter's hands were free—had not had to fire a shot.

It was mysterious; it was almost ludicrous. And as the formidable Dixon mob vanished into the dark of the night, Bud Trainor, his nerves giving way under the strain, began to laugh hysterically.

It seemed ridiculously easy, a thing that children could have done as well, but the girl, sitting quietly there in the dark of the night, understood perfectly. None but heroes could have done such a feat—and heroes they were, little Davey Trainor most of all, and Bud, and her own father. A tremor went through her, pulsing as if from the sound of a deep, friendly voice at her ear.

There were other men of the Dixon-Shay outfit to be accounted for, and, above all, there was the imminent danger that the fugitives, learning how small a force had struck at them, would return to blot out this insolent little group.

What could they do?

The inspiration came to her, then.

She drew the wire nippers from her pocket. Three clicks, three sounds like the snapping of bowstrings, and there was a gateway made. Like piled-up water at a breaking dam, the cattle poured through. Three more clicks and another gate. And then—for the guards had fled from this side of the fence line— the other cattle, maddened by the sight of their companions getting through toward the water, pressed forward in masses. They put their tough chests against the barbs. Down they went. There were cuts and gashes, but what of that? Water was more precious than blood to these starved creatures, and sweeping in hordes through a dozen gaps, they galloped for the water. The creek was black with them!

That was not all.

The stroke at the center of the Dixon camp had dissolved all its force, it appeared. Even from the other fence line to the west of the creek, the guards had withdrawn, and the cattle, inspired by the sight of their fellows drinking on the opposite shore, pressed in on the fence, and it also went down in great sections.

Down they rushed. A vast bellowing arose. It sounded to the girl like the shouting of triumphant armies, legion on legion. Armies of right, which had conquered, and the wrong had gone down!

She reined her horse away from a threatening rush of the cattle. In so doing, she was forced into the small group which had taken shelter from the invading beasts behind a specially strong section of the fencing.

Davey and Bud were secure in another spot.

And here she found herself with her father, and with the Kid. Dolly Smith was near the fire itself, for the brightness of it turned the cows easily, while they still were at a considerable distance.

The Kid was on one side of her now, and her father on the other, and silently they watched the cows flooding down to the river, whose silver, star-freckled face became all black and full of strange movements.

The bellowing died down. There were clashing of horns, and clacking of hurrying, split hoofs. That was all. Even this disturbance grew less. Even for all the thousands on the ranch, there was ample water in Hurry Creek, and the starved animals were rapidly drinking to repletion.

Some of them, filled to bursting, lay down on the bank, unable to move farther. And a quiet, profound joy and trust grew up in the girl as she watched the thirsty cattle.

"Chapin," said her father, "I've promised to tell Georgia. I want to tell you, also. That day when you were six years old and the thieves came at you out of the night—"

"Milman," said the Kid, "you don't need to tell me. Tonight has told me by itself. When I saw you jump your horse over that fence, then I knew that I was wrong."

"Do you think that?"

"I know it."

"I'll tell you this much more. I'd gone north to buy cattle for the ranch. We had a chance at a bargain in a big sale, up there. I made the purchase. I started south on horseback, to see a huge section of the range, and look out for likely places to buy grazing lands for the southern drive. And, on the way, I made a fool of myself at a small town; I met those fellows you found me with. I drank too much. And that same night I rode south with them. They blundered onto your little outfit. I think I was half foolish with liquor. It merely seemed to me a silly practical joke. Then, the next morning, I realized. There was one of the thieves named Turk Reming. He seemed a decent sort of a fellow. I had to go on south. But I bought the entire lot of the cattle they had stolen, and Reming swore that he could get the money back to the man who had been plundered. I can only give you my word for that, my lad; and that I left the cattle with a dealer in the next village, and that I went on south, taking the mule along to carry my pack and make the going lighter for my horse. I can't really ask you to believe such a cock-and-bull story. It's the truth, but I know that no jury in the world ever would believe it!"

"Georgia," said the Kid, "how about you, if you were on that jury?"

"She's a prejudiced juror," said Milman, "but——"

"I'm prejudiced, too," said the Kid. "Georgia, have I got a good reason to be?"

John Milman grew suddenly hot with discomfort, and very tense, and then he heard his daughter say clearly, and in such a voice as he had never heard from her before:

"Ben, you have all the reason in the world. All the reason that I can give you!"

THE KING OF ADULT WESTERN ENTERTAINMENT,

ZEKE MASTERS